CONTEMPORARY AMERICAN FICTION

MONKEY BAY

Elaine Ford is the author of three previous novels, *The Playhouse, Missed Connections,* and *Ivory Bright*. She is professor of English at the University of Maine and lives on Maine's coast, where *Monkey Bay* is set. She is married to Arthur Boatin and has five children.

MONKEY BAY

ELAINE FORD

PENGUIN BOOKS

PENGUIN BOOKS
Published by the Penguin Group
Viking Penguin, a division of Penguin Books USA Inc.,
375 Hudson Street, New York, New York 10014, U.S.A.
Penguin Books Ltd, 27 Wrights Lane, London W8 5TZ, England
Penguin Books Australia Ltd, Ringwood, Victoria, Australia
Penguin Books Canada Ltd, 2801 John Street, Markham, Ontario, Canada L3R 1B4
Penguin Books (N.Z.) Ltd, 182–190 Wairau Road, Auckland 10, New Zealand

Penguin Books Ltd, Registered Offices: Harmondsworth, Middlesex, England

First published in the United States of America by Viking Penguin,
a division of Penguin Books USA Inc., 1989
Published in Penguin Books 1990

10 9 8 7 6 5 4 3 2 1

Grateful acknowledgment is made for permission to reprint excerpts from the following copyrighted works:
"Waiting for a Girl Like You" by Mick Jones and Lou Gramm. © 1981 Somerset Songs Publishing, Inc.
All rights administered by Intersong-USA, Inc. All rights reserved. Used by permission.
"What Have I Done to Deserve This?" words and music by Allee Willis, Neil Tennant, and Chris Lowe.
© Copyright 1987 by Texascity Music, Inc., Streamline Moderne Music, 10 Music Ltd, and Cage Music Ltd. Rights of Texascity Music, Inc., and Streamline Moderne Music administered by MCA Music Publishing, a division of MCA, Inc., New York, New York 10019. Rights of 10 Music Ltd and Cage Music Ltd administered in the United States and in Canada by Virgin Music, Inc., Los Angeles, California 90069.

LIBRARY OF CONGRESS CATALOGING IN PUBLICATION DATA
Ford, Elaine.
Monkey Bay/Elaine Ford.
p. cm.
ISBN 0 14 01.2057 2
I. Title.
[PS3556.O697M66 1990]
813'.54—dc20 89-78392
Printed in the United States of America

FOR EARL LOWELL

It is a time for dancing

Although set in Maine, this novel is about the experience of living, rather than the experience of living in Maine. The characters and events are entirely creatures of the author's imagination and are not intended to celebrate Maine, to explicate it, or to reflect negatively upon it.

The author is grateful to the National Endowment for the Arts for the generous grant that made possible the writing of this book. She thanks also her husband, Arthur Boatin, for his devoted attention to her and her work, and Sanford Phippen for reading the manuscript and making many helpful suggestions.

MONKEY BAY

September

When she comes home from work she finds him laying the carpet in the loft, finally. The nails are puncturing the floor and making a double row of spikes over the couch.

She climbs the stairs and asks him, "Why are you using such long nails?" He's kneeling on the gray carpet, part of it still unrolled behind him. He turns and just looks at her.

Marilla bought the carpet three or four years ago, on a sale. She lugged the rolls up to the loft, where they sat for weeks on end. One day they disappeared. "Where'd those rolls of carpet go?" she asked him.

"Down cellar," he said.

Every once in a while she'd mention how rough the floor was in the loft. Or cold. A splinter went into her foot right through the sock.

"Stop nagging me, Marilla, for Christ's sake."

She could have put it down herself, but they'd always understood it was his house. Tucker bought the land when his grandmother died and left him some money. Two acres of sand and rocks and scrub on Monkey Bay, four miles from Route 1.

Marilla held the hammer or carried the other end of the board when he was building the house. "My house," he'd call it, talking to people. And although she's lived in it more than ten years, ever since it was nothing more than a one-room shack over a cellar hole, even she thinks of it as Tucker's house.

The house is some fifty yards from the water at high tide, up on a bluff. From the stoop Marilla can hear water lapping the cordgrass if the tide's in, and if it's out, she can see clam diggers out on the mud flat, so far away they're the size of gnats. In September the bay's apt to be woolly with mist, and though it may be sunny in town, some days the sun never does burn off the fog on the peninsula. Sea heather grows down on the beach, poking up around the rocks. September is when it blooms, tiny blue flowers on delicate branches like sprays. Marilla gathers it to put in a jug. She bought the jug at a yard sale and discovered afterward that it has a slow leak through a crack in the bottom; but it's all right for sea heather, because you don't put sea heather in water. It dries and stays pretty all winter.

September's also the month Marilla brings in all the green tomatoes and fries some and stores the rest under layers of newspaper, hoping they'll ripen before they rot. The cabbages stay out, and so do the potatoes, until after the first frost. By now the peas are long gone, and the beans. One year, to please Tucker, she tried to grow muskmelons, but they never amounted to much, though the seed catalog claimed they were specially developed for short growing seasons and cold climates. She never seems to have luck with lettuce, either. If the cat doesn't dig it up, slugs eat it, or grasshoppers, or some kind of fly.

The garden patch has other problems. The soil's thin and poor, and the woods are so close there's no section of the garden that's not in shade part of the day. It's a challenge to get anything to grow there, and maybe that's what she likes about it.

Tucker also is what you might call a gardener. Most of his cellar is devoted to the cultivation of his crop. He plants the seeds in late winter, transfers the seedlings to large pots in the spring, and harvests and cures the mature plants in the fall, all under ground. No chemicals—he fertilizes with composted fish guts and seaweed. He has his own generator for the Gro-Luxes in case the power fails, which it does often in winter, ice weighting down the wires.

In almost every way Tucker considers himself self-sufficient. If Marilla hadn't come to live with him and brought the ability to earn a living with her, he'd still make out okay. He has quite a bit put by for emergencies.

He trusts the people he does business with, he trusts Marilla. She's not one of those women who wash the family laundry at every ladies' aid meeting. Not that she goes to meetings, anyway.

Tucker Burchard came from Lubec, his father and grandfather worked in a sardine factory. But Tucker used to spend every summer here in town, in Stony Harbor. He didn't want to can sardines, or clam or dig worms, either. So he stayed with his grandmother Retter in the old white house on Main Street, next to Trumble Hardware, and worked at different summer jobs.

He worked as a stock boy in Blodgett's the first summer. He was thirteen, and so was Marilla. She was doing some errand for her mother, picking something out from the sewing notions rack, when she saw him for the first time. She watched him slit open a carton and begin to take little girls' underpants out of it. He took his time about it, arranging them by size and style in the green wooden counter bins instead of shoving them in any old way. Some had polka dots, others had narrow bands of elastic lace around the leg holes. He patted each stack when it was done, molded it with his hands. Watching him do this made her feel so peculiar she thought she was going to topple over.

He began to whistle a little, a tuneless, rasping sound between his teeth. His hair was a very pale sort of brown, like a wood chip or dried hay. Cut short then. She thought how nice it would be to touch it, then shoved her hand hard into her jacket pocket. He wouldn't be as tall as she was if they were standing side by side—she noticed that right away. He was slight, but he'd have the muscles he'd need to haul a trap, she thought, or to swing a maul. His eyes were dark. Brown, maybe, though she couldn't be sure in the dim, dusty light at the back of Blodgett's.

She fingered bolts of material, cards of ribbon and eyelet, watching him as best she could from the shadows. Then all of a sudden he was gone, just picked up the empty carton and disappeared. She waited there a long time, staring at the needles and straight pins in their little packets. In the front of the store Miss Blodgett dozed next to the cash register. He didn't appear again. Probably he went out the back way and was sitting at his grandmother's kitchen table eating a baloney sandwich while she still stood there like a lunatic.

When Marilla got back with the straight pins, her mother wanted to know what had taken so long to pedal half a mile to Blodgett's and back. She'd felt faint in the store, she said, and had to walk her bike home so she wouldn't fall off. Was it her period coming on? her mother asked. Had she asked Miss Blodgett to give her a glass of water? No, no. Her mother sighed and sucked on her cigarette and went on applying neutralizer to the customer's hair bundles.

The fifth summer Tucker Burchard didn't come back. Marilla didn't have the nerve to ask Mrs. Retter what had happened. She married Lyle Pratt not too long after that and didn't see Tucker or hear a word about him for nineteen years.

Hannah sees her mother even before she gets to town. On Route 1, right after the turnoff for Monkey Bay Road, she notices a new building covered in garish aquamarine siding. MONKEY BAY REDEMPTION CENTER AND VIDEO, the homemade painted sign says. Her mother is standing in a little cindery clearing in front, talking to the driver of a Pabst beer truck. Marilla's tucking loose hair into her knot; her cotton skirt flaps around her calves. The driver's grinning down at her from the cab. Hannah lifts her foot from the gas pedal for an instant but can't make the decision whether to stop or not in time, and so drives on past.

When Hannah was a year and a half old Marilla got herself a job. Lyle didn't like it much, but they needed the money, so what could he say? They were living in the trailer on Seal Neck Road then, on a swampy piece of land snarled over with wild raspberries. She tried to hack out a garden, but you rip up a bramble and ten more spring up where the first one was. The roots go all over, threaded through that squashy clay. The raspberries aren't even worth eating, all seed.

She'd leave Hannah with her mother, plunk her down in a corner and give her plastic curlers and rollers and snakes of cotton to play with, and then drive into town in the old Mercury her brother had left behind when he went into the service and never bothered to reclaim.

That job was at Blodgett's, where she'd fallen in love with Tucker Burchard, but that's not why she went to work there. At the time the only other jobs to be had were in the cannery, and like Tucker, she wasn't going to can sardines. Or else drive to Ellsworth and be a checkout girl in a supermarket, but she wasn't going to do that, either. Forty-five minutes each way, more in the winter. The old Mercury wouldn't have made it.

The truth was, she hated working at Blodgett's, haunted by Tucker and all the kinds of feelings he used to make her have. There were still cartons to be opened and new clothes to be laid out in the counter bins, except now it was Marilla doing it. When she touched that soft material, she couldn't help thinking about Tucker's hands, and that was painful.

So she kept her ears open, and she heard the Brass Lantern needed a waitress. She did that for a couple of years. The money was all right. But the hours were bad, with a kid, and with Lyle complaining that the only one in town that didn't get waited on by Marilla was him. So she quit, and they got along as best they could on what he earned.

For the last couple of years she's been bagging up empty bottles and cans and handing out the redemption money, and renting out videos for two dollars a day each, one dollar on Wednesdays. So there's money going both ways across the counter, but there's never so much business that she's in any danger of becoming confused.

On Poplar Street Hannah lets the Pinto come to rest some distance from the house and turns off the ignition. She yanks the leather gloves from her hands and drops them on the seat beside her but doesn't move from behind the steering wheel.

The name is Poplar Street, though everybody in these parts calls the trees popples. For a long time Hannah thought that popples were common ungainly trees that grew in ditches and fields, like weeds, and that poplars were majestic, like elms. And she'd wondered why the street she lives on had the name it did when not a single poplar grew in any of the yards. Maybe like the elms they'd been killed by a plague. She refused to believe it when Frances told her that "popple" and "poplar" are one and the same.

The house hasn't changed in three years. It's a frame house, white with green trim. Beside the walk there's a whitewashed tire with shrimp-colored geraniums growing inside, and on the lawn is a small sign that says PRATT and, next to it, the painted wooden whirlybird Frances bought the time they took the overnight trip to Augusta and stayed in a motel, the three of them in one room. In the night she'd heard them, her father and Frances, grunting under a quilted sateen bedspread. That was a long time ago.

As she carries a white jug of sea heather into the big room, for the hundredth or thousandth time Marilla's eyes are drawn to the nails in the ceiling over the couch. *Tooth and nail* are the words that spring into her mind. *Hard as nails.*

Over the years Tucker collected pounds of them. He found them on construction sites, near the foundations of old houses, lying in ditches, driven into the poles and planks that washed up on the beach. He straightened them with a hammer and dropped them into a burlap sack on the floor of the shed. Some were already rusty, some rusted in the sack.

Those were the nails he used to lay the carpet in the loft. He used only the long ones, the three-inchers. He had to have known they'd go through the floorboards, right through the ceiling below. She's angry. He did it to even the score with her for nagging, and she's not a nag, not like other women.

The odd thing is, though, he wasn't hammering in anger. He tapped each nail carefully, deliberately, almost gently. With resignation, it seemed.

Holding the jug, she has the sudden thought that he was hammering them as though they were coffin nails.

* * *

Frances sits on Hannah's bed and knots her hands together. "Did you ever think about how much you were hurting your father?" Frances asks. "Did you ever think about that, even once?"

Frances's body seems to spread out on the mattress, in bundles, like groceries settling inside a plastic supermarket sack. The room has been stripped of Hannah's belongings, right down to the mattress ticking. They must not have expected her back.

Hannah slips a dress, the only one she brought with her, onto a wire hanger. "Everybody goes away."

"Not everybody." Her schoolteacher voice, all in her nose, rises in pitch. "The selfish ones, they take off without caring a fig about what or who they leave behind."

You don't have to be a genius to know Frances is talking about Hannah's mother as well as Hannah. The funny part is that if Marilla hadn't left, those many years ago, Frances wouldn't be here. But Frances has learned her husband's lines so well, on almost every subject, she now knows them better than he does.

"You have to go if you want a better life for yourself." To defend herself, Hannah sees, she also has to defend Marilla. But their cases weren't at all the same.

"A better life," Frances says scornfully.

"Oh, of course I thought about my father."

Frances unclasps her hands. Her plump fingers, Hannah notices, are now mottled in this unheated room. And the thumbs are bent at odd, ugly angles. Arthritis. Hannah feels a stab of pity.

"He cried when he found you were gone, Hannah. He just broke down and wept like a baby."

"Well . . . I'm sorry."

"I don't think Lyle would want you to know that. But I'm telling you anyway.'

Hannah hangs the single dress in the closet and takes some underwear out of her overnight bag. The top bureau drawer still sticks. The newspaper that lines it is dated some three months after she left home—that must have been the point they gave up on her.

She raises the shade and looks out at the backyard. There are some cabbages in the garden plot near the tool shed, and a faded quilt sags from the wash line.

"I've always wondered why my father was content to have all his eggs in one basket."

"Eggs, Hannah?"

"Why you and he didn't have children," Hannah says, turning away from the window.

"Why, you know the reason," Frances says.

"Do I?"

The truth is, the possibility of Frances and her father having children together has never before crossed her mind. She doesn't even know why she brought it up.

Frances clasps those ugly, mottled hands. "It's your mother you should be asking that question. She could have had more, after you. She wasn't too old, the way I was. She was just too selfish, in my opinion."

Yes, her mother was selfish. But it irritates Hannah to have to agree with Frances. She goes on unpacking without saying anything more.

Sometimes tourists come into the redemption center with their empty bottles and want to know where the name Monkey Bay came from. Probably they imagine monkeys down by the water swinging through the spruce and birch.

But Monkey wasn't an animal. He owned a big boat, fished

for cod out beyond Great Wass Island, built a house back of where Clarence Elvin's trailer is now. The house burned down around the turn of the century, but if you know where to look, you can find the stone foundation in the woods, all overgrown with lilac suckers. Monkey was supposed to have been a hunchback, and he had two wives, and God knows how many children. A lot of his descendants, Gibbens and Elvins, still live around here.

One night Monkey got himself shot. A story you hear is that he was smuggling spirits in that big boat of his—the state was dry back then—and one of his henchmen had some private bone to pick. Another story is that it was over a woman, and her husband was the man who shot him. Anyway, the clam diggers found him on the beach in the morning, dead as a herring, and for reasons of their own didn't want the law poking around, so they buried him in the woods and didn't say any more about it. His widow must have been just as glad to forget the whole thing. But Monkey's name stuck to the spot where he was killed, like it or not.

Marilla doesn't tell all that to the tourists. She lets them think whatever they want.

October

Marilla was married to Lyle Pratt for seventeen years, and she still carries his name around with her. There are Pratts all over Washington County. There used to be several families of Pratts on Seal Neck Road, and another lot across town on the Flag Road, and yet another lot—boat builders—up the river in Dudbridge. There'd always be a Pratt on the Board of Assessors. But for some reason they seem to be dying out. Lyle had sisters, and most of his cousins were girls, too. Lyle and Marilla had no son. His present marriage is childless.

Lyle got his job in the only insurance agency in town, after he graduated from business college, because he was a Pratt, but that didn't mean they had to pay him anything to speak of. Marilla didn't know what he did in that office all day long, but it probably wasn't worth being paid much for. After a few years they built a particle-board partition around his desk and gave him his own telephone extension. Then the year Hannah was born he had to study and take some kind of test up to Machias so he'd be qualified to stamp documents. The first time he took the test he failed it. Marilla thought he was going to have a breakdown he was so humiliated. The next time he took it he passed.

Up to the time Hannah was born Marilla worked at seasonal things, raking blueberries and making balsam wreaths. That's how they lived, really.

It has been ten years since Marilla's been Lyle's wife, but she sees him just about every week of her life. Not to talk to—they just pass in the post office and she gets a whiff of his Brylcreem. It would be more often if he didn't send his wife to the redemption center with his empties instead of bringing them in himself.

It was terrible when she left him. He said he was going to take his father's rifle into the woods and kill himself. In town, people thought he looked deranged. Marilla's friend Mittie saw him buying Trojans in the drugstore. He wasn't making any secret out of the girl he'd found at the checkout counter in the Shop'n Save, everybody knew about her. Anything female would do, apparently. He was too stubborn to drive to Ellsworth or Machias to get his rubbers, figured if people wanted to blame somebody, they could blame Marilla. It was only just, after all. She felt miserable for Hannah's sake, but there wasn't anything she could do for her.

Lyle wasn't a bad man at all. Everything that happened she brought down on her own head by marrying him in the first place. Why did she do it? He wanted her so much, and she didn't have the heart to say no.

Every year in October, the anniversary of the founding of Flowers Insurance, the company takes out a full-page ad in the Machias weekly that features photos of each member of the firm—all five of them, from Billy Flowers, the president, down to the high-school girl who comes in on Saturdays to file and run the copy machine. The secretary, who owns a Polaroid camera, personally takes all five photos, including her own, since the camera has a timer.

Although only his face will be in the photograph, Lyle

straightens the print of a rock washed by waves that hangs on his particle-board wall. He shifts the forms and letters and documents on his desk into neater piles and puts on his suit jacket.

He hears the camera going off on the other side of the partition and Billy and Roz, the secretary, ragging each other, kidding around. Suddenly she's inside his cubicle and her sharp perfume stings his nasal passages. His facial muscles constrict as she manipulates the big black contraption, getting ready to point it at him. "Say cheese," she yells, and he feels the way he does when a client is hovering over his desk, waiting for him to unsnarl some especially knotty claim, and his brain fails to operate, just plain shuts down.

He is aware that his lower jaw is jerking into a maniacal grin, like a skeleton's. He can't sit still for the click, but instead gives a sudden involuntary twitch that sends his eyes popping and his teeth clacking together. Roz is evidently too busy with her equipment to notice, and when the ad comes out Frances will say it's the flashbulb and the terrible quality of the newspaper reproduction. But he imagines Marilla idly leafing through the newspaper, coming upon that image of him, knowing the truth about him without even having to study it, turning the page.

One year a midget came to visit his class at school. He did a comic dance with a stuffed parrot for a prop and led the class in singing "Our Boys Will Shine Tonight." At the end of his act the midget asked the second-graders who had a birthday in March. Lyle raised his hand, and because his birthday was closest to the midget's, the midget presented Lyle with an autographed photo of himself. It was black and white, the size of a Get Out of Jail card, and showed the midget full-length. His second-grade teacher, he hopes she's rotting in hell, checked in her record book and bellowed, "Oh, Lyle, your birthday isn't in March at all. It's in May."

The midget gave Lyle a kindly smile—poor pea brain, seven years old and taller than I am and doesn't even know when his birthday is—and said it was all right, Lyle could keep the picture anyway. He autographed another snapshot for Aileen Franey, born in February, who was rightfully entitled to it.

Lyle brought the photo of the midget home to show his mother and father. He told them the midget had given it to him because they had the same birth month, May. He kept it for years, and every time he looked at that stumpy song-and-dance man he felt again the humiliation. So he was prepared when he found out that Marilla was screwing Tucker Burchard. The midget had prepared him.

In spite of living a decent life, Lyle suspects that somehow he is an impostor. He thinks his unholy dread of the camera has something to do with this, but he's not sure what.

The girl was twelve when Marilla left Lyle and went to live with Tucker in the shell of a house he was building on Monkey Bay—a bad age for a girl to be without a mother. Marilla knew that, but she had to go.

During those terrible days when she was making up her mind Lyle talked about what he called "home truths." There really was such a thing as honor. Sin was not something vague out of the Bible but as real as a poison mushroom and could make you just as sick. Or kill you, he said.

Even though she'd sinned with Tucker Burchard, if she'd stay Lyle would find it in his heart to forgive her.

He actually used those words, "find it in my heart." They nearly drove her wild. She wished his fat, pale, pulpy heart would shrivel into a pebble. She wished he'd choke on his own sanctimonious words and fall over dead.

No, she said quietly, she didn't want to be forgiven. Yes,

she'd gone to bed with Tucker—more than once, lots of times—and she'd lied about it. Not to save her own skin, but to spare Lyle's feelings. Too bad he'd found out. But there they all were, and she wasn't going to ask Lyle's forgiveness.

He ranted some more about honor. He used the word so many times that later on in the summer, when she knew how much Hannah was grieving, she was able to turn the word back on Lyle and make him give Hannah the choice, which parent to live with.

Marilla used the pay phone outside Mawhinney's Exxon to call the house on Poplar Street. No, Hannah said, she'd rather stay with her father. Her voice was faint, as though she didn't want to come close enough to the phone to touch it.

"Are you sure?" Marilla asked. From the pay phone she was watching a truck on a hydraulic lift being lowered slowly, painfully, to ground level. One side of the truck was bashed in.

"That's not my home, where you are," Hannah said.

Marilla didn't blame her, but it was hard. The worst of it was that she couldn't get Tucker to understand how she felt.

Tucker's crop lies on the plywood kitchen floor, neatly stacked so that the tips are all together at one end and the roots together at the other. They remind him of the chickens he and Marilla used to raise for their eggs. In early winter when the old hens had quit laying he'd wring their necks and stack them the same way. Then Marilla would pluck and clean and boil the bodies and can the cooked meat. Nothing makes a better chicken pie than a tired old layer. However, he's just as glad they don't raise the birds anymore. Smelly, brainless creatures drawing rats and weasels and other vermin.

Tucker can tell that Marilla is excited about something, the way the color rises in her cheeks and her eyes take on a watery, glazed sort of look as if she has a high fever. She's always expressed emotion that way, ever since he first knew her. But there's no point in trying to coax whatever it is out of her. One thing he admires about Marilla is her private nature. He hates women who can't help spilling their guts all over everything and everyone.

He's separating the plants into males and females. The tops of the females are the best grade. While he works he watches Marilla out of the corner of his eye. She's peeling vegetables at the sink. Her shoulders are rounded and her waist is a little thicker than ten years ago. Strands of gray in her dark hair now, too. It's not in its usual knot but hanging carelessly down her back, a rubber band around it just at the top knob of her spine. Tucker can actually feel that knob under his hand. He knows her body so well, but not always what's in her head. That's okay with him.

He goes to the drawer for a knife to cut the tops off the stack of females. As he stands beside her she sighs, almost soundlessly, and drops the peeler with a clatter into the sink.

Women have secrets. They eat chocolates when you're out of the house, and when you come in unexpectedly, they shove the candy box into a dresser drawer. They have little caches of money. When they bleed they wrap the evidence in newspaper. Sometimes they hang up the phone in a hurry when they hear your footsteps. They flush babies down toilets.

Lyle trusted Marilla, he thought she wasn't like the rest of them, but it turned out she was.

Now Lyle is wary. Especially of Hannah, who has been away for three years, who has lived six or seven different places and has probably slept with more than one man. Lyle can tell by the easy way she sits on one end of the sofa, her knees close to her chin, painting her toenails. Her dark brush of hair falls down over her face. A hundred things have happened to her, but she says nothing. It's like she's wrapped them up in newspaper, all those bloody pieces of evidence, but has not discarded them.

He should have had sons. Everything would have been easier if he'd had sons.

Marilla was fourteen when she started going out with Lyle. He'd just graduated from high school and wasn't doing much that summer. First of all his father died, and then the rest of the family was arguing over whether to send him to business college in the fall. He was waiting for them to make up their minds.

He picked Marilla out from among the younger girls. She guessed he noticed her because she was so tall she stood out from the rest and because she had a bosom. He took her to a carry-out place in Unityville and bought her a fried haddock sandwich. Then he drove to a spot he knew about, but it took him a long time to find it, a trail off in the woods leading to somebody's hunting camp. It was dark and foggy, no moon. She could smell something musty, like toadstools, and whatever it was he put on his hair then. He said, "Marilla, please let me, please let me . . ." but he didn't say what he wanted her to let him do, and she didn't say yes or no. She didn't say anything at all. Finally he struck a match to light a cigarette, and she could see how the flame trembled. It surprised her that he should be scared of her. He turned on the car radio to a country-and-western station and finished the cigarette and then drove her home.

She thought that would be the end of it right there, but no. Every Saturday night he'd treat her to a fish sandwich and then they'd go to that same camp road and he'd listen to country-and-western and smoke a cigarette. One night he brought along two cans of beer. Marilla drank the one he gave her and it went right to her head, but still nothing happened. He must have expected her to start things off, figuring that because she had big bones and big breasts she'd automatically know what to do. And he couldn't understand why she wouldn't go ahead and do it.

"Hannah's back," she says to Tucker. He's stripping leaves off stalks, and the kitchen is filled with their smell of wet straw and cat pee.

"Did she call you?"

She sets a bowl on the zinc tabletop. There's a chip on the rim of the bowl. "Mittie called me. She saw her in town."

He doesn't say anything. Does he know how much she's been willing to bear on his account? They've never talked about it, and she guesses it's too late to begin now.

Her father has changed in the three years she's been gone. He's shrunk. Not in size, exactly, but in his sense of himself. Or become frozen or mummified, to the point that he has difficulty opening his mouth wide enough to speak clearly. As if his face might actually crack if he raised his voice. And when he laughs it seems to Hannah like a false laugh, without any mirth behind it.

She pretends he's the same. And maybe he is; maybe she just never looked at him with any care before. But he says, "I'm old, Hannah. My life's nearly over, and what have I done with it?" Does he want her to agree with him and sympathize, or to argue? *Of course your life's not over, and you've done lots of things. . . .* She can't make herself do either, and so in a way she's as lockjawed as he is. It's Frances who does all the talking.

Hannah wonders whether her mother foresaw the way he'd turn out—not only pitiable but asking for pity—and that's why she ran off when she had the chance. Or would he be different if she'd stayed?

Standing at the window in her room, Hannah remembers how he got down on his knees in the mud and systematically pulled out Marilla's tulips by their stalks. As though he could root her out of their lives that way. And not long afterward, that same summer, he was fucking that awful woman on the Gilley Road.

Over and over he said to Hannah, "Think of your mother as dead."

When he wasn't looking, she gathered up the tulip bulbs into a paper bag and got on her bicycle to take them to the half-built shack on Monkey Bay. But when she got there, she saw her mother's lover nailing shingles onto the roof. He stared at her, without knowing who she was, Hannah was sure, but not smiling. His face was in shadow, and there was something menacing in the way he crouched there, holding the hammer, staring at her. Maybe he guessed. She turned and left and dumped the bulbs into a swampy place by the side of the road.

Marilla was on Gaspar Pier jigging mackerel. Tucker came in a blue punt. "Want to go for a ride?" he asked, even though he'd never said a word to her before in his life. She left her rod on the pier with the Christmas-tree hooks still tied to the end of the line and climbed down into the boat.

He rowed to an island far out in Bucks Bay where there were cranberries. They looked ripe on top, where the sun had touched them, but they were pale yellow underneath. She was fourteen, and so was Tucker.

Somebody swiped the rod, and when she got home without it, she had to tell her mother that so many mackerel jumped on the hooks all at once that the rod flipped out of her hand

and was now in the bottom of Bucks Bay. Her mother pursed her lips but had to believe her. Marilla wasn't one to lie. It was Rolf's rod. Luckily he'd already gone into the service.

Years later, after they were living together, Tucker said offhandedly how surprised he'd been that she was a virgin. "I knew you were young," he said, "younger than you looked, but I'd seen you around with Lyle Pratt. I assumed you were putting out for him."

"Were you sorry?" Marilla asked him.

"Sorry? Why sorry?"

"Because you might feel more responsible for me, then."

"No, I never thought I was responsible for you, Marilla."

"When I was getting ready to leave Lyle, he said, well, at least we were the first for each other, at least he had that and I could never take it away from him."

"Did you tell him the truth?"

"I didn't have the heart."

Tucker howled at that.

Hannah comes in with a grocery bag full of empties. Her dark hair is fixed in a new way, Marilla sees, cut short and brushed to one side. It makes her jaw look even squarer, that jaw she got not from Lyle but from Lyle's side of the family. A tax assessor's jaw.

"Are you surprised to see me?"

"I heard you were back." Marilla looks inside the bag because she doesn't want to seem to be giving Hannah the once-over. "Have you counted these?"

"Counted them? No."

Marilla takes the cans out of the bag in twos: Bud, Sprite, Diet Pepsi. "Somebody told me you were out west. Seattle?"

"For a while."

Hannah tugs at a pair of unlined leather gloves. They can't have any warmth to them, Marilla thinks.

"I bounced around quite a bit."

"Ninety-five cents." Marilla puts the coins on the makeshift wooden counter so that Hannah won't have to touch her.

She scoops the coins into her purse. "Thanks."

"Frances send you here with the empties, did she?" Marilla asks, wondering what mischief Frances could have had in mind.

"I knew you were here," Hannah says. She's examining a poster taped to the rough plank wall. It shows a girl with pigtails holding a soft-drink can and balancing on a skateboard.

"Oh."

"The other day I was driving past and I saw you outside. You were talking to a truck driver. He was leaning out of his cab. You weren't wearing a sweater or a jacket, and it was pretty cold that day, so I figured you must work here."

"Mittie Labbett got me the job. You remember her."

"Sure."

"The drivers pick up the empties and take them back to the different companies. The Dr Pepper driver takes the Dr Pepper cans to the Dr Pepper plant and . . ." Hannah's rattling her car keys. "I guess they grind up the metal and make more cans."

"You don't have to explain."

"Are you back for good? Or is this just a visit?"

"I don't know yet."

Out of habit Marilla collapses the grocery bag, folds it, smooths out the wrinkles. She leaves it on the counter where Hannah can pick it up. "Sometimes I worried about you."

"Did you?" Hannah shrugs. "That wasn't necessary." She walks away past the rack of video boxes, leaving the folded bag behind.

A man Tucker knew when he lived in Boston shows up out of the blue. He brings a bottle of rum with him, and he and

Tucker sit up drinking it most of the night. He's a Canadian by birth, and that's where he's headed, but he doesn't seem in much hurry to get there.

During the nineteen years Tucker was gone he installed central vacuuming systems, glued wigs on dolls in a doll factory, sold tickets in a roller-skating rink, delivered corsages and sprays for a florist, and probably did a lot of other things Marilla hasn't heard about yet.

"How were those jobs any better than canning sardines?" she once asked him. At times she can't help resenting those years he was gone and the mess she made of things on account of it.

"When you work in a cannery you can't ever get the fish stink out of you," he said.

Plenty of people who work in the sardine factory walk around town without cats following them, but no use saying that.

The Canadian sleeps on the folding bed in the lean-to that will someday be the laundry room if Tucker ever puts the plumbing in for the washer.

When she and Mittie drive to Mull Harbor with the laundry on Sunday morning they see snowflakes mixed in with the rain. Not even the middle of October yet. Going to be a hard winter, maybe.

Mittie comes by with half a squash casserole. Her husband Harold wouldn't eat it, and she thought Tucker might.

"Tucker's gone to Montreal."

"What? You didn't tell me he was going to Montreal."

"It was a spur-of-the-moment decision."

Mittie shoves the cat off a chair and sits down at the kitchen table. It's an old pine table that somebody nailed a sheet of zinc to when the boards began to warp and crack. "I wish Harold would go to Montreal. That lump of lard never goes anywhere."

Marilla switches on the electric ring under the coffee pot.

"Serve him right if I went someplace myself and left him behind, left him right in the lurch. For good."

The kitchen is quiet, except for the oozing and shifting of logs in the wood stove. Mittie, realizing that what she's said has cut too close to the bone, says quickly, "He wouldn't eat it because it has nuts in it. How does Tucker feel about nuts?"

"It's seeds that bother him. Like in huckleberry jam, you know—they stick between his teeth."

The cat, Mackerel, is scratching at something in the mud room; she's probably seen a spider run under a boot. Suddenly Mittie says, "Remember when the kids gave Harold and me the silver anniversary party in the Veterans Hall? A mountain of tinny silver-plate ashtrays and coasters and a cake that said 'Congratulations Harold and Mittie,' like we'd survived something."

"You had."

"Damn right. Now every year I get even more credit for having lived with Harold so long. It wouldn't be worth it to leave him now."

Tucker once said that Mittie reminded him of a ferret. It made Marilla angry at the time, but she knew what he meant. She has a small face and sharp-looking teeth, and she speaks fast, and intently, the way a ferret moves in its cage.

"Even if some man was begging me to, which they aren't."

"If you're talking about Tucker, he didn't beg."

"Well, I wasn't—but since you brought him up, I might as well admit I always knew how you felt about him," Mittie says, spooning sugar into her coffee. "Right from the beginning. When he came back it was like somebody'd handed you the one thing in the world you wanted. You'd have to be awful numb not to grab it and run, wouldn't you?"

Marilla's hardly listening. She's thinking about Hannah, and how she looked when Marilla told her. They were at supper, and the girl set her jaw and picked up her plate with the food half-eaten, put it in the sink, and went to her room. If Marilla could go back to just before that moment, would she?

"That's why," Mittie goes on, "I stayed your friend when everyone else in town dropped you flat. I knew I'd have done the same thing you did."

They stare at the squash casserole between them on the table. Beads of water have collected under the plastic wrap, making the surface look pocked, like the moon.

"But it's too late now, of course. For me, I mean."

"My mother used to say, what's done is done. She said that the day I married Lyle. But it isn't true, really. I feel like I'm still marrying Lyle, still leaving Lyle, still longing for Tucker, still . . . Nothing's ever done."

"Until the grave. And even then . . ."

"I saw Hannah. At the redemption center."

"What did she have to say for herself?"

"She still hates me, Mittie."

"Don't tell me she came right out and said that."

"No. But I knew."

Tucker and Marilla slept together for three summers, and nobody ever knew, not even Mittie—never mind what she says now. All that time Marilla was also going out with Lyle. He'd try to put his hands on her and she'd calmly shrug him off, like you do a cat that wants to climb into your lap but you're about to start supper so you don't let the cat settle. Now it seems strange to her, but at the time it didn't. It was as though there were two different Marillas, and what one did had nothing to do with what the other one did.

Tucker and Marilla made love in boats, in the woods, in

sheds and barns, once in the weeds behind the state liquor store, right in town. Nobody saw them or talked about them, and she never got pregnant, although they didn't use anything. Could she have dreamed it?

In the long winters she used to think maybe it *was* all a dream. Of course Tucker never wrote to her or came down from Lubec to see her. He wasn't the type to write letters, and he was too young to have a driver's license, or when he was old enough he didn't have a car, and there wasn't any bus.

And in the meantime Lyle was going to business college, commuting back and forth to Bangor, and trying to get his hands on her. Marilla's mother said he'd never marry her, she might as well put that idea right out of her head. It was the last thing Marilla wanted, but she couldn't convince her, even though the fact was that Louise Geary never cared much for Lyle. She didn't say why, and Marilla didn't ask. At times Marilla wonders if her mother would like Tucker any better.

In a way Marilla lived for the summers, when Tucker would come back, but in another way the winters were what was real—shivering in the cold, pulling on galoshes, figuring out algebra problems, shoveling snow, peeling potatoes. In warm weather she was detached from those things, floating almost.

Then, the summer after she graduated, Tucker didn't come back. Every day she told herself, He's just coming a little later, that's all. But Tucker had graduated from high school, too, and he wasn't about to hang around Lubec any longer than he had to, so without telling anybody where he was going, he hit the road. In Machias he hitched a ride on a Pine Tree Paper Products truck that brought him right around the bend at Trumble's, half a mile from Marilla's house and a few feet from his grandmother's, heading west. It was half past eleven at night, and neither Marilla nor Mrs. Retter had any idea. So even if Marilla had been able to work up the courage to ask the old lady about him, she wouldn't have been able to tell her.

The truck let him off in Boston, where he found the job in the flower shop. On the floor of the loft, before they had any kind of bed except for a pile of quilts and coats, he told Marilla about delivering sprays to funeral homes, and a brawl in Fenway Park, and the ride on the truck full of paper towels. They were stories, strung-out jokes. He never spoke of the women he knew in Boston, then or later.

Of course he had women in Boston. One time he looked at Marilla suddenly and asked, "Why do you scrape your hair back that way?"

She was holding something level so he could drill a hole in it in the right place, and she said, "I've always done it that way. Remember?"

He grunted, maybe only with the effort of turning the drill handle, and that's all there was to the conversation. But at that moment she knew that somewhere in the Boston area was a woman who didn't scrape her hair back. Fluffy-haired. Small-boned, like a field mouse or a vole.

She didn't try to change anything about the way she looked. In his own way Lyle's stubborn; Tucker's stubborn; and Marilla is, too.

Before she goes up to the loft to sleep Marilla calls in Mackerel to keep her company. While she's waiting for the cat to come out of the woods she stands on the stoop and looks up at the Milky Way. Suddenly one of the stars comes unhitched from its place and begins to skid westward. Then she realizes it's a plane, so high it's hardly bigger than a star.

She doesn't sleep well when Tucker's gone. She's never lived alone in her life, and she's not used to it. Went from her mother's house to Lyle's and from Lyle's directly to Tucker's.

The house makes all kinds of peculiar noises at night.

Tucker pieced it together out of odds and ends he'd swapped for, or swiped from abandoned buildings and construction sites, or haggled out of a wrecker. So there are plenty of corners that don't fit together very well. Not that they have many drafts—Marilla stuffed in great wads of pink insulation as Tucker was building—but the house settles unevenly or something. Especially up in the loft she can hear cracks and pops, sometimes as loud as a gunshot.

When Tucker was building the house Marilla asked him why he didn't build it from a plan like everybody else, with regular materials from a lumber store. She'd be happy to pay for it. It would be so much easier. He looked at her as if she was a lunatic, so after that she kept her mouth shut.

The hard freeze killed all the potato tops. Time, Marilla thinks, to dig them up and store them in the cellar.

Her father's hair was thinning, even then. He put something on it, something out of a tube. It smelled like parsnips. He bought a new suit, a summer suit, baby-blue striped gabardine. The trouser legs were too long and he asked whether she could shorten them. He stood in the doorway of Hannah's room, holding the trousers, and asked if Hannah knew how to do it. No, she said. His mouth trembled, but she turned her head away.

He wore the suit like that, bunched up on his shoes. She wondered if he knew how ridiculous he looked. She wondered if he knew and was doing it on purpose to make people feel sorry for him. To make Hannah feel sorry for him.

She saw the box of Trojans on a shelf in the bathroom, between the dish with his shaving soap on it and his razor. At least he could hide them, she thought. At least he could keep them in his own room. Sometimes he walked through the house in his underwear. There were thick pads of fat above his hips that pressed upward into his back. He almost had breasts. His boxer shorts lumped in front, like he had a potato in there. He must not have understood how repelled she was. Or else he felt she had no right to be repelled—he was her father, he owned this house, he could go to the refrigerator for a glass of milk in his underwear if he wanted to.

She did feel sorry for him, she couldn't help it. Once she woke up in the night and heard him sobbing, gasping to catch his breath.

He brought two lock kits home from Trumble's. He ripped out the old locks and installed a new one on the front door, a new one on the kitchen door. They were a special extra-secure kind that you needed a key to work on the inside as well as the outside. Before, they'd never even bothered to use the old locks. Now she was supposed to keep the house locked all the time. He threaded a string through the kitchen key and hung it around her neck. It was to keep her mother out, he told her. If her mother came to the door she was to say that she wasn't allowed in the house. She was to telephone her father at the office and he'd call the state police and have her arrested for trespassing or harassment. Her mother didn't come, though.

They were having noodle soup for supper the night Marilla told her. She'd put lettuce thinnings in it, and the noodles were like worms swimming around in algae, in a swamp. Hannah couldn't eat it. She got up from the table and put her bowl in the sink, still nearly full of the awful soup. When she got home from school the next day Marilla was gone. She'd left a letter, but her father wouldn't let her read it. He held a match to the corner of the envelope and dropped it into the toilet when it flared, and she heard it hiss, hitting the water. He flushed the toilet. She hadn't wanted to read it, anyway.

Over the soup Marilla explained she had to leave because Lyle was making her life impossible, and her father said that wasn't true, she'd made life impossible for herself, and now she was going to have to lie in the bed she'd made. Hannah didn't understand at first that her mother had a lover, but when he said "bed" that way, she was on the edge of guessing. Mittie Labbett phoned one afternoon and told her where her mother was. How to get there, in case she ever wanted to know. She said Marilla was staying with somebody she'd known for a long time, ever since she was only a little older than Hannah. "A man?" Hannah asked, and when Mittie said yes, then she knew.

At night, hearing the scrape of the key in the locks, she felt uneasy. She felt like they kept her in more than they kept her mother out. But she knew that wasn't what her father intended. None of this was his fault.

The swamp maples are bright red now. They're so red they look artificial, Tucker thinks, like something plastic from Hinckley's variety store.

Lyle came to Monkey Bay three times that terrible summer after she left him. The first time he delivered some plants in pots. He took them from the backseat of the Malibu and set them on the pebbly driveway. A rex begonia, Marilla remembers, a spider plant, a grape ivy. "Nobody wants to water them," he told her.

Lyle looked up at the house. It was just a shell then, one room, raw beams and naked pink insulation. From inside came the sound of hammering. *Wham, wham, wham, wham.* Pause. *Wham, wham, wham, wham.* Pause.

"Hannah's not willing to water them?" Marilla asked. They looked dry all right, nearly on their last legs.

He didn't answer that. "I told Hannah she should think of you as dead," he said, his words heavy as lumps of clay. Drops of sweat were oozing from his high forehead, but his face was pale.

She gasped. "Lyle, you can't tell a child a thing like that."

He just revved up the engine of the Malibu and bounced away over the rocks and potholes.

The second time he came to ask for her wedding ring back. Maybe he thought she wouldn't be able to do it, hand it over in cold blood, maybe he thought she'd come to her senses and come back to him. But that was never a possibility. She had Tucker, she couldn't get enough of Tucker to make up for all the years without him. She went into the house and got the ring and gave it to him without blinking an eye. He looked sheepish then, but he dropped it into his pocket and took it away.

The third time he brought documents: the Malibu and the house on Poplar Street were in joint ownership, and Lyle had hired a lawyer to draw up papers for her to sign, releasing any claim to them. In return, he wouldn't sue her for abandonment.

He happened to come when the battery in the pickup was dead. From a window in the loft Marilla watched Tucker say something to Lyle, and then Tucker got the jumper cables out of the pickup and the men hitched the pickup battery to the Malibu battery. Tucker brought the papers inside, got a couple of beers out of the cooler—they didn't have electricity yet—and went back out with them. Marilla could see Lyle and Tucker walking around the chicken coop Tucker was building, beer cans in their hands. From inside, it almost looked like they were friends. She signed the copies, multiple copies, everywhere the lawyer had made a large red *X*. She didn't mind signing. She didn't want anything of Lyle's.

Marilla raised chickens for several years, until one morning she went out to feed them and found that something, a fox maybe, had killed every single one, including the evil-tempered old rooster.

"I'm going to pick up the mail," Lyle says, pulling on a rubber. It snaps against his heel. "Won't you come with me?"

Hannah takes her coat from the front closet and flings the wire hanger into a chair. It must be a new coat, or anyway, Lyle has no memory of it. The belt is made of the same material as the coat, and ties in front as a bathrobe does, but in spite of that informality, in Lyle's eyes it's a city coat. The light color, the same as Billy Flowers's Labrador, wouldn't be practical in mud season.

It's a foggy day, one of those three or four days in the year when you could swear you smell a paper mill, though the nearest one is forty-odd miles away, as the crow flies. "You'd think you were in Millinocket," Lyle remarks, as they are walking past the elementary school, but Hannah doesn't seem to catch his meaning. She turns her head and looks at the school, as though that must be what he's talking about. Although it's Saturday, a teacher is taping a paper jack-o'-lantern to the inside of one of the windows. "The smell," Lyle says. "Don't you smell it?"

The silver popple leaves are still hanging on to the branches, not ready to let go. They don't change color, they shrivel and turn dull and begin to look a little rusty. Hannah's head just reaches Lyle's shoulder. She'll never be as tall as her mother.

"I have high blood pressure," he tells her suddenly.

They turn the corner onto Cottage Street and are passing the lot where the new bank is being built before she says anything. "Is it dangerous?" she asks at last.

"Not if I take my pills. Which I do."

She thrusts her hands into her coat pockets.

Bricks for the new bank are stacked on the lot. They have steel bands around them and are partly covered by tarps. Even so, it's a wonder people don't help themselves to them in the night. Tempting, just sitting there that way.

"Trouble is, the pills take a lot out of you."

Now they are crossing Main Street; straight ahead of them is the movie house, where something called *Fatal Attraction* is playing. Before he knows what he's doing, Lyle is telling her *how* the pills take a lot out of you. They've made him lose his manhood. The look on her face is as though she's finally aware of the paper mill, and then she laughs. It's a nervous laugh, though, and she begins to walk faster. An RV pulling away from the pumps at Mawhinney's Exxon has to brake sharply to keep from running into her.

What was wrong with telling her? She's not a little kid anymore.

On account of the fog it looks as if the world ends just beyond the state liquor store. Flowers Insurance seems to have fallen off the edge. Lyle knows the tide is out, though, by the sounds of gulls shrieking over the river. He's hurrying to keep up with Hannah, who is taking the short cut to the post office behind the Busy Bee luncheonette, through a field of dead weeds. He feels a headache settling in, just as the fog has.

When he turns the key in the mailbox, he finds a Colonial Garden Kitchens catalog addressed to Frances and a reminder from his dentist that he's due to have his teeth cleaned.

"Nothing for me?" Hannah asks.

"Are you expecting something?"

"No."

Marilla has the same dream she's dreamed a hundred times. She's struggling to get a place cleaned up. All around her, people—not her family, strangers—are dumping clothes on the floor, spilling food out of containers, pulling bric-a-brac off shelves, emptying out closets and cupboards. The harder she works the worse the mess gets, because there are more of them than there is of her. She wakes up exhausted. The dream always has the same setting: the trailer she and Lyle lived in on Seal Neck Road the first seven years they were married.

In some ways the trailer is more vivid to her than the house on Poplar Street, though she lived on Poplar Street longer. In the winters there was always the smell of sex, and kerosene from the heater, and wet wool, and the musty brown couch that came out of Lyle's mother's attic, and cooking fat, and—after Hannah was born—diapers. She'd wash Hannah's diapers by hand and hang them on a plastic cord that stretched, sagging, from one end of the trailer to the other and then looped back again. The diapers picked up all those smells as they dried. Mostly kerosene.

Hannah was a good baby, not a whiner, but she had such tender skin. Her first winter she got an awful rash in her crotch. Marilla bought an ointment to put on her, but it didn't get any better. Some places the skin was rubbed raw and bleeding. Now Marilla says to herself: What was *wrong* with you, that you couldn't manage to get her to a doctor? But at the time she was too tired, or the roads were too icy, or she'd have to impose on a neighbor to take them to town, or she didn't have the six dollars for the doctor, or she thought the rash looked a little better that day.

Then a public health nurse came to the door. Just a routine visit, she said, checking up on how the baby was getting along. But nobody had come to visit Mittie's babies, and Mittie had three of them by then, so Marilla wondered what was going on. But she had to let the woman in. The nurse ducked under the wet diapers and sat on that couch that smelled of mold.

The nurse wasn't a bad person. She had a gentle, doughy

face and thin hair done up in curls, that metallic yellow that comes out of bottles, and some animal had shed on her navy-blue coat. She was kindly, and when she got an eyeful of those sores, she sucked in her breath and said, "Oh, heavens, we'll have to do something about that, won't we, dear?"

For years Marilla was sure it was Lyle's mother who had sicked the public health nurse on her, which was so unfair, because the main reason they were so poor was that Lyle was giving his mother money every month and his useless sisters weren't lifting a finger.

After they moved to Poplar Street, though, Marilla's mother revealed, with satisfaction, that she'd written an anonymous letter to some county official in Machias. She thought Hannah got colds all the time on account of them living in that trailer out in the puckerbrush, and she wanted to shame Lyle into providing better for them. It never entered her head that Marilla would be the one she'd shame, not Lyle. Of course Marilla hadn't told Lyle, or anybody else, about the public health nurse.

A call comes from the Greyhound station in Bangor, and Marilla drives there to pick Tucker up.

He's grown a mustache in Montreal, and he seems nervous, restless. His pea coat is buttoned wrong. She doesn't ask him why the plan changed, why the Canuck didn't bring him home as they agreed. Since he clearly has no money on him, she figures something must have gone wrong with the sale.

She knows he's been with a woman.

After they make love he sleeps against her, the stiff new mustache hairs in her armpit.

It rains like the devil all the next day, and a limb of the mountain ash Marilla planted the fall of the year she moved to Monkey Bay tears off in the wind. When the wind turns around to blow from the south, the old leak around the stovepipe in the big room begins again. Marilla hauls out her rag collection to wrap the pipe. She knows that's not going to fix anything, not permanently, but it's better than nothing.

He leans in the doorway, smoking, watching her.

"I talked to Hannah," she says from the stepladder.

"While I was up north?" If he's surprised, she can't tell from his voice.

"Before."

"How come you were keeping it such a deep dark secret?"

"No secret, Tucker," she says, running her hand over the damp place on the plaster. "I didn't get a chance to tell you."

"She come to the house?"

Marilla sits on the top of the stepladder and smooths the rag out across her knee. "To the store."

"I suppose she wanted to rent a video."

"I think she came to see me."

"So what did she say?"

Marilla has gone over the conversation endlessly in her head, but now, when it comes to telling Tucker the gist, she can't put her finger on it. "Not much, really. I asked her if she's back for good."

"And?"

"She hasn't made up her mind."

"Well," he says, coughing, "no point in hanging around here."

"You came back. You're here."

He walks over to the wood stove to get rid of the butt. When he opens the stove door an acrid, charred smell flies out with flakes of cold ash. He slams it shut.

"Plenty of people come back to stay," she says.

"After they've made their first million. Like me."

He's smiling. His teeth are small for his jaw. The mustache has gray in it and looks tentative and unplanned, the way a child's scribble sometimes does.

"What's she going to do," he says, "live in her old man's house and hold his hand for him?"

Marilla begins to wrap the rag around the pipe. It's part of a dress she brought with her from Lyle's house, green cotton with a narrow white stripe. Once upon a time, when she was still an honest woman, she used to wear it to church. She came to Tucker with two laundry bags of clothes, that was it—her dowry and trousseau. She was crying. Tucker looked at the bags in the back of Mittie's car and said, "A matched set of luggage, I see. I admire a woman with style." He said it to cheer her up, not to humble her. But she did feel bad he wasn't getting more of a prize.

"She might find somebody and get married," she says, tying a double knot in the rag.

Tucker laughs. "You didn't have much luck at that, did you, Marilla?"

Rain crashes on the roof, and the striped rag is damp already. "I'm not complaining," she says, and climbs down from the stepladder.

"Good-looking girl, though, that Hannah Pratt."

The berries on the black alders are bright red now. You notice them because the leaves have fallen, and only the berries are left on the branches. Another name for black alders is winterberries. If you want to cut some branches to bring into the house, you have to wear waders or clam boots, because the only place they grow is bogs.

At this time of year people decorate their porches with dummies. They stuff an old shirt and overalls with straw to make a body. The head is a jack-o'-lantern, sometimes carved out of a pumpkin, sometimes bought in the five-and-dime.

The dummy doesn't stand the way a scarecrow does but sits floppily in a porch chair or lounges on the steps.

To Marilla there's something unsettling about pumpkin men. At first glance, passing by, you might think it's a real person. But then you realize it's only a fake. And at night all you see is candlelight glowing inside the hollow head.

When she was a child, she and her big brother, Rolf, made a pumpkin dummy every year. One November her father was burning brush in a clearing near their house on the Gaspar Road. The dummy was still on the porch, but his head had rolled off his body, and his eyes and mouth were sunken in and blackened from the candle flame. She and Rolf were standing on the porch, watching the bonfire, and all of a sudden Rolf grabbed the dummy's body and dragged it over to the fire and heaved it in.

"Damn it, Rolf, what in hell do you think you're doing?"

He yelled so loud it scared them both. Marilla doesn't know whether he thought Rolf was going to hurt himself in the fire, or he was mad because the old clothes might have been saved and used the next year, or whether for an instant he thought the dummy was a real person. Marilla, maybe.

Her father had been sick a long time when that happened. Sometimes he felt well enough to get out of bed, and he'd do something around the house that needed doing. Changing the oil in the car, repairing the Mixmaster, burning brush. She was too young to know he was going to die, but she thinks Rolf understood. She thinks he was exchanging the pumpkin dummy for his father. Killing it so that somehow his father would be spared. But it didn't work out that way.

November

After Marilla left them, Lyle burned her cookbooks with some other trash. He brought home a spiral-bound cookbook put out by the elementary school booster club and began to fix things like Hong Kong burgers and quick crab quiche. By the next year, when he married Frances, the saucepans and baking dishes had grease fused onto them and their insides were scorched and pitted. Frances was a schoolteacher who hadn't been married before, and she'd cooked only for herself. Lipton's Cup-a-Soup, frozen chicken pie. She gave the old pots to the Congregational church for their rummage sale and bought new ones and took over the kitchen. It was her duty, she said. Sometimes, though, she lets Lyle cook on the weekends.

Hannah sits in the breakfast nook drinking a Diet Pepsi while her father fries up a pound of hamburg. As a treat for Hannah he's making his specialty, pizza casserole. She can feel the molecules of fat settling on her arms, although the fan over the stove whirrs away at top speed. It doesn't vent to the outside, all it does is circulate the smoke and grease through a mesh screen in the hood. Before she went away, Hannah never noticed how cramped the house is, the utensil drawers stuffed so full you have to jiggle them to get them open, the closets packed. You can't walk more than a couple of feet in a straight line or some piece of furniture will give you a kidney punch.

Hannah feels worn out. The first week she was home Frances reached over and pulled down her lower eyelid, told her her blood was low, told her to take iron pills. Well, maybe she should. She's beat. Too many apartments belonging to other people, too many jobs that weren't ever going to make her rich. "Bounced around quite a bit," she said to Marilla. For sure.

What she really wanted to say was: "The kid you left in the lurch grew up okay without you. She's been around, seen the sights. She didn't need you after all." Is that why she came back—to say those words? Then why didn't she?

"Won't you give me a hand, sweetheart?"

Hannah leaves the half-drunk Diet Pepsi on the table and picks up a vegetable knife. The onion is one of those yellow ones with a tough, tight skin. Peeling it back, she thinks about how bitter she felt when Marilla folded up the grocery bag and smiled at her. That shy, sudden, graceful smile. She took it away from them and gave it to that worm digger.

Her father is sprinkling egg noodles from the package onto a layer of hamburg. The dry noodles rattle as they fall. They hadn't deserved what she did to them, damn it. They hadn't.

•

Marilla's mother was known for her knack with hair. She was always giving somebody a Toni Home Permanent in the kitchen, the table littered with curlers and end papers, a brassy smell seeping relentlessly into the rest of the house. She'd stand at the magazine rack in the drugstore and study the hairstyles, trying to figure out how the cut was done and what size curlers they'd used. Then she'd try out those styles on her friends.

After Marilla's father died she heard about a barbershop in Machias going out of business and selling off its equipment. She moved all the furniture out of the front room and screwed one of those secondhand barber chairs onto the middle of the floor. After that her friends had to pay for their hairdos.

They wondered, those friends, why her daughter had such plain, limp hair when Louise Geary had a gift like that. Too bad the girl's so big and gawky, but at least her hair could look decent. The reason was, Marilla wouldn't let her mother near her with her lotions and potions. She knew she wasn't the type to have a crimpy head. The struggle went on for years. Finally Louise was so exasperated she said Marilla would never find a husband if she refused to submit.

Sometimes Marilla thinks that's why she married Lyle, to prove her mother wrong. To shut her up.

The chainsaw's making such a racket Tucker doesn't notice the marine patrol officer until the guy's standing practically on top of him. He's a big red-faced fellow in a bilge-brown uniform, and he's carrying a box of Christmas cards. Tucker finishes slicing through the log before he flicks the switch to off.

"Mornin'," the guy says. He looks foolish, holding the little box, and he knows it.

"Mornin'," Tucker answers, blowing sawdust off the chainsaw teeth.

"The wife in?"

"No." He doesn't take the trouble to explain that Marilla's at work over to the redemption center. Or that she isn't, in actual fact, his wife.

"She ordered these."

"That so?" Tucker smiles a little, thinking of the guy moonlighting by going from house to house peddling Christmas cards. Maybe holiday wrapping paper, too, and scented candles.

"From my daughter Cheryl. But Cheryl's got the flu."

"Has she."

"So I'm making her deliveries for her."

After a pause Tucker says, "We don't send out Christmas cards much."

The guy fumbles in the breast pocket of his uniform and pulls out a rumpled wad of order slips. They are smudged with carbon, and he has to sort through them twice before he locates the one with Marilla's name on it. "Item number X-nine-seven-three-Z. One box. There's two dollars and seventy-nine cents due on that."

Tucker, playing dumb, scratches his head and examines the order slip. Probably the guy thinks he can't read.

"I can come back another time."

"Naw, what the hell. Come on in."

As they're walking toward the house Tucker asks, "What did you say your name was?"

"Holly. Fred Holly."

"Don't recall seeing you around here before."

"I've only been on the job three months."

"Bet them clam diggers keep you hopping."

"Work the tides yourself?" he asks as Tucker ushers him in through the mud room.

"Naw. Let me get you a beer," he says, before the guy has a chance to develop an interest in what it is he does do. "Take a load off," he says, steering him to the recliner by the wood stove in the big room. He goes back to the kitchen to get a couple of beers and some money. Counting out the change from Marilla's stash in the Crisco can, he mutters, "Who you planning on sending Christmas cards to? The governor? The president?"

Still, it gives him kind of a charge to have the marine patrol officer sitting directly over his entire cash crop, which is now sealed in eighteen-dozen quart Mason jars.

"It's a regular bed of nails." Mittie's looking at the double row of nails pointing down over the couch. "Like they lie on in India."

"Except it's upside down," Marilla says. "And I don't lie on it."

"You lie on it in your head." Every time she sees the nails Mittie gets angry at Tucker all over again, for Marilla's sake.

"I've stopped seeing it, even," Marilla says, though that's not the truth.

"You know what you could do, Marilla? You could pound those nails from down here, pry them out upstairs, and replace them with carpet tacks."

"Tacks wouldn't hold. Not in those big holes."

"Fill in the holes with plastic wood. What's the matter with you, Marilla? You didn't used to be so numb."

She wouldn't be able to explain it to Mittie, but now, somehow, it seems right for those nails to be there.

Drizzle today. And a warmish, unsettling wind blowing out of the south.

It was at the house on Poplar Street. She was hanging the wash out on the line and somebody came around the corner of the house by the hydrangea bush. She thought at first he must be the man to read the electric meter, but then she saw who it was. She took the clothespin out of her mouth and stared at him as though he was a man come back from the dead, which in a way was so.

"Hello, Marilla," he said, calm as a clock.

There'd been a lot of snow the winter before and now, in early April, some patches still lay in the shade, behind the tool shed and on the boggy end of the lot where nothing would grow but moss and bunchberries. But the sun that day was warm, and she hadn't bothered with a sweater, and her arms were bare. She remembers how the wet sheet she was holding felt against her bare skin in that long moment she was looking at him.

"How did you find me?" she asked at last.

Tucker shrugged. "Simple. I figured you probably married Lyle Pratt. So I asked at Mawhinney's where Lyle's place was, and here you are."

Yes, simple. Tucker would know exactly what she'd do, and wouldn't care one way or the other.

"What do you want?" she asked, folding a corner of the sheet over the line and shoving a clothespin down over the fold. The hem of the sheet dragged on the grass, but she didn't bother about it.

"To see you. What's wrong with that?"

He was wearing a mustache in those days, too, but there wasn't any gray in it then. He didn't have a pot over his belt the way Lyle did. He had on a pigskin jacket that was worn soft, stained, as though it had been around and about for a long time.

"Do I have to tell you what's wrong with it?"

There were bits of dead grass sticking to the hem of the sheet. She left it that way, and yanked a dress shirt of Lyle's out of the heap of wet clothes, and hung it up by the tail.

"Come on, Marilla, don't be that way. We're old friends, right?"

Her throat felt so sore and choked she could hardly get the words out. "Not in my book we aren't."

"We never had a single fight."

"How can you have a fight with somebody who isn't there?"

Tucker didn't have an answer to that. He took a pack of cigarettes out of his shirt pocket and lit one. He hadn't smoked when she'd known him before.

"You look the same, Marilla."

"After nineteen years?" she said, pinching a row of Hannah's socks onto the line. "What's that supposed to be, a joke?"

"No joke." He flicked some ash into a forsythia bush, which was beginning to show signs of budding. She didn't care much about the bush, it was an overgrown and straggly thing even when she and Lyle bought the house, but she thought Tucker ought to show more respect for their property. "Well, aren't you going to say something?" he asked finally.

"Like what?"

"Like welcome home, I don't know."

She hated him then. She hated that he'd gone and done all those things, been all those places, and here she was, hanging out Lyle Pratt's underwear. She'd rather he'd been working in the cannery for nineteen years, married to her or not.

"Stony Harbor isn't your home."

"You know what I mean."

"I don't think I do, Tucker."

He tossed the butt over by the shed. "Marilla, I wrote you a letter the day I left Lubec."

"I never got a letter." The laundry basket was empty now, and she was beginning to feel chilly. She rubbed her arms.

"I know. I didn't mail it."

"You left it at a pit stop. You threw it away with your sandwich wrapper. It fell out of your pocket and blew away in the wind."

"I decided it wasn't fair."

"Fair?"

"I didn't have any idea what I was going to do, but I figured it might take a long time, whatever it was."

"And you figured I'd be better off marrying Lyle than waiting around for you."

He looked sheepish or rueful, she didn't know which.

"And what do you think now, Tucker?"

"I don't think any different."

"Well, now I understand how things are," she said, and picked up the empty basket and went into the house.

Hannah wakes to find a thin wet coat of snow stuck to everything. From her bedroom window she sees her father in the yard, making black footprints as he carries a bag of trash out to the can by the tool shed. Something about the way he walks catches her attention. It's stiff, halting, as though he's afraid of falling, the way a much older person would be. She wonders if high blood pressure would do that. Or if he might be sick in some other way, a way that pills couldn't necessarily fix.

Lyle never struck Marilla, except once.

It was the summer Tucker didn't come back but went to Boston on the paper products truck instead, and she was grieving. Lyle knew something was up with her, but of course she couldn't tell him what.

She didn't want Lyle to touch her—in fact the idea had come to disgust her—but in a kind of fog she kept going out with him. Maybe she was lonely. Or maybe she was afraid of what would happen to him if she broke it off. "You're my girl," he said. "I need you, you know that." He swore he wouldn't be able to take it if she stopped seeing him, and she believed him. She didn't want to be responsible for . . . who knows what.

He was determined, though, to get inside her. Not for the fun of it, the way it was with Tucker, but because he thought he'd own her then. He'd wheedle, and grab, and wheedle some more.

"He'll never marry you," her mother said, "when it comes down to it."

Marilla was raking blueberries that summer, making pretty good money.

"You'd better think about your future," her mother said. "Maybe I could get enough money together to send you to beauty school in Bangor."

"I don't want to go to beauty school."

"Suit yourself. I wish somebody'd offered to send me, that's all I can say. I'd have been grateful."

"I am grateful. I just don't want to go."

"Well, don't expect *him* to support you."

It was awful, she kept on seeing Lyle and saying no. In an odd way she cared about him, because he was a nice person and he felt things. She just didn't want him to touch her, that was all.

Mittie got married that fall, married Harold Labbett who worked the tides when he felt like it and drank too much and got Mittie up a stump. She put a good face on it, had a proper wedding, and Marilla was a bridesmaid.

The next month, on an October Sunday, Marilla and Lyle drove out to Oak Point. The paved road gives out before you get to the end, and the road narrows, and the trees are so close to the road that their branches get woven together overhead and block out the sun. Also, it's boggy. The road is under water in places, and you expect at any moment to break an axle or sink without trace.

But they made it all the way to the point. Lyle parked the car and they got out and sat on the pink granite boulders that are piled there. The sky was low, overcast. The tide was out, the clam flats exposed, and dead oak leaves blew all around them. The only sign that anybody was within a hundred miles of the spot was a red mooring buoy, like a beach ball, bobbing in the channel.

Lyle began to talk about how much he needed her. Some people thought she was deliberately teasing him, he said, and he couldn't understand why she'd want to do that.

"What people?" she asked.

"Just people."

"What you and I do is private, Lyle. You can tell them, whoever they are, to go screw themselves."

Maybe it was the word that unhinged him. He tried to clamp his hand on her arm, but she was wearing a baggy string cardigan and she pulled away from him, pulled herself partway out of the sleeve.

Then he began to hit her. Not slaps, more like a pounding, on her face, breasts, stomach, everywhere he could reach. She didn't try to run away: Maybe she deserved it. Or she was so sore already from longing for Tucker that it didn't make any difference how much Lyle hurt her. He was sobbing as he pounded her, using both fists, and she was crying, too. Not so much from pain as from sheer misery. Out in the channel the red buoy kept on bobbing, with each lap of the tide straining to cut loose, and each time yanked back by its rope.

Finally he stopped. She didn't have a tissue with her, so she wiped her nose on the sleeve of the string sweater. When she got home she washed the sweater out in the bathroom sink, and she and Lyle never spoke again about what had happened. It didn't solve or end anything. It was almost as though it had happened in a dream or to two other people.

Frances and her best friend, Bev, are eating sandwiches and drinking coffee in the breakfast nook. Bev is a squat woman, older than Frances, with stiff gray hair that looks as though it was styled with a meat cleaver. She's a schoolteacher—Miss

Purkis—Hannah had her in eighth grade. She kept an iguana named Larry in a tank at the back of the classroom, and the boys would torment it with pencils when Miss Purkis was at the blackboard working out fraction multiplication.

For a long time Hannah stands at the refrigerator with the door open, gazing at packets of luncheon meat and individually wrapped cheese slices. Finally she takes out a can of diet soda and shuts the door.

"Aren't you going to eat?" Frances asks Hannah, rolling her eyes at Bev.

"I'm eating out," she says, though the idea has only popped into her head this minute.

"Out?"

"With a friend."

Frances puts down her sandwich. "What friend?"

"Tina Franey," Hannah says, thinking quickly. From the sidewalk she's seen Tina inside Hinckley's variety store, working at the checkout counter. Maybe she *could* have lunch with Tina. Invite her out to the Busy Bee or the Brass Lantern. Tina would know all the dirt about her old high-school classmates.

"She isn't Tina Franey anymore," Bev says. "She married that fella works over to Mawhinney's pumping gas, one of Chubby Maddock's boys, the one with the warts. Worst case of warts I ever saw."

"That boy's not a Maddock," Frances says, "he's an Oxberry. I had him the year I was in charge of the Christmas play and he fell off the stage and broke his leg and had to be in a cast for six weeks."

"That wasn't an Oxberry fell off the stage, it was a Pilcher, and *I* produced the Christmas play that year," Bev says.

Hannah leaves them arguing over the Christmas play and slips out the back door. It's a bright day, chilly, with the sky so luminous it's like the inside of a delphinium-blue bowl.

Hannah feels sprung, free. She smells wood smoke, a smell she realizes she missed in Boston, without knowing she was missing it.

She wonders whether Tina really did marry the boy with the worst case of warts in the world, Tina who was going to be a famous country-and-western singer and even did sing with a group at the Longhorn in Ellsworth while she was still in high school. Hannah and some other classmates drove to Ellsworth to hear her one night. Tina wore a white spangled cowboy shirt and strummed a guitar and sang in a nasal, sexy, overripe way that was astonishingly different from her speaking voice. When she came over to their table after the set, Hannah noticed that one of the pearl buttons was missing from the spangly shirt; Tina had pinned the shirt together from the inside with a safety pin. Hannah hated herself for noticing things like that, because they spoiled everything, but she couldn't help it. Even with a group of friends she was always really on the outside, watching.

By the time Hannah reaches Hinckley's, she suspects it would be a mistake to have lunch with Tina Franey or Tina Maddock or whoever she is now. It would be more of the same, only worse—noting Tina's varicose veins or shabby coat or missing back tooth. She's relieved when she looks in the window and sees that the person at the checkout counter is a man, Mr. Hinckley himself.

But she can't go home yet, to be cross-examined by Frances and Bev. She wanders along Main Street, idly looking at blouses in Blodgett's window and fishing tackle next door in Stout's. At the bakery she buys a doughnut and eats it in front of Mawhinney's, watching Tina's husband pump gas. She wonders if there are warts under his coveralls. She wonders what it would be like to go to bed with him and feel the tough little nubs everywhere.

Around the corner from Mawhinney's, on Water Street, is

Flowers Insurance, where her father has worked for more than a quarter of a century. The office occupies the ground floor of a frame house, between the state liquor store and the marshy west bank of the Burnt Mill River. Both establishments are gray clapboard and could stand a coat of paint.

She finds her father in his airless cell, distractedly kneading his thighs with his palms as he stares at a four-page stapled report. Billy pokes his head in and says with a grin, "No babies yet, Hannah?"

"I wonder if I'll live to see them," Lyle mutters.

When Hannah was newborn Marilla began taking pictures of her with the Brownie Hawkeye she'd had since high school. Stark naked on the rickety card table, dressed up in an organdy dress Louise bought her and propped up between pillows on the couch, outside in her carriage, her head lolling to one side and sun in her eyes. When the Brownie died Marilla bought an Instamatic. She kept the photos in a shoebox, hundreds of them, all of Hannah.

When she left Lyle she had to leave the shoebox.

"Go ask him for them," Mittie said. "He has Hannah. The least he can do is let you have the pictures."

She went into the insurance office and asked.

"They are family records," Lyle said, "and you are no longer part of the family."

"March right over to the house and take them," Mittie said. "He'll never notice the difference."

"He told me he had the locks changed. After I left."

"The bastard," Mittie said, outraged.

"I'd have done the same," Marilla said.

"No you wouldn't, either."

Today in her mailbox Marilla finds a brown envelope with a return address in Boca Raton, Florida. Inside are some snapshots with bent corners, unsorted, all of Hannah. They are from Marilla's cousin Nancy. When Hannah was little Marilla sent the photos to her mother's sister every Christmas, and now her aunt has died and this is her inheritance.

There's Hannah, four years old, bundled up in a snowsuit that is too big for her. The day is so blustery she's leaning at an angle, and snow is whirling all around her, but she's grinning at the person holding the camera. She was a spunky kid.

December

When there's ice on the bay and the ice is covered with snow, you're not aware of the action of the tide moving underneath. From the shore the bay is grayish, blurred by mist, tranquil, dull. It might as well be a field under snow. When that happens, Tucker begins to feel closed in. He's not sure what he's doing here.

Returning to this place was nothing but a fluke, anyway. He happened to run into a Lubec girl in Park Street Under. Funny him turning up that way, she said, because just the week before she'd seen his name in the legal-notice column of the hometown paper her mother gave her the subscription to. She thought he'd inherited some money, or something like that. When he wrote he learned it was sixty-five hundred dollars after taxes, his share of his grandmother Retter's estate. Well, he wasn't especially sorry his grandmother was dead. She'd lived a long life, and besides, he didn't agree with most of the opinions she'd held when he was alive.

Still, he had a sense that the money ought not to be simply frittered away. It had been earned in Stony Harbor, earned the hard way, and it should stay there. So without thinking much about the consequences—that it would root him here—he exchanged the money for the piece of land on Monkey Bay. And then, because he needed a place to stay, he started to build the shack out of scrounged lumber. But first he had the cellar hole dug. So he must have known, somewhere inside him, that the shack was really a house.

He hired the backhoe for the cellar hole before he went looking for Marilla. He never doubted he'd find her, and at the same time he never imagined she'd be free just to walk away from whatever life she'd been living. When he saw her hanging out clothes in that cramped little yard, out by the school, it seemed to fit exactly some image he'd had. And yet he can't remember having thought of her much at all, those years he was away. It wasn't even true, what he told her, about writing a letter and not sending it. Maybe he thought of writing—he can't be certain now—but for sure he never did it. He probably hasn't written more than half a dozen letters in his whole life.

He found her in Lyle Pratt's backyard and he knew, without her having to say so, that she still felt the same way about him. He knew on account of how angry she was. And that scared him, made him want to back off. He wasn't afraid of her anger, of being hurt by it, but of her love, and how that might hurt him.

He tried to leave her alone, but he couldn't. For some reason, when he was sawing endless planks and nailing them together with an endless number of nails, he kept thinking about how she still hadn't learned to pluck the hairs between her eyebrows, and that damn near drove him nuts. He thought, if only that place between her brows was smooth, he'd be able to walk away from her, whistling.

Now, when the bay freezes over, he almost wishes he had.

Frances and her girlfriend Bev had it all planned. Together they purchased a condominium in a retirement village in

North Carolina, and the minute Bev hit sixty-two they would leave the ice and snow forever. Frances would take early retirement. In the meantime, the condominium corporation was renting out their unit for them, and that way it cost them only a small fee each month to have their futures settled and secure.

Frances was forty-three when she and Bev made their pact. A little young to be thinking about retirement, maybe, but she'd been teaching seventh grade ever since she was twenty, and the truth was, she was tired of it. Eleven years to go, and she and Bev, who taught eighth grade, were counting off the minutes.

And then one fall afternoon she was leaving the school late because she'd been preparing an experiment on photosynthesis, divvying out the bean seeds, and her car refused to start, and Lyle Pratt happened to be passing the parking lot on his way home from the insurance office. She knew him, because she'd had Hannah in her class the year before. And of course she'd heard all about the scandal of his wife leaving him and going to live with that scalawag without benefit of clergy. One thing led to another, and after he got Frances's car started, he invited her out for a meal.

In the teachers' lounge and at the Busy Bee lunch counter the girls thought her lucky. As though landing a husband at her age was like winning the lottery.

But it wasn't like that. She didn't tell anybody, not even Bev, but she wasn't sure it was luck at all, or at least not good luck. She had an uneasy feeling about Lyle. He was a good man, respectable, with a year-round permanent job, and not too bad looking. Not even forty yet. But a man that another woman leaves, there's something tainted or spoiled about him. Like a carton you see in Zayre's that's been ripped open and taped back together—well, you know somebody's returned it, and you feel nervous about paying full price for it yourself. Even though there's probably nothing defective about it, it's just that the cassette player or whatever didn't suit the previous owner for some reason.

Frances wasn't desperate for a man or anything like that. In fact, Bev is a better friend to her than Lyle will ever be. If she and Bev could have gone off to North Carolina right then, she probably wouldn't have given Lyle Pratt another thought. But ten and a half more years! Now that an alternative had presented itself to her, she wasn't sure she could last it out. The truth really was that she hated those kids. She couldn't hardly stand it anymore.

Still, she felt terrible about letting Bev down. Bev suggested that maybe Lyle was so hot to get married again because then his custody of Hannah would be more secure in case Marilla should marry that beachcomber, and that gave Frances pause. It wasn't easy to say yes to him. But the more she hesitated, the more determined Lyle got. For Christmas he gave her a pearl ring that he said she could consider a friendship ring if she wanted, no obligation, but once she'd accepted it, and worn it, and people noticed, she realized there *was* an obligation. Gradually, as he pressed more things upon her—a potted azalea at Easter time, a clock radio for her birthday, an electric carving knife for no reason at all—she saw there was less and less chance of ever saying no.

She almost hoped Hannah would be an obstacle. It wasn't hard to imagine that she'd resent Frances moving in on them. But Lyle just assumed that Hannah would be glad to have a mother, and if Hannah put up any fight before the marriage, he must have closed his eyes and ears to it.

In class Hannah had been a cool customer, sure of herself, popular with the other girls. One day, though, Frances caught her cheating on a social studies test and tore up her answer sheet in front of the class. Gave her a nice big goose egg in the record book. Hannah pretended she didn't care, but

Frances knew better. Of course Hannah must have remembered the humiliation. Maybe she decided Frances had something on her. Maybe her shame kept her quiet, not that Frances would have dreamed of saying anything about it to Lyle.

So Frances said yes, finally, and broke the news to Bev, and handed in her resignation to the superintendent of schools. She's been a good wife to Lyle, she's backed him up one hundred percent. This coming June, at the end of the school year, Bev will be taking off for North Carolina. They haven't been quite so close since the marriage, but still, it will be hard to see her go.

No one from the Pratt house has come to redeem empties since Hannah was here the one time, and that's been two months. Maybe Lyle has gone on a diet and given up beer; maybe Frances has cut out soft drinks on account of some cancer scare. Or maybe they're driving right past her place and depositing the empties in Taunton. Or maybe they're not doing anything at all about the empties. Marilla imagines the house filling up with cans and bottles, in one end and not out the other, like constipation.

She hasn't seen Hannah in that time; the only way she knows Hannah hasn't gone back to wherever she came from is that Tucker saw her in town Saturday. He was driving across the bridge on his way to make a delivery, and he saw her just standing on the bridge, looking down into the water. Watching the chunks of ice hurtle along with the tide, probably. Even when you're used to it, you can still be surprised by how fast the tide runs.

Maybe Hannah plans to stay over Christmas.

Briefly it crosses Marilla's mind to give her some kind of Christmas present. But it's harder to receive a present than to give one, Marilla knows, and she doesn't want to make

Hannah feel uncomfortable. Anyway, she wouldn't know where to begin choosing something. It would be bound not to fit or be the wrong color or style or in some way embarrass her. Hard to believe that once she chose all Hannah's clothes and toys without a second thought. Hard to believe she knows her own child so little, now.

Idly Marilla turns one of the revolving video racks and repositions some of the boxes. Some video stores segregate the various kinds—horror with horror, love stories with love stories—but Marilla believes in mixing them up. She likes to think of people finding surprises in their video boxes, something they hadn't counted on, something to shake them up a little.

It was a surprise, as a matter of fact, that Tucker thought to mention that he'd spotted Hannah on the bridge. Probably he was doing it to get some kind of rise out of her, and she didn't oblige.

Rain has begun to fall, turning the road in front of the redemption center to slush. A pickup loaded with brush for wreaths swings wide at the curve, going too fast, kicking the slush behind it onto a little hatchback. It's a yellow car, like the one she watched Hannah pull away in that day. Maybe the car *is* Hannah's and she's leaving, not hanging around for Christmas.

Marilla has a sensation of loss as she thinks of Hannah inside the yellow car heading west. Tucker produces the same feeling in her, which is odd, because she *has* Tucker, and he's not likely to go anywhere. Not for good, anyway.

Frances is sitting in the center of the sofa, the carton of ornaments open in front of her. Though it's two in the afternoon, she's wearing a quilted housecoat in a floral pattern, huge purple morning glories. A number of quilting threads have caught on things and snapped, and there's a suggestion of a stain on her bosom that she doesn't know is there because she has trouble focusing on anything that close. On days she doesn't have to go out anywhere, Frances doesn't get dressed. It goes back to all those years of teaching, she says, when she had to stuff herself into a girdle every day of her life. She's forever explaining this, as though embarrassed about the housecoat. She has the impression, Hannah figures, that there's something not quite respectable about it.

She's unwrapping the decorations one by one and placing them on the sofa beside her. Hannah drops sideways into an easy chair so that her legs dangle over the chair arm and pops open a beer. The room is stifling, choked with Frances's lily-of-the-valley bath powder, though upstairs in Hannah's bare room the temperature is so cold it makes her nailbeds turn blue.

"I'd watch that, young lady," Frances says, looking over her eyeglasses at the beer can. "You could land yourself in big trouble."

Hannah wonders if there's anything worth watching on the television at two in the afternoon. She reaches out and presses a button so that a picture comes on, but no sound. It's an operating-room scene, and the camera zooms in on a hand in a rubber glove brandishing a scalpel.

"I mean it, Hannah. Drinking alone is a bad habit to get into."

"I'm not alone."

"Don't be smart."

The irritation Hannah feels tells her that what Frances said has some unpleasant truth to it. Not about drinking—she's sure she's in no danger of becoming a lush—but about bad habits and how one falls into them. Out of boredom, or laziness, or weakness, or spite even. Being in this house is somehow sapping her energy, as though her father's mummylike condition is some kind of disease, and it's catching.

"Remember this?" Frances asks, coming upon a box of angel chimes. Of course Hannah remembers. She remembers Marilla carefully fitting all the brass pieces together, lighting the little white candles so the angels would circle and the chimes ring. How stupid of Frances not to realize that's what she'd remember. Fat Frances, sitting plumb in the middle of the sofa in her dirty housecoat, as though she owned the place.

Hannah takes a swallow of beer, but it's room temperature and rather flat, and it makes her feel sick. She's not sure she has the strength to live with the angel chimes, the wax candle choirboys, the plastic Frosty the Snowman for the next two or three weeks. But she's not sure she has the strength to go anywhere else, either.

Marilla was on a pier, just like the first time. But this was the town dock, not Gaspar Pier, and she wasn't jigging mackerel, she was just sitting. And he didn't come in a boat but on foot across the wide, muddy parking lot. She saw him coming a long way off, but the only escape route would have been into the river. In April that water is cold.

She could feel her cheeks burning when he stood over her. The wind was blowing her hair so that it had come partway out of its knot and the ends of her scarf flapped. Her boots were caked with dried mud.

"I'm surprised you didn't jump in the river."

"I thought about it."

He sat beside her on the splintery wood and felt in his pockets for cigarettes. "I was in Trumble's and I saw you walk by. I decided to follow you."

"There's no need of that, Tucker."

"No? How else am I going to see you?"

"I mean, there's no need for you to follow me *or* see me. You'll only make trouble."

He cupped his hand around the cigarette and sucked at it until he got it lit.

"He a jealous sort of guy? Lyle?"

"I've never given him any reason to be," she said, but she remembered how Lyle hated her working at the Brass Lantern, serving meals to other people, putting the tips they left her in her uniform pocket. He was jealous, all right.

"So what are you worried about?"

"I didn't say I was worried. I just think we'd all be better off if you left me alone."

The cigarette smoke twisted around in the wind so that it stung her eyes.

"Sorry."

She picked up a weathered Popsicle stick from the dock and began to jab at the caked mud on her boot.

"I'm not about to rape you, Marilla."

She knew her cheeks were burning, and she jabbed more fiercely at the mud. There it was, right out in the open. She felt buffeted by the salty wind, the smoke, his words. She felt her eyes tear.

He got up and walked to the other end of the dock, and she thought he was going to leave her, but then he turned and walked back. He tossed the butt, and they both watched it disappear in a swirl of foaming river water.

"I have a kid, Tucker."

"I know that."

She wondered, stricken, if he'd been asking around town about her. How long would that take to get back to Lyle?

"How did you know?"

He laughed, standing over her, so that she had to look up into the sun to see his face. "It would be the natural thing to do. Besides, some of the clothes you were hanging on the line were kids' clothes."

"Tucker the detective."

He sat beside her again, closer this time. "How old is your kid?"

"Twelve."

This seemed to surprise him. Maybe he'd wondered if the kid could be his own. "You must have waited a while."

"Five years, almost. I was working and . . . I was working."

Casually he took one end of her scarf in hand. The scarf was the same light gray as her eyes, made of some slithery material. She'd bought it at a yard sale.

"Lyle give you this?"

"Yes."

"I guess I never gave you anything," he said, fingering the soft cloth.

"You never even bought me a hamburger."

"All I gave you was me."

She snorted, but she saw the two of them locked together, years ago, in a field of high dew-soaked grass.

"I could still give you that."

"No, Tucker."

"Nobody would have to know. I have a place on Monkey Bay. It's private. I could show you where you could leave your car and walk in."

"No."

"Nobody knew before."

"All the more reason the odds are against us now."

He smiled and let the end of the scarf slide out of his fingers. He'd heard the word "us"; she knew he was thinking sooner or later she'd come. She dropped the Popsicle stick and pulled herself to her feet.

"The kid named after Lyle?" he called after her.

She half turned. "No. Her name is Hannah. She's a girl."

Frances's friend Bev gave her some kind of bulb the size of an onion. Frances packed dirt around it in a flowerpot, and after a while it began to send up a thick green stalk with a stumpy tip. No leaves or anything, just the stalk. Every day it grows taller and the tip fatter. The stalk leans toward the window, searching for light. With the light behind it you can see that inside the tip something, a flower head, is forming. It must be curled up tight inside the tip, like a fist or an embryo.

Lyle can hardly believe that when Frances waters it, turning the pot so that the stalk will grow upright, she doesn't notice how obscene it is. There are times when he thinks Frances has told Bev all about his condition, that the two women are in cahoots, that the plant is really some loony joke between them, meant to shame and humiliate him.

The first time he did it was with Marilla, in the trailer on Seal Neck Road, the night they were married. Now he sees, as if in a vision, two jerry cans in the prefab shed they had back of the trailer. One had kerosene in it, the other gasoline. If ever he'd filled the heater with gasoline by mistake, he'd have blown them up, himself and Marilla and the trailer and everything in it. But he didn't make the mistake, and it's too late now.

All day Christmas it rains hard, soaking into the six or so inches of shopworn snow that lie in the yards on Poplar Street. Hannah is wild to get out of the house, which reeks of desiccated turkey and fake pine from the centerpiece candle; and in the late afternoon, while her father's in the john, she seizes an umbrella from the front closet and makes a run for it. She couldn't have borne his company. The guilt she feels over his mental state makes her itch with impatience. Sharp words keep leaping out of her mouth. And why should she feel guilty, for God's sake? It's not Hannah's fault he has high blood pressure, or is impotent, or is sad about his life.

It's always been that way, the pointless guilt, ever since

she was twelve and watched her father's fury collapse into desperation. His shame rubbed off onto her. She was ashamed that he was so weak, and she was ashamed that she couldn't prop him up. The only way she could have done that, she sees now, would have been to have become a sort of second wife. She probably sensed that, even then. And she wouldn't. She shrank away from his terrible need, and she felt bad about it.

When he married Frances she was relieved, though she couldn't understand why he'd want to marry someone that old and plain and boring. But maybe he figured somebody like that wouldn't be as apt to leave him. And to give Frances credit, she's stuck to all her vows like glue. The discouraging part is that Frances's loyalty doesn't seem to have made him any happier.

Marilla. Marilla is at the bottom of it, still.

Sleet is mixing in with the rain as Hannah turns onto Cottage Street and heads into town. Her feet, in tight leather boots, are already wet. The chill is almost a pleasure, though, after the stifling house.

Most of the houses on Cottage Street have electric candles lit in the windows or colored bulbs looped around the bushes in the yard, but one of the houses is dark. There's a FOR RENT sign nailed to the siding, the steps sag, the sidewalk is broken in places. Inside, a dog is barking. The family, renters, must have gone to spend Christmas with relatives and left the dog behind. The bark is steady, patient, hopeless. If only it would gather its forces into one loud howl of lament, Hannah would feel better about it. She moves on, toward town.

She's thinking of the dog they had for a while after Marilla left. Somebody threw him out of a car up by Pilcher's garage and her father heard about it and brought him home. Marilla didn't like dogs and would never have one in the house, so her father probably thought this is the one thing he could do for Hannah that her mother wouldn't, give her a dog. Hannah named him Lucky. But he didn't work out. Maybe his owners had beat him, or being thrown out of the car depressed him, or maybe he just didn't care for his new home. He chewed things under the couch; he sulked; he made messes in dark corners.

Finally, after he bit her father in the leg, they took him to the animal shelter in Ellsworth. Hannah remembers watching the man lock the dog into a wire-fenced run out back of the shelter building, and she watched knowing that no one would ever adopt him, because he wasn't cute and didn't try to make himself agreeable. He turned tail on them and nosed a plastic bowl that had a little kibble in it. She felt sorry for him, but not enough to beg her father to give him another chance. If she had, he would have.

When she reaches Main Street Hannah pauses, undecided whether to head in the direction of Gaspar, past the Methodist church and the cannery, or to go the other way, past the Congregational church to the bridge. It's almost dark at four in the afternoon, and the sleet has changed back to rain.

As she's standing there under the umbrella, a battered pickup truck pulls up across from Hinckley's variety store, and a man in a pea jacket slams the door and hurries into the store, out of the rain. He's wearing a mustache, but right away she knows who he is. She moves toward Hinckley's, and through the plate-glass window, which is nearly obscured by notices of pets lost and things for sale and church baked-bean suppers, she spots him gazing into the dairy cabinet. After a moment's thought he takes out a carton of eggnog. Then he disappears down an aisle where she can't see him. When he reappears he's carrying a couple of cans of something along with the eggnog, and at the counter Tina Franey adds a pack of cigarettes to the other groceries.

Hannah decides to turn back up Cottage Street. It's pitch

dark now, and she realizes that her hands and feet are freezing. The dog has stopped barking. Into her mind comes the picture of Marilla and the man in the mustache sitting in their ramshackle house on Monkey Bay, drinking Hancock County Creamery eggnog. Suddenly it hits her that she wants to be with them. Lifting a glass, saying "Merry Christmas." The desire is so strong it amazes her. She turns and almost runs after him, as though she'd be able to catch him before he pulled away from Hinckley's, as though he'd actually take her along, when they've never spoken a word to each other in their lives.

January

Before the house was finished, Tucker lost interest in it. When she's working in the kitchen Marilla tries not to notice that the floor's plywood, that the sink needs a splashboard, that the cabinets he built out of scrounged wood that turned out to be green have warped and cracked so they don't close right. On days like this, when the temperature outside never makes it above zero, all the crevices that could use caulking send in blasts of air as sharp as blows, as relentless as searchlights. Marilla wears three sweaters and wraps a thick wool scarf around her neck like a poultice. Tucker laughs at her. He doesn't feel the cold. Even when he goes tramping in the woods or down by the water in the middle of winter, all he wears is his pea coat half buttoned or not buttoned at all. No cap, no gloves. Sometimes Marilla wonders what it is about him that protects him. Or maybe it doesn't, really. Maybe one day he'll freeze solid and never realize what hit him.

She hears him in the mud room flinging his boots in the general direction of the boot box. There's somebody with him, which surprises her, because no car is parked in the clearing by the alders, and people in their right minds don't walk in, not in the winter. The driveway is long, uphill, and slick with ice.

Marilla looks up from the rack she's hanging wet socks on and sees that it's Fred Holly, the marine patrol officer. Marilla's heart clamps tight when she sees the brown uniform and leather holster, but she turns the knob under a ring on the electric range and fills the kettle. Fred Holly is not a local man. You couldn't be raised here and do the job, because you'd be partial to your kin, or they'd expect you to be, and people would assume you were whether you were or not. People get themselves shot over things like that. It's an easy way to make enemies, being a marine patrol officer. The only way to do it is to be evenhandedly mean to everybody.

But Fred looks genial enough, on the surface anyway. He and Tucker must have come up to the house together from the beach. The men pull chairs up to the table and she sets mugs down on the putty-colored metal surface. Tucker offers Fred a cigarette, and his accepting makes her relax a little. She doesn't think he'd allow himself to be in Tucker's debt if he was here on official business.

She's getting out mixing bowls and listening to their talk. It's about clams, and how there are less every year, and how the greed of the clam diggers is not only going to be their undoing but their children's and their children's children's. It's downright biblical the way Fred Holly is talking—the sins of the fathers visited upon the sons—and as she pours coffee into their mugs she sees that Tucker is apparently taking all this seriously, is genuinely grieved for the sake of the clam and the fate of the clam diggers. But Tucker is a poker player, and you can't always tell.

"Ever dug clams?" Fred asks him.

"Never have."

If Fred is skeptical, or is wondering how, in fact, Tucker does make a living, he doesn't wonder out loud. As she's taking eggs out of the refrigerator the conversation shifts from overfishing and poaching to other kinds of recklessly immoral behavior, and again Marilla begins to feel uncomfortable. Now her scarf is too warm, and she unwraps it a couple of loops.

Tucker is telling Fred a story about a woman he used to know up to Lubec who had nine children, only four of them her husband's, and the reason her old man didn't kick her out was, he was the sort of fella that liked to have a hot breakfast on the table every morning.

It's not hard to understand why the men laugh: They are putting themselves in the lovers' shoes, not the husband's. Suddenly, breaking eggs into a bowl, she thinks about Lyle, and knows he wouldn't find the story funny at all. Even before she ran away, he could only have stood in the husband's shoes. Absently she turns the beater in the eggs and watches as the yolks burst and are smeared into the slippery whites.

Mud season was hardly over when Marilla went to Tucker's shack. She didn't hide the car and walk in through the woods. She drove right up to the house, or as near to it as she could get, with the heaps of planks and shingles, and sawhorses, and lengths of pipe and tubing strewn everywhere.

She let the engine idle and waited for him to notice the car and come down out of the house. When he came, she saw that he'd shaved off the mustache. He was wearing a pair of ragged dungarees with a splatter of oily stains on one knee and a crudely sewn patch on the other, but no shirt. The hair on his chest was sparse. She'd forgotten that about him. It made him look more boyish than he was, now. He put his hands on the roof of the car, Lyle's Malibu, and ducked his head to look in the window.

"Aren't you cold?" she asked him.

"You work up a sweat."

His face was so close to hers she could feel his breath. It was warm and smelled like he'd been eating sweet corn.

"You'll catch something."

"Maybe I need a woman to take care of me."

She stared ahead through the windshield, beyond the shack, to the bay. The tide was out, and three or four clam diggers were bent over the mud. "Terrible on their backs," she said. "I don't know how they stand it."

"Turn off the ignition," he said.

She looked down at the key. It seemed that if she did that she could no longer pretend she only came to have a look at him, to see how he was. The engine chugged patiently, waiting for her.

"Go on," he urged in a low voice, almost a whisper. "Wouldn't want to waste his gas." Her fingers reached out and turned the key. The engine shuddered for a couple of seconds before it stopped.

He opened the car door and stood back while she got out. He didn't touch her or help her pick her way across the junk littering the yard. He was going to take his time. He was going to make her be an accomplice, not a victim.

Outside the house, grass grew in random unplanned clumps, evidently where they had been dropped by some piece of heavy machinery and then rerooted themselves in the clay or sand. She stopped there and looked out at the mud flat. Dead low tide.

"Marilla?"

She looked down at her hand. There was a pale, shiny, constricted place on her finger where her wedding band should be. She'd pulled the ring off before she left home and hidden it in a kitchen cupboard, inside a teacup. She closed her other hand over it.

"Marilla, I shouldn't have said what I did about needing somebody to take care of me. I don't need a woman that way."

"No."

"It might look like I do, but I don't. Never have. Never will. I wouldn't want to lay that on you."

Out on the flat the clam diggers inched along, like snails, over the mud.

"It was a joke, that's all," he said.

"I understand, Tucker."

When she left the shack the clam diggers were gone and the bay was filled with smooth gray water. Even the cordgrass had disappeared.

Lyle's black box sits on the table in the breakfast nook. Stamped on the Leatherette case are the words BRISTOLINE ELECTRONIC SPHYGMOMANOMETER. He unsnaps the cover, wraps the cuff around his left arm just above the elbow. Across the table Frances sets her coffee cup in the saucer and watches as he pumps the black rubber bulb. The needle on the gauge slowly swings around the dial.

From the window seat Hannah also watches, but her eyes are not on the dial, they're on her father's face. This is part of his morning routine now, the way other people have a cigarette or use the toilet. His expression is so absorbed, yet so rigid, he's like one of those people buried alive, in a bog in Denmark or somewhere, and when they're dug up ten thousand years later everything, skin and all, is intact. Some chemical in the mud preserved them.

Lyle presses the switch on the blood-pressure machine, and almost at once a red light flashes and a shrill beeping begins. It's like the alarm that goes off in the movies when some complicated apparatus is about to go haywire, a nuclear power plant is on the verge of exploding. Gradually the needle flickers downward and the beeps die out. When the needle reaches zero Lyle records some numbers in a spiral notebook, removes the cuff. The ripping sound of the Velcro makes Hannah think of the way her mother used to yank off old Band-Aids. No point in giving you time to fret over it. One big quick pain is better than a lingering lesser pain. Hannah winces, remembering.

"Well?" Frances asks.

"Under control." His mouth barely opens as he speaks.

Frances is spreading jelly on a piece of toast. Clouds of lily of the valley emanate from her, the way a pillow gives off dust when you punch it. Her housecoat is floral polished cotton, and because the sleeves are only three-quarter length, she's wearing a cardigan underneath.

"I'm hitting the road today," Hannah says suddenly, as though the pilling Orlon sleeves sticking out from the housecoat are what have forced the decision.

They stare at her, Frances holding the half-slice of toast with one bite out of it, her father frozen in the act of snapping the sphygmomanometer case.

"They're predicting snow," Frances says in her schoolteacher voice. "They said on the radio there's a travel advisory posted for Washington County. Why don't you wait until tomorrow?"

"I can't."

"Can't? Why can't?"

"I've made up my mind to go today, that's all."

Lyle's hand rests on top of the black box.

"You'd kill yourself just to do things your own way, wouldn't you," Frances says.

"That sounds like a soap opera." She walks to the sink and sets her orange-juice glass down on the drainboard.

"*And* your father."

Hannah doesn't reply to that. She runs upstairs and starts

stuffing bras and panties and unironed shirts into her overnight bag.

Snow has already begun to fall when Frances goes upstairs to strip Hannah's bed, empty the wastebasket, deal with the wet towels she expects to find slung over the foot of the bed or balled up on the floor. But the room is as bare and neat as it was in September, when Hannah arrived. It's as though she'd never been here.

The wire hangers jangle together in the draft from the closet door opening, but there's nothing in there, not even dust kittens. Nothing in the bureau drawers, either. Frances lowers the shade so the sunlight won't fade the carpet any more than it has already—not her fault, her predecessor's—and sits for a moment on the mattress. She's out of breath.

The room is the same as before Hannah came, but in fact things aren't the same. They're worse.

She feels an uneasiness that has to do with lost opportunities, things she maybe could have done for Hannah, or about Hannah, if she only knew what they were.

She feels uneasy about Lyle, too. It's not that she's really worried about the high blood pressure. He's taking his medication, doing everything the doctor said. But she senses that something else is wrong, something bigger and more terrifying than anything the blood-pressure machine could monitor.

One thing is, he makes mistakes at work. She doesn't let on that she knows, but she's heard rumors about claims he's botched. One of the girls at a Monday Club meeting started to say something and then clammed up when she realized Frances was within earshot. And not long ago Billy Flowers called Lyle early on a Saturday, and she didn't hear Billy's end of the conversation, but from the expression on Lyle's face she could tell he'd messed something up. Lyle went over to the office, in the Caprice instead of on foot the way he usually does, and spent all morning trying to straighten out whatever it was. He told her it was an emergency, and she guesses it was, but not the kind he'd wanted her to believe.

It frightens her not to be able to trust his word, and it frightens her even more that someday, if things go on this way, he's bound to land himself in big trouble. Get fired, even. Surely he must be losing business for Billy Flowers, people he's aggravated switching their policies to Machias and Ellsworth. Billy may be a kind man, but he's not a fool, and he has his own family to think of.

If Lyle got the axe, she might even have to go back to teaching.

And the truth is, Hannah only rubbed salt in the wound. Not meaning to, maybe, or even realizing she was; but Frances could see him losing heart. Wanting Hannah there, wanting her never to leave, but at the same time not knowing what to say to her. Wanting her to give him something—what?—but too timid or shy or clumsy to ask for it. In fact, he was actually afraid of her, it occurs to Frances now. As if he expected Marilla to jump out of Hannah like a jack-in-the-box and thumb her nose or make a rude noise.

He looked almost happy when she drove away in her yellow tin can of a car. And now there are just the two of them again, Lyle and Frances.

Frances pulls the sleeves of her sweater down against the chill. The radiator in here never has worked right. The valves need to be bled or something like that, but you can't expect Lyle to do anything about it—he's worse than useless at anything practical.

At this moment she wonders whether she shouldn't have followed her instincts and not married Lyle Pratt. She looks down at her hands, which pain her, and which are becoming more crippled every day, the thumbs bent into hooks, the knuckles so swollen her rings might have to be sawed off if she ever wanted to remove them. Not getting any younger, and nothing to look forward to. No jumping into a yellow car and taking off, like Hannah. You'll never budge Lyle from this town where he was born.

No condo in a warm climate, not even a cruise. But never mind. She knows her duty, and she'll do it.

There are two things Hannah can do. She can sail along Route 1 going west, hit I-95 at Bangor, and keep driving south as far as her stamina will take her. Or she can turn left on Monkey Bay Road, drive as far as the cemetery, and take another left toward the bay. She's gone that route a million times in her head, but maybe she remembers wrong. Well, if she can't find it, that will be that.

Dry snow skids across the road, blowing too fast and not enough of it yet to stick. Hannah punches the radio knob. *Waiting for, waiting for, a girl like you, waiting for, to come into my li-ii-ife, a girl like you . . . Currently light snow at thirteen degrees with KISS 94 FM . . . How'm I gonna get through, whudd've-I, whudd've-I, how'm I gonna get, whudd've-I, whudd've-I, whudd've-I done to deserve this, whudd've-I, whudd've-I. . . .* She punches the knob again and listens to the wipers wheeze, scraping the snow.

She's behind a rusted-out boat of a Buick, and when it signals for the turn onto Monkey Bay Road, she takes that for a sign. She's right behind it as they leave Route 1 and pass a grove of white pines, a trailer, a frozen field with bunched corn stalks sticking out of the snow, a farmhouse, the evangelists' quonset hut, another field, a pink bungalow with a TV dish and a stack of lobster traps in front, another trailer, a stretch of woods.

At the cemetery, though, the Buick barrels right on, and

Hannah lets the Pinto slide to a stop. For a while she sits there and looks at the old tilted gravestones. There are around sixty of them, inside an iron fence. GIBBEN, she reads. ELVIN. A bunch of Elvins in their graves, and some of them still walking around town. Gibbens, too. She went to school with one, a boy named Harry. She wonders if he's here in town or whether he's gone off someplace, joined the coast guard, maybe, or the navy. Or become a trucker and is at this very minute pushing a semi along a highway in Ohio or Texas or California. As she watches, snow is beginning to stick to the plastic wreaths and ribbons on the gravestones.

The unpaved road that goes off to the left has a small cluster of posts just at the turn, but they have RFD numbers, not names. Still, she's sure this is the right road. The question is, shall she take it? She waits there, letting the engine idle, as though expecting another sign. For a long time there is nothing, no movement except the falling snow, which rolls around on the hood in dry little pellets, and the clacking wipers. No other traffic on the road—the Buick long gone—no birds, or weasels, or porcupines, not even a house cat. In spite of the cold she cranks her window down partway. No sign of life at all.

And then she sees, above the tips of the spruce trees, a faint delicate curl of wood smoke winding up into the falling snow. But then it's gone. Maybe she only imagined it, or it was a trick of the atmospheric conditions. Without thinking about it anymore, she puts the car into gear and takes the turn.

The road goes up a rise and then down again, across a marsh and over a frozen stream. She remembers the boulders in the road from ten years ago—worse now, if anything—and between the rocks are uneven patches of ice where there's been melting and refreezing. Now there are birds, ravens, croaking on the wing overhead. She can't see the water yet, but she knows it must be near. Ravens are sea scavengers, like gulls.

At the top of the rise there's a fork, and again no names on boards posted to trees, not even any strips of crimson plastic to mark boundaries. These must be private people in here, who know their own way and aren't expecting any strangers. She can't remember how she decided which fork to take when she was here on her bicycle. Maybe Mittie Labbett told her, and she's forgotten. Or possibly the choice was obvious: One way became so boggy her bike wheels sank down into the mud and so she backed up and took the other. Or maybe it was just a lucky guess.

She takes the right-hand fork, for no particular reason except that it seems the more traveled. There's just the suggestion of tire marks under the thin coating of snow. And now she can smell it, the wood smoke.

She parks in an open place near some alders. The house isn't at all the same. When she was here before it was like a shack, but a queerly shaped shack, a lot taller than it was wide, like a big ugly shoebox sitting on end on the lip of the bay. Now there are various additions stuck onto the central building, so that the proportions aren't so odd, but it's odd in other ways. None of the windows match. One is round, like a porthole; another has stained glass in it. One chimney is made of chunks of pink granite and the other is brick the color of creamed corn. Nothing is at right angles. Only a crazy person could have designed this house.

She's come this far, she can't turn around now. She touches the car door handle and it's cold, icy cold. Her feet seem frozen to the gas pedal and the clutch.

She sees him open a side door. He has pulled on a pair of boots but not bothered to lace them, he's not wearing a coat, and snow is falling on his hair. The loose shoelaces, thongs, lash the thin snow as he heads toward her car. He ducks his head to peer in the window.

"I'm looking for my mother," she says, her fingers gripping the door handle.

"Come on in," he says.

At first Lyle thought Marilla would come back after a few days, or at most a week. He would have taken her back. He promised her that, when she was pulling clothes out of drawers and packing them into a laundry bag. She could have taken regular suitcases, there was the matched set his parents gave him for his high-school graduation. It sickened him to think of her doing it with that little bastard Tucker Burchard, sickened him so much he didn't want to touch her. But he would have forgiven her.

She refused to take the suitcases. She said she didn't want anything that belonged to him. She left behind the pins and bracelets he'd given her on special occasions. Later on, he sold them. Took them to Beal's in Ellsworth. Didn't get anywhere near what he'd paid for them, but it gave him satisfaction to get rid of the lot all the same. He hoped some friend of hers saw her starburst pin in Beal's window and told her, he hoped she felt a pang.

Give her a week, Billy said. But the week went by, and then another, and she didn't come. She was stubborn. Lyle sees now that no matter how difficult she found life with Tucker Burchard, how disappointed she was, she'd be too proud and mulish to admit her mistake. So that's how it goes. So many lives wrenched on account of one woman's foolishness.

He didn't sell Marilla's wedding ring. He threw it in the river.

One Sunday afternoon in July he left Hannah at his sister's and drove to the Gilley Road. He parked the car by the side of the road a quarter of a mile from the girl's place and walked the rest of the way. That orange flower called hawkweed was in bloom, Lyle remembers. He picked some of the hairy stalks to give her, but the plants had a coarse sort of smell and didn't look like much close up, so he gave up on the idea and tossed them into the ditch. The road was unpaved, still is, and his shoes were scuffed and dusty by the time he got there.

She lived in a trailer that had been painted a luminous blue at some time in the past, but it was a flat paint evidently intended for wood or plaster, and large patches of it had peeled off, revealing the rust-streaked pale green underneath. When he arrived she was sitting on a concrete block stoop, filing her nails. She looked not much older than Hannah, but she must have been, because she'd been working as a check-out girl in the Shop'n Save for years. A hand-painted sign, BEWARE OF THE DOG, was attached to the side of the trailer with electrical tape.

"You have a dog?" he asked.

"It ran away."

"I'm sorry."

She shrugged. Her freckled shoulders were narrow, and because she was wearing a loose cotton top that gaped open at the neck, he could see her collarbones. They stuck out as far as—farther—than her breasts. She was also wearing shorts. As she sawed at her nails she clapped her knees together and then apart, together and apart, as though moving them in time to a radio in her head. She was thin, extremely thin, but the flesh on the underside of her thighs waggled a little.

He wanted to get inside the trailer, in case someone should drive by, but he didn't know how to ask. She went on filing her nails as though she had no idea why he was there and didn't much care. Maybe Billy had it wrong. Maybe she didn't do it just like chewing gum, the way he said.

"I'm Lyle Pratt."

"Oh, I know who you are." She looked up at him and blew nail dust off her fingers. Her lips were surprisingly thick, the rest of her so thin. "You work for Billy Flowers and your wife left you."

He put his hand on his hair. Dust had stuck to his Brylcreem. He wiped his hand with his pocket handkerchief, which had a border of purple stripes, some wide, some like ruled pencil lines. He'd had the handkerchief forever and never especially noticed it before, but now it struck him as ugly and old-fashioned, an old fogey's handkerchief. He stuffed it, unfolded, back into his trouser pocket.

After a while he said, "Billy told me you like company sometimes."

"Sometimes." She was using the tip of the nail file to scratch her thigh. The file had a pearly-pink handle.

Down the road he heard the pop of a rifle shot, and then a couple more. Somebody lazing away his Sunday afternoon putting holes in tin cans for target practice. "Hot out," he said. It was so hot, in fact, that he felt dizzy standing there. All kinds of junk littered the clearing in front of the trailer, including an overstuffed sofa, but he couldn't bring himself to sit on that.

"It's hot all right, but no use complaining. Ain't going to do us no good to complain, anyhow." She examined her nails. "You got something?"

Something? He wondered if she meant money. Billy hadn't said anything about money. She wasn't a whore, Billy said, she just liked to do it. But maybe for different men there were different arrangements. He had only four or five dollars in his wallet, he thought. Probably that wouldn't be enough.

"You know, rubbers. You don't expect me to provide them, do you?"

He felt in his shirt pocket to make sure. It was there, the small square of foil. "Yes, I've got it."

"Then you might as well come on in out of the heat."

He told her to make herself at home and went to some other part of the house—where, Hannah doesn't know. It's warmest in the kitchen, which is heated by a wood stove, so she settles there at the table. He didn't take her coat, and she keeps it on, for warmth and because she's not sure she's going to stay long. The house is dead quiet, except for a striped cat licking itself and the hissing and shifting of logs in the stove. The cat pays no attention to her.

After a while she gets up and looks around for something to occupy her as she waits. All she finds are a couple of four-or-five-day-old newspapers. There are no books about, nothing like a deck of cards or a jigsaw puzzle. No television set, and when she turns on an old Philco portable radio, all she can get out of it is static.

She tries to remember what Marilla did in her spare time when she was at home, living with them. She sees Marilla with a mending basket, Marilla stirring rhubarb in a big dented pot. She sees her standing at the ironing board set up next to the kitchen stove, testing the heat of the iron by spitting on it, unrolling a dampened shirt and spreading it out on the board, pressing the tip of the iron down on the collar. After she left, Lyle tried to do his own shirts for a while, and then he started taking them in a big bundle to a laundry somewhere. And then he asked would she, Hannah, do them. She said she didn't know how, which was true—Marilla hadn't encouraged her to do things around the house—but the real reason was she didn't want to touch his things in such a familiar way. He made it plain how hurt he was that she wouldn't try. Finally Frances came, thank goodness.

Marilla didn't go to club meetings, like Frances, or look at magazines, or give herself perms. In fact, she didn't give herself anything, Hannah realizes—not because they were so poor but because that was her nature. How astonishing, then, that Marilla should all of a sudden have indulged herself in a lover. Have made a quick grab for it all, you might say.

Hannah can't help being curious about him.

Around noon he comes into the dim kitchen and puts a frying pan on the stove. He heats some margarine in it and then lays two slices of bread in the fat. On top of the bread go two slices of American cheese. The cat rubs against his leg, but he ignores it. He puts two more pieces of bread on top of the cheese and presses them down into the burning fat with a spatula, then flips them over. As they sizzle in the pan he takes jars out of the refrigerator and sets them on the table in front of her: catsup, mustard, mustard pickle, relish, pickled onions, bread-and-butter pickle, black olives, green olives. Finally, at pickled beets, she begins to laugh. It's as though he read her thoughts about Marilla grabbing it all and is demonstrating to Hannah exactly what it is she got.

He slides each sandwich onto a plate and then sits down across from her. The plates don't match. His is squarish aqua melamine, hers is willowware, with a chip on the rim.

"You don't look at all like her," he says, holding his hot sandwich in both hands.

She feels uncomfortable under his gaze. "So people say."

"Don't you know?"

She unscrews the pickled beets and spoons a whole beet onto her plate. Right away the pink juice begins to creep toward the sandwich. "I look at myself in the mirror, like anybody else. I don't look at her."

The edge of her sandwich is pink and wet, sour from the beet juice. She picks it up and puts it down.

"Why don't you look at her?"

"For one thing, I'm not in the same room with her very often." He should know whose fault that is, and if he doesn't, too bad.

"And for another?"

She shrugs and tries to eat the beet with a spoon, but it slides away on the plate.

He leans forward, over the uneaten part of his sandwich. His mustache has an orange bit of melted cheese stuck to it. "I bet you've got a big kick out of hating her all these years."

"I haven't. I don't."

"Nursing your grudge like a cozy little pet."

"What am I doing here, then?"

He smiles in an unpleasant way. "You tell me, miss."

Ice chokes the river in great slabs. Sailors' coffins, Lyle heard somebody call them once. Underneath, the cold water churns with the tide, but you can't see it.

He stands on the bridge and looks down at the ice. This is where he threw Marilla's wedding ring. He imagines that it's still there, flashing like a shiny fish amid the stones, half-decayed wood chips, mussel shells.

The ring was what gave her game away, finally. That day he came home early from work because he had a headache. He thought he'd have a cup of tea. Marilla was out somewhere, so he put the kettle on to boil himself. When he was taking a teacup down from the cupboard he heard a rattle, and there inside was her ring. He'd never seen it off her finger since the day they were married. He knew right away that something was wrong.

He put it in his pocket and made his cup of tea. When she came in he didn't ask her about it right then. He sat in the breakfast nook and waited. As she unpacked groceries and put them away he could see the white place on her finger where her ring should be. He pretended to be picking up grains of sugar. She thought he wasn't paying attention and opened the crockery cupboard. No, Marilla, the teacup isn't there. Her eyes fell on the table then and she saw it, with the dregs of milky tea inside it. Afterward, days later, she smashed the cup in the sink, but he remembers it all right, though she only had one like it, pink and white, with a vine-like design in gold that had worn partly off.

"I have it," he said matter-of-factly, though his chest was so tight he could hardly breathe.

When she looked at him her eyes were like flat gray stones. "Have what?" she asked, calm as could be, but color flamed in her cheeks, so he knew he was right.

"You know."

She leaned back against the counter and rubbed the naked place on her finger. "It's begun to pinch," she said. "I must be getting fat."

He felt like smashing his fist into her, that she could lie to him so coolly. But he stayed where he was. There was a box of Quaker Oats on the counter, he remembers, and a bunch of carrots with the feathery tops dangling limply over the edge. To this day the smell of raw carrots makes him sick.

"Where were you this afternoon?" he asked.

"Shopping. As you see."

"Before that."

As he was waiting for her to answer he took the ring out of his pocket and placed it on the table. It looked surprisingly small.

"I visited a friend."

"What friend?"

Her eyes were on the ring. He thought she might try to rush to the table and snatch it, but he'd be quicker. He wouldn't let her have it just like that. She'd have to beg for it.

"What friend, Marilla?"

She shrugged. "Just a friend."

He was amazed at his own calm. He thought about Billy Flowers's yellow dog watching a woodchuck hole. That dog would wait all day, if necessary.

"Anybody I know?"

She let out a sigh, like a tire with a nail in it. "I don't want to tell you, because I don't want to hurt you."

"Go on, Marilla."

"All right, then. Tucker Burchard."

Lyle couldn't believe it. What did that little scumbag have to do with his wife? He couldn't believe he wasn't dead somewhere, murdered for his wise lip. Of all the men in all the world, Burchard was the last one Lyle would have guessed.

"Did you sleep with him?" he asked, very quietly.

"Yes."

He looked at the ring. FOREVER, it said inside, with their initials. "One time? Just today?"

"No."

"No? More? How many times did you do it?"

"I don't know," she yelled. "Lots of times. What difference does it make how many times?"

They heard the storm door bang then. Hannah came in with her schoolbooks and dumped them on the table, without noticing the ring. She opened the refrigerator door to take out a carton of milk, and Lyle could feel the chill on his damp shirt. He realized then how much he'd been sweating.

"What's wrong?" Hannah asked, pouring milk into a glass.

"Nothing's wrong," Lyle said.

"What are you doing home so early?"

"He has a headache," Marilla explained, although Lyle couldn't remember telling her that. But of course, the only time he ever drank tea was when he had a headache. It was his mother's foolproof cure.

Later on Marilla just slipped the ring back onto her finger, and he let her. He felt worn out, exhausted.

He stares down from the bridge, and all he sees is ice.

The snow never amounted to much, hardly more than a dusting. At four, when Mittie comes to relieve her, the roads are clear and Marilla decides to drive to the Flag Road for eggs, and on the way home stops at the post office for the mail and at the Shop'n Save for yellow-eye beans. She buys a cauliflower on sale and a sack of navel oranges. With one thing and another, the sun is setting behind the bog as she navigates the pickup over the bumpy unpaved road. The sun turns the frozen stream red.

At first she doesn't notice the little car parked by the alders. Mackerel streaks between her legs as she's juggling eggs and oranges and trying not to slip on the ice, and she's reminding herself to put the beans up to soak for tomorrow. Then, out of the corner of her eye, she sees a splash of yellow. She knows it's Hannah's car, but she doesn't let herself think about what it might mean.

The house is quiet. She leaves her boots in the mud room and begins to unpack the bags of groceries. Eggs are smaller at this time of year, and one is cracked.

"Hello," Hannah says from the doorway. Her dark hair is mussed so that part of it sticks up in a cowlick. She's wearing an old pigskin jacket of Tucker's and a pair of thick woolen socks that are pulled halfway up her legs, over her jeans. The socks also belong to Tucker.

"Hello," Marilla answers, holding the styrofoam egg box.

"I was sleeping when you came. On the couch in the other room."

Marilla can't think of anything to say.

"I borrowed these things—I found them in the mud room. I hope you don't mind."

"They're Tucker's, but he won't care," she says, opening the refrigerator door. She tucks the egg box in the only place it will fit, under the little freezer.

"I don't usually sleep in the daytime, but I suddenly felt so tired, I had to lie down."

Like Goldilocks, Marilla thinks. She pries open the iron door of the wood stove and finds that the fire is nearly out. Tucker must have forgotten to feed it, or else he expected that Hannah would. "Has he gone off somewhere?" Marilla asks, throwing a handful of kindling on top of the embers. She wedges in a fat split log and then some smaller logs around it. Chips of wood and bark flare as she slams the door.

"I don't know. He didn't say."

"He never does."

From the top shelf of the cupboard Marilla takes an earthenware bowl and empties the bag of yellow-eyes into it. Then she covers the beans with water from the tap. She's waiting for Hannah to explain why she's come, but instead Hannah dips her hand into the water and plays with the beans.

"I don't know why," Hannah says, "but this kind of bean makes me think of an old lady."

Marilla's moving about the kitchen, getting things ready for supper. She feels clumsy, her body overlarge and awkward. Spaces in the kitchen have contracted, with Hannah sitting crossways on a kitchen chair, her feet in Tucker's wool socks close to the wood stove, her elbow on the table. "What old lady is that?" she asks.

"I don't know who she was, but I'll tell you what else I remember about her. I think I was in her house. You put me to bed in my clothes, and the bed was two chairs pushed together, with pillows so I wouldn't fall out, but I did fall out. It was dark and I was crying."

One of her many sins, Marilla thinks. One she'd even forgotten about.

"Now do you know who she was?"

"I suppose that must have been when we took you to visit my old granny, my father's mother, up to Eastport. We got caught in a storm and had to spend the night. You were a baby—I'm surprised you can remember."

"Like how old?"

Mackerel mews and jumps for Hannah's lap.

"Let me see. It was after we moved out of the trailer, I know. You were around two and a half or so."

"Why do yellow-eyes make me think of her?"

"Maybe we ate them for supper."

"No, I don't think that was it. I connect her with the raw, hard bean."

Marilla shrugs. "Who knows why we remember the things we do? Odd things stick in the mind."

"She was very old, wasn't she?"

"Over ninety. Outlived all her own children, and she had seven of them."

"That must be terrible, outliving your children."

"It was hard on her."

Mackerel's on Hannah's lap, she's stroking the lean, sleek body. The cat flattens her ears under Hannah's fingers, but after each stroke they snap up again.

"Hard the other way round, too," Hannah says. "Either way, you don't get any more chances."

"No, you don't." Marilla wipes her hands on a towel. "Will you be staying to supper?"

"If it's all right. With him, I mean."

"Don't worry about him," Marilla says, breaking open the cauliflower.

* * *

On the Cotter District Road there's a rimwracked old farmhouse, sitting on thirty-odd acres of land. The property can't be sold because it's heirship property; nobody can get clear title to it. Every year the fields become more choked with weeds and scrub, more shingles blow off the farmhouse roof, another porch step rots out, while the heirs argue away unto eternity.

One day when Tucker happened to be driving by to make a delivery he stopped to look the place over. Might be something he could scrounge. Boards were nailed across the front door and windows, but he had no trouble getting in the back way. He found some rubbish the family or the auctioneers hadn't bothered to haul away: a musty overstuffed armchair, a cheap coffee table with weewaw legs and maple veneer shriveled by the elements, a homemade bookcase put together out of scraps of plywood. He loaded these things onto the back of the pickup and took off.

Down in the cellar he sits in his overstuffed chair, which has a pink chenille bedspread draped over the bird droppings. He puts his feet up on the rackety table. Next to his chair, separating him from the rest of the cellar, is his bookcase. He has books there, paperbacks he picks up three for a quarter at yard sales, and stacks of articles clipped out of newspapers. He saves items about such things as quasars, the ozone layer, the supercluster complex, genomes, the birth of stars. When he plugs in his electric heater the fan makes a wall of noise that is companionable, insulating. He reads a good deal. But a lot of the time he just thinks.

He's in his third-floor flat near Inman Square fucking Irene Lapolla or Sarah Stephansky. He's on the Lechmere bus drinking Jim Beam out of the bottle at one in the morning. He's listening to a girl with long brown hair play a flute, down in Park Street Under, letting six E cars go by because he likes the music, even though he has no idea what it is. He's gluing wigs on dolls, pleasurably numbed by the feel of their rubbery naked limbs, by their pert, foxy faces. He's watching lights slither on the surface of the river, a joint in his hand, and there was a girl earlier, but he's all by himself now.

He hears footsteps thump above his head, but he doesn't pay them any mind.

It has begun to snow again. They can't see it, but they can hear it, mixed with freezing rain, blowing against the window glass. Hannah picks a plate out of the drainer and carefully wipes it. The towel seems to be at least partly linen, worn smooth with many washings, and it has a ragged hole in the center and faded green stripes along the sides. Hannah has never seen it before. Nor, as a matter of fact, has she seen the caramel-colored bowl the beans are soaking in, or the tin canisters on the counter, or the Philco radio with the cracked ivory case, or this blue-rimmed plate. It's odd and depressing to think of her mother living—for years—with all these possessions that Hannah has never laid eyes on.

"Do you have . . . things with you?" Marilla asks, scrubbing a cup and holding it under the tap.

"Things?"

"Clothes and such."

This is the first time either has spoken of the possibility of Hannah's staying here.

"An overnight bag. In the car."

"You'd better bring it in before the weather gets any worse."

Hannah turns the towel to find a dry spot. "I don't want to intrude."

With her soapy hand Marilla lifts a strand of hair that has escaped her knot and hooks it over her ear. A fluff of suds stays on her hair. When Marilla's rounded shoulders bend again over the dishpan, Hannah realizes the significance to Marilla of what she's just said. Where your mother lives is supposed to be your home, and there's no such thing as intruding on your own home. Well, if Marilla wants to take it that way, Hannah can't help it.

"I mean," Hannah says, laying a serving spoon on the linoleum counter, "I'd like to stay, but—"

"When people stay, they stay in there." Marilla nods toward a room off at the far end of the kitchen. There's no door, but a limp cotton cloth hangs from a wire strung across the door frame. "It's not much, but at least it's warm and dry. More or less."

"What about him, though?"

"Oh, Tucker likes company."

Hannah remembers what he said over the cheese sandwich, accusing her of wallowing in her grievances. He was closer to the truth than she liked, and that makes her nervous, but she doesn't see how she can say all this to Marilla. The conversation would sound too intimate in the retelling, as though she'd confided things she hadn't. And wouldn't ever, to him.

"All right, then," she says, hanging the towel over an arm of the wooden rack by the wood stove.

In the mud room she has to remove Tucker's socks to get her own tight leather boots on. She wonders now at her own impudence, appropriating the socks after the things he'd said to her. Of course she didn't know they were his—or the pigskin jacket, either—but she might have guessed. The jacket would be snug on Marilla, and it smells of stale cigarette smoke. She hangs it on a peg and slips into her own long wool coat.

She has to shove her shoulder against the door to get it open, since an inch of wet snow crowds the sill. The air is much warmer than when she came this morning, must be up around freezing, but the wind has picked up. Though the distance to the car is no more than twenty yards or so, she can't see very well and she feels unsteady, not knowing where patches of ice lie just under the snow or have been exposed by the wind. When she reaches the car she realizes she doesn't have her gloves, and she wipes the snow off the door handle with her bare hand. But now she's got the bag, and the way back should be easier, marked by the light in the kitchen window.

On the north side of the house she sees something move in the shadows. Tucker's just standing there, smoking. The tip pulses as he takes a drag and then another. He doesn't offer to carry her bag for her, he doesn't say anything at all. Her hands sting from the cold, and she hurries into the house.

February

They say that on Candlemas the winter's half over. There's been a thaw, and areas of tan, dun, olive dapple the woods and fields. Ice is melting in the bay.

At night, though, the temperature drops well below freezing. Tucker feeds the fire in the big room, thick logs he took from the woods more than a year ago and sliced up with the chainsaw. Marilla's sewing elbow patches onto an old sweater. The girl also is sewing something. Her fingers are clumsy on the material, cautiously poking the needle through. The thread she's working with is too long, even Tucker knows that. Tucker did his own mending for nineteen years. A long thread is bound to snake itself into knots.

He feels restless. He's in the mood to start something, pry their attention away from their busywork. He lights a cigarette, makes a clatter of getting a glass ashtray down from a shelf. The girl, on the couch, stays hunched over her sewing, and Marilla meditatively sticks her hand up the sleeve, under the hole. The logs crackle in the wood stove.

"I had this friend Wally up to Lubec," he says. "Told me a good story once."

"You and your stories," Marilla says, her eyes on the patch.

"What's the matter with my stories?"

"You never tell true ones."

"This one is true. Honest to God."

The girl glances at him, holding the needle out at the end of a long thread. Her turtleneck is taut across her breasts. They're small, puny, not like her mother's.

"Wally was just a kid when this happened. I mean little, five or six. His family went on a camping trip." To Hannah he says, "You ever been camping?"

The girl looks at her mother. "I don't like bugs," she says carefully.

"They went to Baxter State Park. The whole family: Wally, his little brother, Phil, his sister, Mother, Daddy, old Granny, dog, cat."

"Must have been a tight squeeze," Marilla says, putting a knot in her thread. "They have a bus?"

"Station wagon. Camping gear in the back, big old canoe lashed to the roof. Cat in a cage on the floor. Dog jumping back and forth between the front seat and the rear seat. Everybody singing, except the cat, which is yowling."

" 'A hundred bottles of beer on the wall,' " Hannah says.

"You got it. Finally, after fourteen hours on the road, they make it to the campsite."

"Fourteen hours to Baxter from Lubec?" Marilla says.

"Rough going in those days. Lots of roads weren't even paved, you know. And they got lost a couple times. So they have to pitch their tents in the dark, and it's commencing to rain, and Wally and Phil and the girl are hungry and whining and the dog is barking and running around in circles, waking up all the wildlife between East Millinocket and Houlton, and the mosquitoes are biting, and the old granny is wishing she'd never been born."

Hannah says, "That's how I always thought a camping trip would be."

"Wait a minute. The next day the old granny gets her wish. Anyway, she dies. Without any warning, just up and keels over."

"Stroke?" Marilla asks. "Heart attack?"

"Who knows? You think they've got a physician on the premises? Wally's daddy is madder'n hell, he hadn't wanted the old lady along in the first place. But his wife got her own way, as usual. Now look at the mess they're in. A corpse on their hands, and Wally's old man has to be back to work in the cannery Monday morning. If they start notifying authorities and filing death certificates they'll be stuck in the boonies for a month."

"A fate *worse* than death," Hannah says.

"He'll get fired and they'll all starve. So what they do is, they load the body into the canoe and tie it back onto the top of the station wagon and set out for home. They never even lay eyes on Mount Katahdin."

Hannah, smiling, puts the cloth she's sewing aside.

"But Wally's daddy can't drive as fast as on their way up. He's worried they're going to hit a pothole and the old lady will take off, flying, out of the canoe. So he takes it real slow and easy, and after fourteen hours they're still a long way from home. Everybody's bushed, including the dog. The cat had a nervous breakdown hours ago.

"Round about Baileyville they spot a motel, one of them mom-and-pop operations with the crummy little cabins, by the side of the road. It's got a coffee shop—it's even got TV."

" 'We wanna stay in the motel!' " Hannah yells.

"You bet. Have a good time, too. Eat burgers and fries in the coffee shop, watch a Debbie Reynolds movie on the TV."

Marilla asks, "What about the old lady in the canoe?"

"Next day they're all up bright and early to make the rest of the trip home. There they stand, blinking in the sunlight outside their cabin. They're just staring into space, because there isn't anything else to see. No station wagon, no canoe, no granny."

"Oh, God," Hannah says.

"Wally's old man races over to a drop-off at the far side of the parking area—there's a landfill there they didn't notice the night before—maybe he forgot to set the handbrake and the vehicle rolled off the edge. He gazes down into a heap of baked-bean cans and bottles and busted baby carriages. No station wagon."

Hannah begins to laugh.

"Now Wally's daddy knows he's had it. An hour later he's explaining to the Baileyville constable that his car's been stolen and oh, by the way, there's a dead body in a canoe on the roof."

"Are you sure this is a true story?"

"Listen, that's not all. The funny part is, the state police never found a trace of the missing car. They had to have a closed-casket funeral because there wasn't any body. The old lady was just gone, vanished into thin air."

The wood in the stove hisses and snaps.

"So what is the point of the story?" Marilla asks.

"Point? Since when does a true story have to have a point?"

Stupidly, Marilla thought that was the end of it, when she put the ring back on her finger. She thought Lyle would let it drop, she thought she wouldn't see Tucker again. But she didn't understand Lyle as well as she'd believed she did. She didn't know until then just how dogged he could be.

"I can find it in my heart to forgive you," he said. "But you have to tell me everything."

He'd come home at lunchtime to harangue her, he'd wake her up at two or three in the morning with a new question. Which one of them started it? Where had they done it? How many times, exactly? Did they have clothes on, or did they do it stripped? Did he do things to her Lyle never had? And did she do things for him that she wouldn't do for Lyle?

She thought if she answered him patiently and honestly he'd get tired of it or run out of questions, and they could just go on as they had before. Instead, the more he found out, the more frantic he became.

The truth was, she didn't want to be forgiven by Lyle, and she knew that in spite of what he said, he'd never be able to forgive her. She was going to spend the whole rest of her life in a bog.

When the telephone rang she was terrified it was Tucker, wanting to know what had happened to her. When it wasn't Tucker, she chewed her knuckles in misery.

It amazed her that Hannah seemed oblivious to what was going on.

At first Lyle wouldn't touch her, then he was in a frenzy for sex, at the same time filled with disgust, he told her. And then he wouldn't touch her again. One lunchtime in an icy calm he said he was going to kiss Hannah good-bye and then take his father's Winchester into the woods. When he went back to the office she took the box of bullets from the closet shelf and buried them deep in the swampy place behind the shed. She waited for him to accuse her of stealing them, but he didn't. It occurred to her that he could have bought another box and hidden them somewhere.

Especially at the times when he seemed under a rigid kind of control, she thought he might be dangerous. She could imagine him going to Monkey Bay. He might not confront Tucker directly, but instead wait in the woods and snipe at him when he was on the roof, say, nailing shingles, or dumping swill by the side of the clearing. He'd justify it to himself by saying that Tucker hadn't given him any warning, either.

She sent Mittie to Monkey Bay with a sealed envelope.

She'd written shakily on half a sheet of Hannah's notebook paper: *He knows. Be careful.*

Then the telephone rang and it was Tucker. "I'm in the pay phone at Mawhinney's," he said.

She blurted out, "I think I'm going to have to leave him." She could hardly believe she'd said those words.

But Tucker didn't seem surprised. He just said "Oh" or "Yes," something noncommittal like that.

"I don't know when. I don't know what I can do about Hannah." She began to cry then. She didn't want Tucker to hear it in her voice. She didn't want him to feel sorry for her or to feel that he owed her anything.

Only eleven days had gone by since Lyle found the wedding ring in the teacup. It seemed like a year.

That night after Hannah was asleep she said to Lyle, "I can't stand this anymore."

"You brought it all on yourself."

"You're driving me away."

"Don't think you'd ever get Hannah. No court of law would give you Hannah after what you've done."

"A girl needs her mother."

"You lift one finger to get her and I'll sue you for abandonment. That's a criminal offense, Marilla."

Even though half the time Lyle didn't know what he was talking about, about this she believed him. Those judges up to Machias would think just the way he did. "I can't leave, then," she said, and she thought she'd made up her mind for good.

He said, "Come down to the kitchen with me."

"Why, Lyle?"

"Just do what I'm telling you."

He took the teacup down from the cupboard and thrust it into her hands. "I want you to break it," he said.

"It was my grandmother's. It's all I have that was hers."

"I can't bear to look at it anymore. If you're going to live in this house with me, you have to get rid of it."

"I'll put it in the garbage."

"That's not good enough. Because how can I trust you now? I want to see you smash it into a thousand pieces."

She hurled it into the sink.

"That's that," he said, clamping his jaw tight, and they both thought, once again, that the matter was settled. But the next day at supper she told Hannah she was going to have to leave, and the day after that Mittie picked her up and drove her to Monkey Bay.

Hannah's room is a windowless lean-to, made of planks from an old barn. They are wide and gray, with specks of mustard yellow in the deeper grooves. On a washing machine in the corner there's an amber bottle with branches of winterberries in it. Most of the berries still cling to the branches, but they've shriveled and turned a darker red.

Hannah sits cross-legged on the folding bed, pushing the needle in and out of the cloth. It's hard to say why she's taken up this project, when she's always been uncomfortable with domestic activities. Or with anything that required patience to complete. One Christmas somebody gave her a cardboard box with hundreds of cotton loops inside, and a wooden frame rimmed with nails. She was supposed to make pot holders.

On Christmas afternoon she made one, with green loops going one way and yellow the other, but it didn't work out. The loops were woven too loosely, and Marilla had to fold it over before she grasped a pot handle, otherwise she would have burned her hand. Hannah put the box in the back of her closet and forgot about it. Probably that's one of the things Frances threw out when they thought she wasn't ever coming back.

Another time she started to embroider a dresser scarf. The length of cloth came with a picture already stamped on it in tiny crosses: a basket of flowers. You had to go over the crosses with embroidery floss. She was planning to give it to Marilla for her birthday, and she did all the flowers, but she got bogged down halfway through the basket. The stitches were too tight and puckered the cloth. It wouldn't have looked right, even if she'd gotten around to finishing it.

As she's sewing, Hannah suddenly hears the scrape of a snow shovel on the other side of the wall. It's so close she's startled. Sounds echo and rebound oddly in this house. There are abrupt cracks and you look around, expecting to find a plank or pane of glass on the point of shattering, but there are no visible signs. Marilla doesn't seem to notice, but the cat's ears twitch, so she knows she hasn't imagined it.

The shovel grates as though it's striking cinder block or pebbles, but it's also muffled, maybe by the snow. It snowed hard yesterday—two inches an hour for a while. And it drifted, so now there must be well over a foot in some places. Hannah's glad the naked muddy spots are buried again.

What she's working on is another dresser scarf. Hannah said she'd like something to do with her hands, and Marilla pulled it out of a ragbag. It was once part of a tablecloth Marilla got for free at a yard sale when the woman said she'd rather give it away than bother to fold it and haul it inside one more time. Hannah cut a good piece from between the stains and holes and is putting a hem in it. The cloth is smooth and finespun, the white-on-white pattern more perceptible to the touch than to the eye. Her needle moves in time with the snow shovel. She feels a queer kind of contentment settling over her. She wishes it would last forever.

* * *

"Blankety-blank snow," Bev says, vigorously kicking her boot against the sill while Frances holds the storm door open for her. Bev's short and stumpy, but strong. Sometimes, because of her bangs, she reminds Frances of a gray-haired Buster Brown.

"It's either that or mud," Frances says.

"Holy cow, will you look at that amaryllis!"

The plant's in the center of the kitchen table. It's in full bloom, the four spectacular crimson flowers flaring out from a stalk thick as a broom handle.

"I have to give you credit," Frances says. "I would never have thought of giving somebody a plain brown bulb for a gift. I wouldn't have had the imagination."

"It did come up well," Bev agrees, throwing her parka onto the window seat and unwrapping the waxed paper from her sandwich. She has only a half-hour lunch break and has to eat fast. "But that's because you have a green thumb."

In her heart of hearts, Frances finds the plant ugly, in some unspecifiable way. Maybe it's too showy for this climate. Of course, she'd never confess this to Bev. Though the two friends have much in common, Bev is the more artistic, original one, and sometimes that originality takes startling forms. Bev is also a natural teacher, which—because it takes showmanship—Frances never was or could hope to be.

"Salami again," Bev says, looking into her sandwich with annoyance, as though somebody other than herself had made it.

"I only wish I could eat it. Salami repeats on me."

"One thing I've still got is my digestion."

"You don't know how lucky you are," Frances says, pouring coffee into their cups. Every Friday Bev insists on giving Frances fifty cents to cover the cost of her share of the coffee. It doesn't really cover it anymore, but Frances wouldn't dream of saying so. Bev's company is so important to her she'd gladly give her all the coffee she wanted for free, and besides, she still feels bad about pulling out of the condo. All these years Bev's been paying the rental management fee single-handed.

"Heard anything from Hannah yet?" Bev asks.

"Not one word."

"Hmm," she says, chewing thoughtfully.

"She was supposed to call when she reached Boston."

"Kids are so irresponsible these days."

Frances bites into her egg salad sandwich. "She's not a kid. She's twenty-three."

"That's what I mean. They don't grow up anymore."

"She doesn't do Lyle's blood pressure any good, I'll tell you."

"She planning on staying in Boston?"

"You don't think she'd tell *me* what her plans are, do you? She just tosses her clothes into a suitcase and takes off, as sudden as she came. Right into a snowstorm, too."

Bev unsnaps her purse and fishes out of it a rubber-tipped gum stimulator. Behind a hand she begins to pry bits of salami out from between her teeth. "Maybe," she says, inspecting the rubber tip, "she didn't care about the snow because she didn't expect to go very far."

"What are you talking about? It's so uncomfortable in this house she decided to move to a motel? She can't afford a motel."

"I wasn't thinking of a motel," Bev says, dropping the stimulator back into her purse. She crumples her waxed paper into a ball.

"You don't suppose she's staying with Tina Franey and the boy with the warts, do you? She hasn't seen anybody else, not that I've heard of. Her friends have all moved away, and the ones that haven't, she thinks she's too good for."

Bev pauses for dramatic effect. "Monkey Bay is not ten miles from where we're sitting."

"Why would she do a thing like that? She hates Marilla, and for good reason."

Bev shrugs and drops the waxed-paper ball into the trash bin on her way out. "It was just a thought. Back to the salt mines."

Frances's bulk strains her coat buttons. She's wearing a crocheted woolen cap with a pom-pom that Marilla hasn't seen before. As Frances sets the grocery carton overflowing with empties on the counter, she gasps with relief. Immediately her eyeglasses film over. She takes them off, and it's almost as though she's taken her clothes off, she looks so exposed. There's an inflamed pinched place on the bridge of her nose, and the whites of her eyes are almost yellow, the way cheap paper yellows with age.

"I already counted them," Frances says, as Marilla's beginning to unload the box. "You owe me two dollars even."

Might as well take her word for it. She punches open the cash register and takes out a new two-dollar bill.

"Would you mind?" Frances says. "I always think there's something not quite legitimate about those."

"Haven't seen you in a while," Marilla says, exchanging the bill for a pair of ones.

"I've been busy."

"I thought you might be taking your empties somewhere else."

Frances puts her glasses back on. "Why would I do that?" she asks, as though Marilla should be the one to want to stay out of her path, not the other way around. "You people all pay the same deposit. Don't you?"

"That's right."

"That's what I thought," she says, beginning to rotate one of the video racks.

Marilla wonders if they've acquired a VCR. Maybe a Christmas present to themselves. Into her mind flashes the ancient Motorola console she and Lyle had in the trailer on Seal Neck Road. Lyle's mother gave it to them when she bought her color set.

"These boxes are all empty," Frances says.

"I keep the tapes behind the counter. When you decide the one you want, you give me the box and I give you the tape."

"It's not likely I'd want any of these," she says, smiling. It's a smile Marilla knows. Frances was the eighth-grade monitor who came into the kindergarten room on Fridays to collect the milk money. If you forgot your money or lost it, or your mother didn't have it that day, you didn't get milk the next week. Of course, Frances didn't invent that rule. It was the way she smiled when she enforced it that made you want to kick her.

"I don't have any trouble renting them."

"I'm sure you do very well. Most people will look at anything." She's still taking this box and that one off the rack, though, and studying the illustrations of hanky-panky, terror, mayhem, and sudden death. All at once it occurs to Marilla that Frances has some other reason for being here than collecting her deposit and ogling the videos. Probably she's waiting for Marilla to say something about Hannah. Well, she can wait until hell freezes over.

"I don't suppose you've seen Hannah lately," Frances says finally.

"Yes, I've seen her."

"Where?" She can't help jumping in with the question, though she'd like to be able to play it cool, of course.

"Here. And other places."

Frances pauses, a video called *Jagged Edge* in her hand. "I wasn't sure she'd been in touch with you."

"Oh?"

"Well, you know, Hannah tends to be secretive."

"I guess she gets that from me."

"Lyle . . ." she begins and stops. Apparently she's decided that whatever she had in mind to say would be too personal or giving away too much. The pom-pom on her crocheted cap jiggles a little. "Her father worries about her. And worrying isn't good for him. In his condition."

An electric-blue van with curtains in the windows pulls into the plowed space in front of the redemption center, and Fred Holly, the marine patrol officer, hurries in out of the cold. "Ain't never gonna make it above zero today," he says, blowing into his cupped hands. "Got anything new, Marilla?"

She wishes he hadn't called her by name in front of Frances. "*Tin Men* came in yesterday. It's there on the rack."

"Any good?"

"Supposed to be funny. I don't know."

With Fred twirling the racks, his revolver at his hip, Frances moves closer to the counter. "The doctor told him he has to quit worrying," she says in a low voice.

"What condition is that, Frances?"

She glances back at Fred. "Blood pressure. You haven't heard?"

"No. How would I?"

For some reason, her saying that reassures Frances. At least it's clear she's not going to plague Marilla anymore today.

"Did you want that?" Marilla asks. Frances is still holding the box for *Jagged Edge* against her tight brown coat with the orange-and-cream nubbles in it.

"Oh, no. We don't have a machine."

She leaves the box on the counter for Marilla to put away and heads for the door.

Down cellar, inside a Mason jar, a hundred seeds swim around in lukewarm water. Each seed has sprouted a little white tail. Tucker dips into the water with a pair of forceps and seizes one. He plants it in a tiny hole in a tray of soil, tail side down. That's the root. The soil is a mixture of one-half composted rockweed and fish guts and one-half Kitty Litter. This formula Tucker has developed himself over the years, and it's a secret. Another of his secrets is germinating the seeds in sea water instead of tap water. Every winter before the bay freezes over he carries a jar full of sea water up from the beach and saves it until time to plant the new crop in February. He gets one hundred percent germination and he figures that's why. Everything came out of the sea in the beginning and everything's going back there. When he thinks of the end of the world he doesn't think of ice or fire or nuclear explosions. He envisions the continents slipping gradually down into the ocean. He sees the tide lapping the tip of Mount Everest. That's all that will be left.

Back in seventh grade they showed a black-and-white movie about the facts of life. They showed it to the girls one Friday afternoon and the boys the next, which was nutty, because it wasn't about fucking at all. You'd never know how to do it if you had to depend on that movie for information.

It was a scratchy old print that kept sliding sideways in the projector, and you could hardly make out the narrator's words. But, Tucker thinks, dipping into the Mason jar and capturing a seed, all the same there was something eerie about all those tiny sperm flailing around that giant egg. Unforgettable, even in black and white, even in sixteen millimeter. The seeds in the jar always make him think of those sperm, though their tails don't wiggle, and there isn't any big egg they're hoping to get inside.

In February, when he's doing this job, he often thinks about his own sperm. He knows there's something wrong there, because he never got a girl pregnant. He fucked Marilla hundreds of times when they were kids and nothing happened. If he thought about it at all then, he assumed it was because he was too young, or she was. But later on, in East Cambridge, he began to wonder. Practically everybody he knew either knocked somebody up or got knocked up sooner or later, especially if they didn't use rubbers. That was before the Pill, before much of anything in Massa-goddamn-chusetts. But no girl ever said to him, "You have to marry me," or "You've got to give me money to get rid of it." That made him free. He didn't want to have some crabby wife on his neck, a bunch of whining kids. After a while he knew he couldn't be tricked that way.

Still, he felt a little odd about himself. As if he wasn't complete somehow. Not that he brooded over it. Not that he ever cared enough to consult a doctor. But still.

He's got each seed in its own hole now. Very gently he spreads a thin layer of moist soil over the top and tamps it down with his fingers. Then he slips the tray into his incubator, which is a fruit crate lined with Reynolds Wrap. He switches on the bulb that dangles down inside. Within a week the seedlings will be up, opening their first little set of leaves.

He remembers lying on top of Marilla, worn out, that summer she came to live here. He can smell wood shavings, turps, fresh-cut planks when he thinks about it. Christ, she couldn't get enough of it then. "I want to have a baby," she said into his ear. She said it fiercely, if a whisper can be fierce. He knew how sad she was, how much she wanted to make up for the kid she'd lost. But all he said was, "I can't."

He didn't explain there was something wrong with him. Maybe she thought he was saying he wasn't sure how it would work out between them, or that he didn't want to take on the responsibility, or he just couldn't be bothered. She didn't try to argue or talk him into it, she just accepted it. Now he's sorry he didn't tell her the truth. Hard to say why he didn't. Maybe he was too proud, or too chicken, to let her know he was defective in that way.

Anyhow, now Marilla's got her kid back. She's invaded the place as fully as any baby could. He can hear the boards creak and thump as she walks around over his head. Suddenly, for no reason, he imagines a great egg inside Hannah, white and blurry and scarred with flecks and scratches, like the one in the movie. It's so enormous it nearly fills her belly, just sitting there waiting.

Something is bollixed up, Lyle doesn't know exactly what. A set of documents he apparently mailed when he shouldn't have, or to the wrong person, or not endorsed properly. His head aches and he's sick to his stomach. A walk might make him feel better, he thinks. Roz clicks her teeth when he brushes by the reception desk to take his coat and scarf from the coat tree. It's not his fault the office is so small they're all right on top of one another. It's not his fault his head pounds so he can't concentrate.

It's cold out, so cold it's a shock to the system. He winds his scarf tightly around his neck, but then has to loosen it, because the pressure makes the nausea so bad he thinks he's going to vomit on the dirty snow. The bottles in the state liquor store look revolting. A Dead River fuel truck backing into Water Street belches a cloud of diesel fumes into his face. It's slippery underfoot. He thinks about falling and breaking something, the crack of bone and the sharp pain, but then after that morphine and white sheets and oblivion.

The storefront that was a craft shop last summer, run by a fat woman from New Jersey who did so little business she took to dozing in the doorway, is now vacant. Wiped clean of crafts, of everything except some empty cartons. Vaguely Lyle wonders what happened to the fat woman, whether she went back to New Jersey, sunk into depression with her failure, or whether she's spending her February plotting some new venture—a vegetarian restaurant, maybe, with live jazz on Sunday afternoons. What's sure is that she won't be back to this town, he thinks, as he turns onto Bridge Street.

There's sea smoke on the river, swirling and steaming, as if it's rising from some other world deep underground. Lyle imagines devils with pitchforks down there. It would simplify life a lot to be able to blame everything on devils. Nausea, malice, lust, blunders, envy, bad blood . . .

Lyle leans against the iron railing and looks down into the channel, where today the ice is broken apart by the current. It makes him dizzy to watch the churning water. A pickup truck passing close to him on the bridge kicks a mush of sand and snow onto his trousers. The pickup is black with a red stripe painted along the side. He tries to memorize the license plate, as though soiling a person's trousers is a kind of hit-and-run. *Three-six-three-three-seven-P,* he recites to himself, though after a few seconds he isn't sure whether he hasn't confused the sequence.

Frances says Hannah's at Monkey Bay, not gone to Boston at all. That's why she never telephoned. Frances says Marilla wouldn't admit it, but she saw it in her eyes. He thinks about those eyes, gray like stones. The palest kind of granite when it's worn smooth by water. At first he didn't believe Frances, but now he sees it must be true. He should have known it would happen eventually, in spite of all Hannah's promises. Marilla is the sort of person who always wins, and Lyle is the sort of person who always loses. Justice has nothing to do with it. It's just written somewhere, and sooner or later it comes true.

But that doesn't mean you have to forgive the people who do it to you. There's no law says anything like that.

He'll have to go back to the office now. He'll have to

endure Billy clapping him amiably on the back and explaining once again what it was he bungled, and then he'll have to make his brain focus enough to try to fix it somehow.

He's cold. Freezes your balls, weather like this. As if it would matter.

Marilla's so tall she has to set the ironing board to its highest position, and the legs wobble. As she irons, her rounded shoulders sloping over the board, its rubber feet make a bumping noise on the plywood floor. Hannah traces a finger around a rusted circle on the zinc tabletop. The circle lacks an inch of being complete, and it's a reddish color, like dried blood.

"What does he do all day?" she asks.

"One thing and another."

"I mean, what does he do to earn money?"

Marilla sets the iron on its heel and turns the shirt so the collar is lying flat on the board.

"Or do you support him?"

"I don't support him."

The tabletop is uneven, rising on one side where the board under it must have warped. A marble placed on it would roll off. The metal is the color of old pewter, and its edge is rough, carelessly cut.

"My father used to call him a worm digger."

"Nothing wrong with digging worms."

"Well, yes, but—"

"Lyle didn't know a thing about it. Tucker never dug worms. Or clams either," she says, unrolling another dampened shirt. The iron sizzles on the cloth.

"Oh, come on. All Downeast men have dug clams."

"Not Tucker."

"What's so special about him?"

"I didn't say he was special. He just did other things."

"I see him leaving the house all the time, but he doesn't bring anything back," Hannah says. "Oh, cigarettes, sometimes. Or a few groceries."

"The work he does is seasonal."

"You mean like raking?"

"Like that. Not exactly that."

Hannah is brushing toast crumbs into a little pile, like an anthill. Though she can tell Marilla's becoming annoyed, she keeps on needling her. "He spends a lot of time in the cellar."

"He reads. Smokes. I don't know, I don't go down there much."

"Because he doesn't want you to?"

Marilla glances up at her. "Because I don't have call to."

This sounds a little like a warning. She picks up the salt shaker and flattens the crumb anthill. After a while she says, "He's not like my father at all, is he?"

"How do you mean?" Marilla asks, maneuvering the tip of the iron around a button.

"They say you keep on marrying the same person over and over, but you didn't do that."

Of course, Marilla didn't marry Tucker. Neither of them refers to that technicality, if it is only a technicality. Three ravens with serrated wings sail past the kitchen window, heading toward the bay. Snow is supposed to begin falling any minute, according to the radio. Turns out it does work, after all, but only Marilla can tune it in.

"Tucker goes off by himself," Hannah says. "My father has to be underfoot all the time, as though he might miss something. Or be left out of something."

"Well, Tucker's not afraid of that."

"What *is* he afraid of?"

She sets the iron down, flips the damp shirt to get at the tail. "If you found that out, you'd know a lot about him."

"If I wanted to."

"If you wanted to."

Hannah feels restless. She wishes the snow would come, it's like waiting for your period or something. The snow will be a wet one, the radio says, the temperature up around freezing. Maybe rain here on the coast.

"Why did he use those long nails to nail down the carpet in the loft? Didn't he know they'd stick through?"

Marilla hesitates before she says anything. "He was sore at me."

This makes Hannah more curious than ever. She'd like to know what her mother does to make him sore. She'd be interested to see him that way, pounding nails like spikes through the floorboards.

"What did you do?"

"I said I got a splinter in my foot because there wasn't any carpet in the loft."

"And *that* pissed him off?"

"It was nagging, he said."

"Ho. He should be married to Frances."

Marilla studies the underside of the iron. This is the first time they've been on the edge of talking about Frances: what she's like as a wife to Lyle, as a substitute mother for Hannah. Marilla's cheeks redden, and Hannah senses that Marilla feels it's treacherous ground.

"I saw her the other day," Marilla says quietly.

"Frances?"

"In the redemption center."

"Did she say anything about me?"

"She wanted to know whether I'd seen you."

"Shit. What did you tell her?"

"Is it a secret, Hannah?"

"He wouldn't understand why I'm here. My father."

Marilla looks as though she doesn't exactly understand, either.

"Well, did you tell her?"

"I figured that's up to you to do."

The snow has started, without Hannah's noticing. They are enormous flakes, artificial-looking. She thinks of the snowflakes you make by cutting into a folded-up piece of paper. It's hard to predict how they'll turn out when they're unfolded. If you don't do the cutting right, you could end up with eight separate pieces.

The storm wedged slabs of ice against the rim of the bay, and now they've frozen together into a crude jagged wall. The surface of the bay's frozen over into corrugations, and in the woods there's a crust of ice over the snow thick enough to walk on. On Sunday morning a big red fox weaves through the spruce right up to the house. Marilla's never seen that happen before in the ten winters she's lived here. She keeps Mackerel inside.

She watches Hannah pace from room to room, as restless as the cat. But there's nothing keeping her here, nothing that Marilla can see. She's puzzled. She thinks the fault must lie in her, somehow, that Hannah's waiting for something that Marilla doesn't know how to give or to do. If only Hannah would ask. But maybe she doesn't know what it is, either.

There's an awkwardness, a raggedness between them. It occurs to Marilla to wonder if they were ever close, the way she'd remembered.

Once Lyle came home from work with a boil on the back of his neck. He'd had them as a boy, he said, he knew what to do for them. He wanted her to hold on to his neck strips of towel soaked in boric acid and hot water, as hot as he could stand it, until the boil came to a head. Then she was supposed to sterilize a darning needle with a match and lance it. On his neck she saw the craters of old boils. She didn't want to, but he said, "That's the way my mother did it. Who else do I have to help me, now? Only you."

So she did what he asked. He flinched when she jabbed the needle into the boil and squeezed it so the pus would run out, but he didn't complain. She almost thought he liked it, keeping her standing there, changing the hot cloths. He sat on a stool in the kitchen and the kettle steamed. In a few days another boil appeared, and another. He wouldn't see a doctor, though. They'd eventually gone away when he was a boy, he said. They would again.

Then Hannah got a boil. Lyle insisted she get the same treatment, and it was terrible. She was only five or six and wasn't used to pain. She cried when Marilla put the cloths on her neck and knocked the pan so the hot water splashed on the linoleum and tried to run away, so that Marilla had to grab her arm and yank her back to the stool and hold her there with one hand while she applied the wet cloth with the other. Hannah screamed when Marilla used the needle and the pus ran out.

Hannah got four or five more boils, and then Marilla had had enough and took her to the doctor in spite of Lyle. The doctor frowned at her for having used a needle on them. That's what spreads the infection, he said, causes the scars. He gave her an ointment in a squat milk-glass jar, which cured them. Lyle was angry at her for going to the doctor behind his back, and in fact his own boils did cure themselves, without any ointment.

The fox is back, lurking at the edge of the woods, stepping lightly, leaving no footprints on the crust. "Look, Hannah," Marilla says, beckoning her to the round porthole window.

"Oh, he's gorgeous."

"I've never seen one so near the house."

"What's he want?" Hannah asks.

They're standing so close together at the small window that their arms touch. They both have heavy sweaters on, but Marilla is sharply aware of the pressure.

"He's hungry," Marilla says.

"Can't we feed him?"

"No. He has to make out by himself, his own way."

"Not even some scraps, some swill?"

"No, Hannah."

"I don't understand that."

"We'd be overrun with foxes if we started feeding them."

Hannah, unconvinced, moves away from the window. Beneath Hannah's short blunt haircut Marilla can see the faint scars from the boils. No use trying to explain to Hannah, then or now, whose fault it was she'd had to operate on Hannah's neck that way. Nobody held a gun to her head and made her do it.

"It's me."

"Well," Frances says.

"I'm sorry I didn't call sooner."

"We thought you must be maimed on the highway. In a ditch somewhere."

"I'm . . . Could I talk to my father?"

"No," Frances says with finality, as though he's under a tombstone. But then she goes on, relenting, "He went to Ellsworth to pick up my vacuum cleaner."

"Vacuum cleaner?"

"We got a new Electrolux. On sale."

Hannah's sitting on the floor, the phone in her lap, the extension cord stretched to its farthest limit. From where she sits she can see a white pitcher filled with dried sea heather, a wooden chest riddled with holes that must have washed up on the beach, a reclining chair with its plastic upholstery cracking open on one side.

"What's the weather like in Boston?" Frances says. "Warmer than here, I hope."

"I didn't get as far as Boston."

"Is that so?"

"I'm at Monkey Bay."

"Oh, Monkey Bay. With Marilla and the worm digger."

"He's not a . . ." A fluff of cat hair is traveling across the floor in little gasps. "There's also a cat."

"Too bad. With your allergies."

"I'm allergic to grass, Frances. Not cats."

"That's why we didn't have a pet, on account of your allergies."

"I don't remember it that way."

"That dog you had. Your father took it to the Humane Society because it gave you asthma."

There's a silence. Hannah can hear rainwater dripping from the eaves, the hissing of the wood stove, a muffled sort of bump beneath her, in the cellar.

"In case he wants to know, how long are you figuring on staying there?"

"I haven't made up my mind."

"You're always welcome to come back here, you know. This is your home."

Hannah thinks of her bureau drawers, empty except for the yellowing newspaper. But maybe Frances has already relined them with fresh.

"Hannah, I don't always say things right. Sometimes I march in with my two left feet. I mean well, but people seem to take offense."

"I don't take offense."

"I want you to know I've done the best I can, in spite of how it might look to you."

Hannah has wound the telephone cord around her finger so that the tip is red, throbbing. "I understand, Frances," she says, though really she has no idea what Frances is talking about.

"Well, I just wanted to say that. For the record."

When she hangs up Hannah feels bad about being so stony-hearted, such a cold fish. At least she could have asked about the arthritis and the blood pressure.

From the kitchen window she watches raindrops stipple a puddle in the yard. It would be good to get into the Pinto and just take off.

The summer after Marilla left, Hannah began stealing money. She doesn't know why, there was nothing much to spend it on. She bought a new kind of plastic curler from a rack in Blodgett's, candy bars in the Shop'n Save, rock magazines in the drugstore. She had to dispose of the evidence, the wrappers and price tags, and that was a chore, and she didn't really want any of those things to begin with. Not past the moment of possessing them, anyway.

Still, almost every night, after her father locked the doors and settled down in front of the television, she'd sneak into his bedroom. In the sour-smelling closet she'd thrust her hand into his trouser pocket—the pants he was wearing that week would be hanging on a hook on the left-hand side—and bring up a fistful of heavy coins: quarters, nickels, and dimes, even half-dollars. She was careful, sensible; she'd never take it all. Just enough so he wouldn't notice.

And yet she couldn't believe he didn't notice. They weren't real poor, but her mother used to buy remaindered bread and cold cuts, and dented cans marked down, and her father nursed the same old car along for years. Every night, almost, she took a dollar and a half or two dollars in change. It was so much she had trouble spending it. How could he not have missed it?

One night he came into her room. Half awake, she felt

him. He pinched and pulled her breasts with his fingers. His hand groped clumsily into the bottoms of her seersucker pajamas. She turned, as if in her sleep, and wrapped herself in her cotton flannel blanket.

In the morning she thought it might have been a dream. He only came again a few times. But she went on stealing money until Frances moved in. It was like some terrible kind of bargain, or blackmail.

Billy's hand covers the dish of peanuts and when he lifts his fist most of them are gone. He eats them one at a time, though, popping them into his mouth like basketball practice shots. "You were a good kid, Lyle," he says, chewing thoughtfully. "Motivated, that's the word." He licks the salt from his lips. "But nervous. You looked like you thought I was going to bite your head off." He laughs and picks up his rum and Coke.

Lyle fidgets with his tie clip. He can feel the skin of his face tighten: This kind of talk is as bad as having his picture taken.

"Thirty years. It's like it was yesterday."

"Twenty-nine," Lyle says.

"You didn't know no more than a goose knows about God. Waste of money, that business school they sent you to."

"My mother wanted it," Lyle says, not really sure anymore if that was the case. What she *didn't* want was for him to be dating Marilla Geary. She turned out to be right about that, but she missed the satisfaction of having her opinion confirmed.

"Well," Billy says, scooping up the last of the peanuts, "there's a lot of things in life women don't understand. Sometimes it's a mistake to listen to 'em."

Billy has a mouth full of shiny white teeth that are round, like pebbles, and when he talks he shows you all of them.

His hair is straight and stringy, almost no gray in it in spite of his sixty-odd years. There might be some Indian in him somewhere, Lyle thinks.

"A course," Billy goes on, "they have a way of wearing you down. They get their own way in the end."

Lyle wonders why Billy ties his necktie in such a small knot, the size of an acorn. It makes his big, horsey face look even bigger.

"Like Mid over Florida," Billy says, as the waitress arrives with his second rum and Coke. Lyle's still working on his first beer.

"Florida? You're vacationing in Florida this year?"

"We're gonna retire there, Lyle. I don't know if I'm gonna care for it or not. It's all Mid's idea."

Somebody has put a coin in the jukebox and the words *lubber zall lubber zall lubber zall lubber zall* blat over their heads, down the backs of their necks. It doesn't make any sense.

"Mid's going down this month to get settled," Billy says, raising his voice over the din.

"What about you?"

"That depends."

"On what?"

"On whether somebody buys me out quick or it takes a while. Or—I could just shut the place down. But that would mean . . ."

Lyle thinks about those movies where they shoot out all the bottles over the bar and booze goes spurting out onto the floor. They shoot out the mirrors, the lights; they plug the jukebox so full of holes it finally shuts up.

"You listening to me, Lyle?"

"What?"

"I was asking if you thought you could scrape enough dough together to buy me out."

Lyle looks at his half-drunk beer. The surface is scummy,

like a stagnant pond, and he knows he's going to retch if he doesn't get out of here. But his feet seem bolted to the dirty plaid carpeting, and after what feels like a very long time, Billy pulls him out of the booth and drives him home.

In the trailer Lyle had to step over a pan of rusty rainwater, magazines lying open, a bathrobe and a T-shirt, a box of Sugar Snaps. The bed was unmade, the top sheet a tangled gray ball at the foot. He had trouble with the rubber; he'd never used one before. After he did it to her, she began to talk. "Ever been to California?" she asked. "I'd sure like to go there. I'd sure like to get out of this hole."

Tucker didn't know her, only that he'd seen her a couple of times with a guy from the town, an older guy who had a car. He liked the way she looked, sitting cross-legged on the dock, jerking the rod to attract the mackerel. She looked like she knew what she was doing. He thought it would be fun to sneak her out from under the guy's nose, like a snake stealing eggs from a nest. So he called up, "Want to go for a ride?" She lifted the rod out of the water, unhitched a hank of seaweed from one of the hooks, laid the rod on the dock, and climbed down into the punt.

She didn't talk in the boat, and he liked that, too. It seemed they were both paying attention to the squeaking of the oars in the oarlocks, the washing of the sea water against the sides of the old punt, the blatting of the gulls. She sat on a plank in the stern, not looking at him. Her hair was dark but not thick, and as he rowed she slowly plaited half of it into a crude pigtail, and then the other half. She was wearing a loose blue shirt that swelled when the wind puffed under it, and he thought her eyes were the same color. It interested him that her eyebrows grew together in the middle and she didn't pluck them out, the way his sisters did.

When they reached the island she didn't wait for him to give her a hand but scrambled out over the gunnels. She helped him haul the boat onto the pebbly beach. It was just a scrap of an island, with a few gnarled jack pines for trees. The rest was boulders, ledge, some scrubby bushes. Bayberry, cranberry.

They sat on a flattish piece of ledge and took off their wet sneakers and socks. She wrung her socks into twists but didn't touch his. He saw that her feet, reddened from the icy water, were bigger than his. Her hands, too. She was bigger than he was all over, but that didn't bother him.

The wind whipped at her hair, and one of the pigtails was unraveling. When she lifted her arms to braid it again, her breasts went up, too. She knew he was watching her and she was shy, but not embarrassed, not in a giggly way.

Cranberries were growing on the ledge. She picked one and rolled it around in her cupped hand. It was red on one side, a pale ivory color on the other. She cut into it with her thumbnail. "Hard," she said.

"Sour, too."

"You wouldn't want to eat them yet."

"You could if you cooked them up with plenty of sugar."

She squinted in the sun, looking at him. A small smile worked around her mouth. He realized she was pretty. She tossed the cranberry and it bounced off the rock and into the bushes.

"Does this place have a name?" she asked.

He thought it was funny that she didn't care about his name, only the name of the island.

"Naw. It's not even big enough to be a dot on the map. Nobody'd bother naming it."

"Been here before?"

The sun was behind a smear of clouds now. She looked at

him levelly, and that's when he saw that her eyes were gray, not blue.

"A few times," he said, lying. For all he knew the island rose out of the sea yesterday and would go down like a stone tomorrow. "What about you?"

"No."

She was sitting hunched on the slab of ledge, the tail of the blue shirt flapping in the wind. He pushed her down, cradling her neck in the crook of his arm. There wasn't room on the stone to stretch out, and underneath them were bumps and ridges, prickly scrub in the crevices, broken mussel shells. He undid the metal buttons on her dungarees, then on his. He thought he was going to swim into her like a fish, but he couldn't, he had to ram her, and she bit his shoulder with the pain, right through his T-shirt. He was the one who hollered. When he was finished he pulled off all her clothes and looked at her. Her breasts were round and hard, the size of those muskmelons bred for cold climates, Minnesota midgets. He saw a dribble of blood run down the inside of her thigh. Her thighs had goosebumps. He stroked the dark hair in her crotch, and right away she came.

When she walked into the house Frances saw a threadbare carpet curling up at the ends, cafe curtains on spring rods, some odds and ends of furniture, a musty couch covered in brown serge. Frances had it all hauled up to the attic. She wanted matching.

Of course she never said anything to Lyle about Marilla. When he talked about her she'd agree, but she carefully avoided bringing the subject up. When you move into a house another woman has left behind, you find out all you want to know about her, and more. Marilla couldn't have cared a bit about keeping house, making a cozy nest for her family.

"Cozy" to Frances meant deep-pile wall-to-wall carpeting. That's the first thing she did, had it put down in the living and dining rooms and on the stairs. She almost wished Marilla would knock on the door, and Frances would generously let her in (but not take her coat) and Marilla wouldn't be able to help seeing how much bigger the house looked with the beige carpeting, how it tied everything together. She might even realize how much more tasteful the new floral wallpaper was, with its miniature bouquets, and how the drapes and the matching valances made the rooms look like real *rooms* instead of bare cells somebody'd absentmindedly hauled a load of rubbish into.

Marilla's mother had always kept such a nice house, even after she had to turn their living room into a beauty parlor. Frances knew that because once when she'd gone for a cut and set she asked to use the bathroom and had a peek into what they were using for a sitting room. Must have been the dining room before. You'd expect just a jumble of furniture crammed in there any-old-how, but it wasn't that way at all. Louise Geary had style, and she knew how to put together a room that could be photographed for *Family Circle* magazine. That's why Frances thought it strange that Marilla couldn't care less about the way things looked. Of course, her father was only a boat mechanic, and some say that disease he had he got from drink.

Personally, Frances thinks Marilla had always been planning on taking off the minute she got the opportunity, so why take any pains? At the Monday Club one or two of the girls said they'd known all along something was queer about Marilla, how silent she was, and how she kept to herself except for Mittie Labbett, and Mittie was all right, but Harold was such a loudmouth, and none of her kids looked like making anything of themselves, especially her oldest boy, Frank, who was always getting into trouble. Probably Marilla'd been thinking about doing what she did for years, too bad all she got was that good-for-nothing bum.

When Frances moved in there were cheese-colored rectangles on that awful sickly wallpaper. Frances assumed Marilla had taken the pictures away with her when she left. She tried to imagine Marilla going from room to room, lifting the wires off the hooks, wrapping the pictures in towels or pillowcases. But it wasn't a scene that formed easily in the mind, particularly since she hadn't taken much of anything else. Frances doubted they were Rembrandts. She doubted they were masterpieces.

For some reason it bothered Frances what had become of them, even after the wallpaper was covered with new, and the rectangles weren't there to remind her.

Offhandedly she said to Hannah, "I suppose your mother took the pictures away with her."

Hannah was sitting in front of the television, sucking on a long hank of hair. It was a habit she'd recently taken up, and it drove Frances wild. Privately she said to Lyle he ought to hustle her over to the town barber and have her hair cut so short she wouldn't be able to get it into her mouth, but she knew enough about kids from her years of teaching not to make such a threat herself. She tried to ignore it as best she could.

"What pictures?" Hannah asked, not turning away from the television.

"The ones that used to be on the wall there."

Hannah just shrugged. Frances felt like marching up to the set and switching the knob off and giving the girl a good swat, but she didn't. She said, "I suppose they were things your mother was especially fond of? Hannah?"

Hannah sighed, as if she was greatly put upon, just to answer a simple question. "She didn't take anything with her. Only clothes."

"Then what happened to them?"

"Why do you care? You've gotten rid of everything else, what do you care about some dumb old pictures?"

"Oh, Hannah. It makes me sad when you talk to me in that tone of voice."

After a while Hannah said, "My father took them down."

"I suppose he gave them away?"

"Why don't you ask him?"

But she could never find just the right way to bring it up. Then, later on in the summer, she went behind the tool shed to dump out a bottle of paint remover she found under the sink, nasty stuff she didn't want to have in the house, and she saw a heap of pictures lying there. The glass was all smashed, the fragments caught in the weeds, and most of the wooden frames were broken. Of course the pictures themselves, under snow and muck all winter, were totally ruined. One looked like it might have been of sunflowers, but the rest weren't recognizable at all.

Frances has never mentioned it to Lyle, but at times like now when he's acting funny, she thinks about it.

Hannah's slouched on the bed, idly tweezing her brows without a mirror by feeling with her fingers where the stubble is, and suddenly he's in the doorway, the blue cloth that hangs from the jamb bunched against his shoulder.

"What do you want to do that for?" he says roughly. "There's no need of that."

The day after the ice cracks up and washes out of the bay with the tide, Marilla sees Lyle for the first time in ages. She's just taken the turn toward Route 1 at the cemetery and she sees somebody walking along the side of the road. If she was in China and saw a man in a coolie hat walking with his rear stuck out and his upper half bobbing, looking at the ground like a duck after grubs, she'd know it was Lyle. Nobody else on the planet walks that way. But she can't imagine what in God's name he's doing on foot, way out here.

She brakes the pickup, leans across the seat, and unrolls the window. "Can I give you a lift?"

He jerks his head up and almost smiles, and she has the odd sensation that his face is about to shatter. "That's all right," he says, standing there in the slush.

"Did your car break down?"

"Yes," he says vaguely, peering down the road as though he knew he'd misplaced something but couldn't exactly remember what.

"Well, get in, and I'll run you into town."

"No, thanks."

"It's seven miles, Lyle. I'm not having you on my conscience."

He opens the door and clambers in awkwardly, flooding the pickup with a sweet oily smell.

"What's wrong with it?" she asks, as they're passing Ethel Erridge's trailer. Old Phil Erridge died last winter, and now they say Ethel's got cancer.

"What?"

"Your car. What happened to it?"

He doesn't answer for a while and then he says, "It was making a funny noise."

On his side of the road is a heap of wooden lobster traps, which are shaped like the quonset hut a little farther on, where the evangelists gather on Sunday mornings and Wednesday nights. Some patches of field are bare of snow now, and three horses are plodding around in the muck behind a wire fence.

Strange he'd be out driving at this early hour. She supposes some on-site inspection had to be done in a hurry, after an ATV accident or burst pipes or a chimney fire, and Billy dispatched Lyle to tend to it. He's not carrying his vinyl attaché case; he must have left it behind in the disabled car.

She's not sure whether to speak about Hannah or not. She has no desire to rub his nose in it, that Hannah's with her, but she doesn't want to appear sneaky, either. She knows that her secrets with Tucker—and being found out—have tainted her forever, and that's hard to bear. Abruptly she says, "You know, Hannah's been with me for a while."

"Yes," he says, but he's still staring out the window, and actually he doesn't seem very interested.

As they reach Route 1 and then go by the redemption center she reflects that she's going to be late opening up; from here it's three miles into town and three back again. She can't just put him out by the side of the road, though. He's rubbing his knees with the heels of his hands, like he's kneading bread, and it's a gesture she knows well. It signals some internal agitation, but she's puzzled, because mentioning Hannah's name scarcely seemed to penetrate. Worried about his car, maybe? Or whatever insurance calamity lies at the other end of Monkey Bay Road?

In the old days she'd have heard all about it, she wouldn't have been able to shut him up. Secretly she scorned the way everything spilled out of him. And she's relieved she's not the one who has to prop him up now. Still, she can't help feeling sorry for him. He's going to wear the ribs off his corduroy trousers, the skin off his palms.

"Knapp's?" she asks, as she slows down to make the sharp turn, downhill, into town.

He takes such a long time to answer that when he says "It doesn't matter," it's too late to pull into Knapp's garage.

"Mawhinney's, then?"

"Just let me off anywhere," he says, taking hold of the door handle.

She stops where she can, next to a filthy snowbank opposite

Cottage Street. He doesn't walk on ahead toward Mawhinney's, though, or in the direction of the office. She watches as he crosses Main Street, narrowly missing being clipped by a van, and starts trudging through the slush down the center of Cottage Street. He's going home, for pity's sake. At ten past nine on a Monday morning.

As they passed a bucket of sea urchins, he said, "My sister has breast cancer." The sea urchins were parked outside a marine biology lab. Hannah couldn't think of anything to say until they reached the elevator. He punched the *4* button and she said, "Did you just find out?"

"This morning. She was operated on this morning."

The cafeteria wasn't very crowded at that hour. Like Hannah, he went to class straight from work and didn't get a chance to eat until afterward. They set their trays down at one end of a long table littered with styrofoam containers and cardboard dishes with scraps of food in them. You got the idea that the students here were too weary from dealing with course work, jobs, families, to finish their meals or clear up after themselves.

Calculus, the class was. She'd enrolled because she wasn't that bad at math in high school and she thought she might get a job with a tax-preparation firm or in tax consulting. Somebody'd told her they were hot fields, those people made good money. He was taking it because he was pre-med. He was easily the smartest person in the class; she couldn't even follow the theoretical discussions he had with the professor.

"She's only twenty-nine," he said, looking at Hannah. "She has three kids."

Hannah stared down at the gray microwaved patty on the bun. She ripped open a packet of catsup, squirted a blob onto the meat, and closed the burger up again.

"They took them both off, but they found malignant cells

in the axillary lymph nodes. I don't think she's going to make it."

"God, I'm sorry, Tim."

"We're very close."

She'd always wished she had a sister, but maybe being an only child has its advantages.

"I feel better now that I've told you."

She felt flattered that he said that. He picked up the package of saltines that came with his chili; they rattled in their cellophane. She liked his hands. She could imagine how competently they'd someday thump a chest, probe for broken bones. He wasn't good-looking. His face she thought of as knobby. He might even have been teased for his odd looks as a child. But she liked his face as much as his hands.

He was quite a bit older than she was, over thirty probably. She gathered from things he'd said over other late meals that he'd been going to school part-time for years, that he was supporting other family members as well as himself.

"What will happen to the children?" She pictured them coming home from school and being told their mother was dead.

He shook his head. "Maybe Paul will marry again."

Hannah's hamburger tasted almost rotten. She didn't know why she kept buying the damn things, except that you didn't have to stand in a long line. You just picked one off the counter, inserted it in the microwave yourself, and set the timer for forty-five seconds. She'd never been patient, and now, it seemed, she was even worse.

"Look, Hannah. A friend of mine has an apartment in Somerville. He's out of town on business and he left a key with me so I could feed his cats."

She watched him break saltines into his cardboard bowl of chili.

"Things are tough at home. Do you understand what I mean?"

"I think so."

"So I'm going back to his place tonight."

"Are you sure it's a good idea to be alone?"

"That's what I'm getting at, Hannah. I thought you might be willing to come with me."

"Oh, Tim . . ."

He put the plastic spoon down on his tray, reached across the table, and took her wrist. He didn't hurt her, but his hand held her firmly, and she could feel the moisture on his palm. "Not to . . . you know. Just to be with me."

"I don't know if I can."

"It's a terrible imposition—of course I see that. But I feel so alone."

She was looking at his fingers on her wrist. His hands were carefully tended for a man's, the fingernails clean and neatly pared.

"Couldn't you spare me some time, Hannah? I don't have anyone else to ask."

"Your family . . ."

"That's what I have to get away from. My mother's so impossible, you have no idea. She thinks what's happening to Karen is the will of God."

She watched his chili congeal in the bowl.

"All right," she said, almost in a whisper.

Lyle hasn't been to the office in nearly a week. He hasn't called in sick or anything. When Roz telephoned the house to ask what happened to him he heard Frances lying, inventing some excuse. Now that he has the blood-pressure condition it's easy to make excuses.

She knows something's up and she's getting ready to

pounce. At one time Mildred Flowers and Frances were thick as thieves, Mildred getting her elected to the Monday Club, and the two of them driving up to Bangor to go shopping in the mall and exchanging house-decorating magazines. A couple of years ago something happened, Lyle never knew what. Anyway, Frances doesn't have a direct pipeline to Mid's plans anymore, so he's safe for the moment.

He could just tell her and be done with it. He'd feel so much better if he could talk to her about it, but there are difficulties. The bargain they made when they got married was all about security, really: She'd always be there when he came home and never leave him, no matter what, and he'd provide a home for her and support her so she could quit teaching. They never signed an agreement to that effect, of course, or even spoke about the bargain out loud, after that one conversation in the Brass Lantern. "I wouldn't want a wife of mine to work," he'd said, "but I would expect her to be faithful."

"Oh, I understand, Lyle," she'd said quickly, and he knew she did. He knows she remembers every word, and the bargain might just as well be typed in triplicate and a copy stowed in some lawyer's safe. So how can he tell her he's going to be out of a job?

Because that's what's going to happen. Even supposing he could get together the necessary wherewithal to buy the business, he couldn't run it. He's not fooling himself. All the money would go right down the drain in short order, along with his health and peace of mind and reputation. If Billy sells out to somebody else, Lyle will have a new boss. Somebody hard-nosed, unforgiving of human error. A person who didn't know about the Pratts—a transplant from New Jersey, even. Or Billy might get tired of hanging around waiting for a buyer while his wife suns herself in Florida and just shut the place down. Already, when Lyle sees the office building in his mind, he pictures the gray paint peeling, yellow shades pulled down over the windows, a FOR SALE sign on the uncut patch of grass in front.

Lyle is fifty years old. What's he supposed to do, take up wreath making? Go to work in the cannery? He feels a hard little cinder of resentment in his chest. It's not so much Billy he resents—Billy has been a good friend to him over the years—but his wife. Imbecilic woman doesn't belong in Florida, doesn't deserve it. She's nothing but a bootlegger's daughter who had the good luck to marry somebody with get-up-and-go. Well, he does feel sore at Billy, as a matter of fact, for knuckling under to her. How's Billy going to go ice fishing in Florida? Lyle wishes he'd thought of pointing that out, but he was too shocked, too battered by the terrible racket from the jukebox. He can still feel it pounding in his ears, the way your heart does sometimes.

"More snow," Mittie says, knocking her boot against the doorjamb. "Just when the chives started coming up."

"It happens every year."

"I know, and every year I think this one's going to be different."

Marilla's in no special hurry to leave. She lingers behind the counter, fiddling with one thing and another, while Mittie strips off her coat and hangs it on a nail. "Take a look at these roots, will you?" Mittie says, peering into a Cover Girl compact. "My hair's the one thing that grows good in this climate. I swear I'm going to chop it all off and get me a wig. Be a whole lot cheaper than perms and tints in the long run."

This is not a new threat, and Marilla ignores it. "Slow day," she says. She runs her finger along the names in the notebook where they record video rentals. "Only six—no, seven—went out today. And hardly any empties in."

"Must be the snow. You give them a little taste of spring and they forget how to drive in the stuff."

"What's in the bag? Smells like a whole deli."

"Bought me a sub at Shop'n Save for my supper. Millard might as well send my paycheck directly to the Shop'n Save—that's where it all goes, anyhow."

Marilla's pulling on her parka.

"I almost forgot to tell you," Mittie says. "Millard's talking about opening Sundays starting in April. You interested in working Sundays?"

"I don't know if I can look ahead as far as April."

"Or maybe Hannah banana," Mittie says slyly. "Maybe she'd like to pick up a little extra change."

"Hannah?" Marilla imagines Hannah's small, neat hands sticky with soda pop. She does up her zipper, reaches into her pocket for her keys.

"Or is she going to be a leech forever?"

"I wouldn't call her a leech," she says carefully, picking out the car key from the bunch on the ring.

"Well, what else is she? All she does is lounge around your house, eating the food you put on the table. A week I could see, but two months? I bet she never lifts a finger to help, either."

"She's my child."

"She's twenty-three, the same age as my Wayne, and Wayne's got a wife and kid and his own place."

"Yes, and Wayne drinks like a fish and Patty has to waitress at the Brass Lantern so they can keep body and soul together."

"He doesn't drink that much—and anyway, what's wrong with waitressing? You weren't too good to waitress, if I remember right."

Suddenly Marilla remembers what Tucker used to say about Mittie looking like a ferret. A ferret with a half-grown-out perm and gray roots.

"You're too soft on her, Marilla. You don't have to go on trying to make things up to her forever."

"I'm not."

"You are, and it's a mistake. I'm just warning you for your own good, that's all."

"Maybe you should stick to worrying about your own kids," Marilla says, opening the door and closing it with cold deliberation.

She'd thought that at least Mittie, if nobody else, understood how it was between her and Hannah. But it looks like she's alone in this, after all. Her boots make black indentations in the fresh white snow.

He smelled of soap and cheap brandy. Hannah could hear a clock ticking, water running in the pipes, the soft thumps of cats moving in the dark apartment, an occasional car on the street. Through slits in the blinds she saw a reddish light, neon diffused in the mist. He turned and sighed in his sleep. The army blanket was rough on her chin.

She felt his breath on the back of her neck. His face was in her hair. His foot, in a sock, touched hers and then moved away.

Later on she was aware of rain on the window glass. A car pulled away from the curb; somebody's footsteps tapped hollowly on the sidewalk. His body trembled. She heard him gasp in his sleep, dreaming.

A cat rustled against the bedroom door, trying to get in.

His hand was on her breast, on the wool of her sweater. She held her breath. His grip tightened and then relaxed; she thought he must have fallen asleep again.

The clock ticked. On another floor somebody flushed a toilet.

He turned her and nestled his head against her breasts. She moved her fingers in his clean hair, stroking it. He made a little cry in his nose, like a cat or a baby.

His hands were under the sweater, slipping inside her bra, his fingers on her nipples. She pulled away from him, out from under the army blanket.

"Hannah, please."

She felt dizzy. The brandy, the fragmented sleep. In the half-light she groped for her shoes. "I can't, Tim."

"You don't like me."

"It's not that."

"Is it her, is that why? The operation?" He was sitting up in the bed. His face looked white.

"No. I don't know."

"Listen, what if I told you there wasn't any operation? My sister doesn't have cancer."

She tied a knot in her shoelace.

"I made it all up so you'd come here with me. I can make you feel so good, Hannah. Trust me."

"Stop. I don't want to hear any more."

She never knew which story was the true one. The next day she got on a Greyhound bus, and a month later she found herself in Seattle.

On the Monday after Billy gave him the news, Lyle woke up at three in the morning. For a while, in the greenish light the clock radio gave off, he watched Frances sleeping. Her hair was done up in some kind of fishnet thing, her mouth was partway open. Without her glasses she had the look of a newborn puppy. He knew he couldn't tell her he wasn't going to work, and he couldn't tell her why.

He bundled together the clothes he'd worn the day before and crept out of the bedroom, so as not to awaken her. He relieved himself, brushed his teeth, shaved, applied Brylcreem to his hair, just as if he were getting ready for a workday—not because he had any plan in mind, but one action led automatically to the next one. His underwear wasn't clean and his corduroys were a little rumpled, but otherwise he was dressed as if for the office. Before leaving the house he took his attaché case from the window seat in the breakfast nook and slid it far under the sofa. He did not check his blood pressure.

It was still dark out, but as he trudged along Cottage Street he began to be aware of a faint light in the direction of the marsh. That particular light reminded him of a time he went hunting with his father as a young boy. He thought about the icy cold, the foreboding, the bone-jarring crack when his father pulled the trigger. The yell of fear bursting out of him. His father edging away, deeper into the woods, cradling the Winchester.

Then, for a long while, Lyle stopped thinking at all. He wasn't even aware where his feet were taking him, he just plodded along, one foot in front of the other. At first there was no traffic, and then, as the sky grew lighter, a fuel truck rumbled by, and then a couple of pickups, and a semi loaded with logs.

He liked the crunching sound his boots were making in the frozen slush. He liked the sting of the cold on his face and the way his muscles ached. He didn't feel a renewal of hope or anything like that. The truth is, saying "All right, that's it, that's the end" can be more comforting than any jeezly little scrap of hope.

He was aware of the building for many minutes—the luminous blue-green color, the rectangular intrusiveness among the spruces—before he realized what it was. A big new sign paid for by the Pepsi-Cola Company announced to one and all PEPSI MONKEY BAY REDEMPTION CENTER AND VIDEO PEPSI. With one hand they were dispensing God's grace; with the other, videos. The sound of his own laughter startled him. It was like an outburst from a mechanical appliance.

There was much more traffic now, one vehicle after another

spraying him with sand and gravel. The slush no longer crunched, and rivulets of water washed around his boots. He left the highway at the next turning, following silence the way a plant leans toward the sun.

He'd never noticed the beautiful stand of white pines before, never walked this road before. After the pines was a rusted trailer, and after that an endless muddy field. Miles went by under his feet. It was like reducing a log to chips by making one tiny cut at a time. He passed more woods and fields, and a farmhouse, and after a while there were gravestones sticking up out of the mud and shrunken patches of snow. A family plot, all Elvins and Gibbens and Erridges, connected to each other in various ways, so intricate even they wouldn't have been able to sort them out, dead or alive. Nothing but bones now, none of what happened to them or what they did to each other mattered a bit anymore, in spite of the plastic flowers people left there. Suddenly the sun felt hot, and for a second it flashed through his mind that he was really in Florida and only dreaming about this sad little graveyard.

But he wasn't in Florida. Slowly he started back the way he'd come, and then he saw the black pickup. It had a red stripe along the side like the one that nearly hit him on the bridge. It stopped just ahead of him, and when he read the license plate, 36337-*P*, he knew it was the same one. So he wasn't surprised when Marilla rolled down the window. What surprised him was that he got in.

Nobody ever told her not to go down cellar, but she's sensed it's off limits. Even when Marilla brings up a pan full of potatoes, or carrots, or a Hubbard squash, there's an odd look on her face. Not guilty, exactly, but secretive.

Cautiously Hannah opens the cellar door and then shuts it behind her. She sits on the top step. The steps are nothing but rough planks. There's a dank smell, like cat pee, though she knows Mackerel isn't allowed down here.

From where she sits, she can see him. He's at the far end of the cellar, in a chair covered with something pink. Over his head a light bulb dangles from a cord. He's smoking, the cigarette cupped in his fingers. It looks as though the light bulb is trying to suck up the smoke, and the smoke is swirling around it, trying to escape. She's sure he heard the door open and close, but probably he can't see her, or if he can, she'd just be a dark shape huddled on the plank.

The other light is in some kind of shiny box. Its inner walls are crinkled, so they reflect the light in strange patterns. Something makes her think of a magician's box, but she's not sure she ever saw a magic show. Maybe at the Blue Hill Fair?

His hair is fine, no particular color, except there's a little gray in it. He has on a loose, ash-colored sweater that Marilla knitted. His mustache is shaggy on his upper lip. His eyes are cast down, watching his cigarette, so she can't see them, but she knows they're brown, like hers. Also, his teeth are smaller than you'd expect in a grown man. They have slight gaps between them, and they're stained from the smoking.

He rubs out that cigarette and, leaning back with his eyes shut, lights another. He breathes deeply. She wonders what his lungs must look like. Sooty, with black pockets in them. Maybe calcified places, hard as coral.

After a while she lowers herself five or six steps, moving as quietly as she can. The new plank has a knothole, under her right hand. She can just fit her finger through it, though it's splintery. The smell of cat pee is stronger now, and she can also smell onions, and the sourness of potatoes that are beginning to shrivel and send out pink sprouts.

From this plank she can see that his feet are propped up on a table, and that one knee of his jeans has a hole in it. The pink thing is an old bedspread with a scalloped edge, which is filthy from having dragged on the concrete, and it has holes in it, too.

He uncrosses his legs and crosses them the other way. What he's using for an ashtray is a coffee cup without a handle. He puts that cigarette out, too, and sets the cup on the bookshelf beside him. He reaches over his head and pulls the light string.

Now the only illumination is from inside the magical box. It's enough light for her to get the rest of the way down the steps, though, without breaking her neck.

When she gets to the chair she wedges her knees between his hips and the chair arms. It's a tight fit. She puts her mouth on his and tastes smoke and salt. The mustache scrubs her upper lip. The edges of his teeth feel sharp, serrated, on her tongue.

She pulls her zipper down, then his. When she yells and digs her fingernails into his back, he mutters, "Christ. Another one."

March

Climbing March Hill, that's what they call it, getting through the last hard month of winter. But Lyle scarcely notices the weather. Every day he's at the office, packing files into cardboard boxes. At the end of the month it's all going to be hauled up to Machias. Some character from a realty was around this morning, stepping over boxes to measure windows and floor space. From the outside he gripped the top of Lyle's particle-board partition and rattled it, to see how easy it would be to dismantle, Lyle supposes. Lyle looked at the fingers dangling down into his cubicle and laughed. He'd thought he was safe, but it was all a trick, an illusion. The hell with it. He has a plan.

He hasn't told Frances about it, and that worries him, because in the going-on-ten years they've been married he's always told her nearly everything. It's all because of the way she carried on when she found out about the company folding. He knew she'd be upset; that's why he wanted to break it to her gradually—bad luck that Roz had to blat it out over the phone. Frances was more than upset. In fact, he wonders if she isn't a little unstable.

Maybe she's been unbalanced all along and she's been able

to hide it from him up to now. Well, now that he thinks about it, he does remember one or two times he thought she went overboard about something. The time she had him install a padlock on a kitchen cabinet so Hannah couldn't ruin her teeth coming down in the night after snacks. And the time she got it into her head that the pin he gave her for her birthday was an old one of Marilla's. He said that couldn't be because he'd sold all Marilla's jewelry, but that didn't mollify her. On both those occasions he wondered if the way she acted didn't have something to do with the moon. His mother believed in the moon as a force. A peculiar notion maybe, but with women you can't tell.

Somehow Frances also found out about Marilla giving him a lift to town that day. It seems like she has spies everywhere. Apparently yet another one of them saw him walking along Monkey Bay Road. He can't think how, since he doesn't recall any cars passing him, until the black pickup came along. Frances didn't believe him when he said he was only going for a walk and he didn't even know it was Monkey Bay Road he was on. It could have been any road. She accused him of going to see Hannah behind her back and refused to take his word for it that he'd forgotten Hannah wasn't in Boston.

"How could you forget such a thing?" Frances wanted to know.

He found it hard to explain. Finally he said, "It's like when you swallow something like a cherry stone or a nickel and it goes right through you."

She looked at him as if he was crazy and then she said, "Or else it sticks in your gullet and kills you."

"Well, I'm not dead, am I, Frances?" he said reasonably, but she wouldn't listen.

Then, when she found out about Flowers Insurance being gobbled up by Shiretown Insurance in Machias, she hardly said a thing about his losing his job, all she wanted to talk about was where Mid Flowers thought she was going to wear her silver fox jacket to in Florida.

He said he'd heard they used a lot of air conditioning in Florida, they didn't care how much energy they wasted, and she told him he didn't know any more about Florida than a pig knows about Sunday.

They never used to have squabbles like this. Dammit, he's not going to use up any more mental energy chewing over who said what to who. He has more important things on his mind.

His plan is to run a permanent yard sale at the house from May right through September. Nothing original about it—half the people who own property on Main Street empty out their attics onto their lawns every summer. Plenty of tourists pass through on their way to the Maritimes, think the natives are so numb they don't know what they have, stop to load the trunks of their cars up with culch. No reason he and Frances can't help them do it. The beauty is it's all cash, you don't have to pay taxes on it like regular income, and you can keep your own hours. They could start with the furniture Frances hauled up attic when she moved in. And it's easy to find rubbish like they peddle in the yards for free, you just have to keep your eyes open.

Only two problems, as far as he can see. One is, their house isn't right on Main Street. But he could rig up a waterproof sign, attach it to the telephone pole on the corner by Hinckley's: YARD SALE, 1/4 MILE.

The other problem is Frances. She's not going to be crazy about tourists trampling the grass, asking to use the bathroom. But she doesn't want to go back to teaching, does she? She'd like to go on eating, wouldn't she? Anyway, she doesn't have to know, not for a while.

He's rather proud of himself for not knuckling under to his bad luck. God helps him who helps himself. At least they won't find him out on the flats grubbing up bloodworms.

Marilla cast the stitches on for her, and now Hannah's got an inch and a half of oatmeal-colored ribbing. The sweater pattern is puckered where something wet dripped on it, taped together at the creases, coming detached where the tape is yellowed and cracking. Following a pattern or a set of instructions is not something Hannah does gladly. But she's determined to do this, though she wouldn't be able to say why.

He's sitting at the other end of the kitchen table, drinking coffee. At his place, pushed back a ways, is a blue-rimmed plate with a scrap of bacon rind and a smear of egg yolk on it. The cup makes a gritty sound when he sets it on the metal surface.

"All right," he says. "Now what?"

She brushes her hair out of her eyes with her sleeve, swallows. She didn't know they'd have to talk about it. She'd thought they'd just do it the once and be done with it. "What do you mean?" she asks, in a voice that sounds to her foolish, limp, like that of a child caught out in some deviousness.

He smiles a little, groping in his shirt pocket for cigarettes. "I'm happy to do what you want, only I have to know what it is."

She sees that she's dropped a stitch, she's going to have to rip out a couple of rows.

"I never turned down a pretty girl yet," he says, still smiling, the unlit cigarette in his mouth, his eyes on her. His eyes don't leave her as he strikes the match, inhales. "Hey, Hannah?"

Carefully she sets the knitting down on the table. "Maybe I made a mistake," she says, returning his stare.

"Oh, I wouldn't necessarily say that. I don't guess your mother would like it, but she doesn't have to know, does she?"

"*I*'m not going to tell her."

He lets the cigarette burn down some, deposits the ash on the rim of the plate. "Not in so many words."

"Not at all."

"Really? It's the perfect way to get even, to settle the score with her, when you think about it."

"I'm not interested in settling any scores."

"Okay, I'll take your word for it. If it's plain old screwing you're after, I'm glad to oblige."

Her face is as prickly hot as if she'd stuck her head in the oven, but she doesn't drop her eyes. "We could just forget about it."

"Maybe we could. Maybe. But sometimes things aren't so easy to stop, once you've started them." He clamps his hand down on the cigarette pack, shoots it across the table at her like a hockey puck. "Like smoking, for instance. Ever smoked, Hannah?"

"Once. At a party."

"Once upon a time I hitched a ride with a guy carrying a load of toilet paper. He handed me a cigarette and I took it. I thought it made me a man. But it's a habit that can give you a lot of trouble."

"Why don't you quit, then?"

He tips his chair back. The only thing keeping him from crashing to the floor are his fingertips under the rough zinc edge of the tabletop. "That's what I'm saying. It's not so easy. You get to craving the lift it gives you, nicotine. You get jumpy when you don't have it. Ruins your temper. You start being unpleasant to people, blatting out things you don't mean."

She looks at the shiny ice-blue package. Trues.

"Of course, not everybody gets addicted to nicotine," he says, letting the chair legs down so softly she can't hear them touch the floor. "Maybe you're one of the lucky ones that don't. Maybe you could just take a cigarette once in a while—at a party—and not even think about it the rest of the time."

"It made me sick the time I tried it."

He laughs, and she can see the gaps in his small teeth. "It made you sick, and you said the hell with it."

"It wasn't like that. The question just never came up again. Maybe nobody offered me one, I don't know."

"Sorry, but that's kind of hard to believe."

"Why?"

"Well, at parties that's what people do. To be friendly."

"I don't go to that many parties."

He reaches across the table, takes the pack of Trues, stows it in his pocket. "Sometimes, when you decide you want company, you find the party's over, and everybody's gone home."

As she's pulling into Mittie's driveway it's snowing, but the temperature is forty-two degrees and the snow is fitful, like gnats circling. Marilla lets the engine idle, waiting for her. She's not in a mood to help haul Mittie's wash—let one of her kids do it for once.

Finally Mittie appears, dragging the canvas duffel bag her oldest boy, Frank, had in the navy. She slings it over the rear gate of the pickup and opens the door on the passenger side. "Just once," she says, slamming it, "just once I wouldn't mind seeing the sun on a wash day, so I could hang it out on the line instead of down cellar."

"Hmm," Marilla says noncommittally. She puts the truck into reverse and backs down the rocky incline. Before they reach the road they have to make a choice, which they argue over every Sunday, whether to go into town or whether to make the trip to Mull Harbor. The laundrymat in Stony Harbor's closer, they can get the chore done faster if they go there, but half the washers are apt to be broken at any one time, and there are no amenities like change-making machines. The place in Mull Harbor is, comparatively, a paradise among laundrymats, but it's a half-hour drive each way from Mittie's house. Today Marilla heads toward town without even consulting Mittie. And Mittie, sensing Marilla's mood, doesn't put up any fight.

"You got any extra quarters?" Mittie asks. "Somebody broke into my quarter collection again."

"Why don't you hide it?"

"I do hide it. They're geniuses at hunting it down."

"You'll have to get change at Hinckley's."

"You know how that little snip that works Sundays is about making change when you don't buy anything. One of these days I'm going to get my hands around her throat and rattle her till her teeth fall out."

"She probably feels the same way about you."

"What's the matter with the heater in this wreck?"

"It's been acting up lately. I think something's wrong with the fan."

"Lucky it's almost spring."

Marilla sighs. "If only."

By the time they reach the parking lot next to the laundrymat the snow has stopped, but the sky's still overcast and there's a rawness in the air. The place is nearly empty, unusual on a Sunday morning. "Better steer clear of that machine," Mittie says, eyeing a suspicious soapy puddle on the concrete floor by one of the washers. She begins to unload her duffel into a couple of machines at the opposite end of the row, as if whatever ails the leaking one is contagious. She sorts as she unloads, jamming blue jeans and socks into one washer, underwear and sheets into the other.

Without saying anything Marilla inserts quarters into the slots in Mittie's machines. They both understand this signals a truce. Other people's kids aren't fair game, and Mittie of all people ought to know that, but she's Marilla's oldest friend. Her only friend now, if you don't count Tucker.

When all four machines are chugging along, they settle into the tippy molded plastic chairs. They've got magazines from the humid pile of reading materials customers have abandoned there. "I guess you've heard about Billy Flowers," Mittie says, opening her old copy of *People* to an article about Sean Penn punching a photographer.

"What about him?"

"You haven't seen the sign in front of the insurance office?"

"I have not."

"Yesterday morning I was going to the state liquor store to pick up a pint of Four Roses for Harold, and I saw two guys ramming the post right down into a pile of dirty old snow. Be easier to nail the sign to the building this time of year, but I guess they don't want to spoil the lovely paint job, ha ha."

"What does the sign say, Mittie?" Marilla asks with exaggerated patience, as if speaking to a mental defective.

"It says 'For Sale,' that's what it says. Run over and take a look right now if you don't believe me. So I ask in the liquor store what's going on, and they tell me Billy's retiring to Florida. Some place called Delray Beach. Ever hear of it?"

"No."

"Me either. His wife's already down there, and good riddance, I say. I never could stand the woman."

"What about the business?"

"A company up to Machias is taking it over. So I suppose from now on I'll have to haul myself over there every time Harold backs into a telephone pole."

The machines, one by one, come to the end of the wash

cycle and start to spin. There's a terrific racket, and the whole laundrymat trembles as if in an earthquake.

"I wonder if Lyle's going to Machias, too," Marilla says, looking down at the puckered face of somebody named Fergie on the cover of her magazine.

"What do you care about him for?"

"Curiosity, that's all."

"Well, the answer is, he isn't. Roz Phillips and that young fella from Taunton Billy took on a couple of years ago, they're going, but Lyle's out on his ear."

Rinse water is whooshing into the machines. Now Marilla understands why he was acting so strange the day she picked him up on Monkey Bay Road. Poor Lyle. She feels a little sick, almost as though what has happened to him is somehow her fault.

Tucker has always been worried that he didn't deserve Marilla. He's felt guilty that he tore her away from her home and family, he's been half convinced that one day he'd be paid back for what he did. That the fates—or whatever—would retaliate and he'd get what's coming to him.

That's why he didn't want to finish the house. Something told him that as long as it was still in progress—no linoleum on the kitchen floor, no plumbing in the laundry room, no carpet in the loft—whatever he and Marilla had together would not be sealed. Certified. Carved in stone. There'd always be the possibility that she could take up her old life again and he'd be let off the hook. By the fates, that is, because he hadn't caused any permanent disruption in the way things were meant to work out.

He never said to himself: If I leave the plywood uncovered I'll save myself. But that was the reason, all the same.

Every nail he pounded into that gray strip of carpet in the loft was bringing him closer to some kind of reckoning.

Tucker wanted her to see what she was making him do, but she looked at the points of the nails jabbing through the floor and didn't understand, and he couldn't explain.

They'd never talked about marriage. When she got her final divorce papers she just put them in a drawer, and that was that. Any other woman would have said: You have to do right by me now. So what if the town calls me a whore, at least I have a wedding ring to flash. Not Marilla, though.

Maybe she was too proud to be the first to speak of it. Maybe she thought if there wasn't going to be a baby it didn't matter. Maybe she'd had enough of papers and documents and legalities and oaths. The fact is, neither of them promised a thing to the other.

In that way, he should feel easy about fucking Hannah. It wasn't his idea, after all. But he doesn't feel easy. He doesn't understand how, exactly, but he senses that a circle is closing in spite of anything he might do, or not do. So he takes her quick—down cellar, or behind the ragged blue curtain in the lean-to, or on the couch under the nails—and he hopes she'll have enough soon, and go.

Frances can't stand it, the thought of Mid Flowers in a condo in Florida, while she's stuck forever in this icy, muddy dump. Even her bones are doomed to lie in the Pratt plot in Dudbridge, under a crust of dirty snow, until the day of judgment. Until Armageddon.

As she dusts the blinds in the front room, Frances imagines herself sitting in Warren Smith's office, directing him to change her will. She wants to be cremated, after all, she tells him, and her ashes sent to Ms. Beverly D. Purkis, who is to scatter them over the man-made lake in Retirement Village, Greenoak, North Carolina.

She folds the dirt into the dust cloth and pictures Lyle—he's bound to outlive her, blood pressure or no—going to the post office to mail her off. Getting mixed up about Bev's address, putting the wrong postage on, neglecting to affix a return-address label. She imagines herself in the dead-letter pile—not even making it as far as Portland—until they sound the trumpet of doom.

What drives Frances crazy is that Mid Flowers does not, any way you want to slice it, deserve retirement in a sunny clime. First and foremost, she has nothing to retire *from*. She did not pound arithmetic, social studies, communication skills, natural science, and hygiene into thirty thick skulls every year for twenty-three years. She didn't do a thing but gallivant around in her tacky fur jacket, and make cheese balls, and buy things she had no need for at the Bangor Mall, and redecorate her house from attic to cellar every five years.

Frances lugs Lyle's footstool over to the next window and stands on it to attack that set of blinds. *And* gossip, she thinks. Thanks to Mildred Flowers it's all over town that Billy was only keeping Lyle on out of charity. And she was supposed to be Frances's friend. It makes her blood boil, thinking about it. She's never been a jealous or spiteful person, not one to hold a grudge, but if she could think of a way to put a crimp in Mid's "retirement," she'd go ahead and do it without a qualm.

Through the slats she sees somebody walking up the street carrying a suitcase. It's Lyle, no doubt about it. She has never laid eyes on this suitcase before—it's plaid, the cheap kind that has a zipper instead of clasps—and momentarily she is frozen with astonishment. One minute she's picturing Mid going off with suitcases and the next here's Lyle marching home with one. He's passing the front door (he doesn't notice her at the window) and going around the side of the house. She climbs down from the footstool and rushes out to the kitchen. Through the bay window in the breakfast nook she watches him round the corner by the hydrangea bush. He's not heading for the back door, though, he's picking his way through the mud and slush in the backyard. When he reaches the shed he fumbles with the padlock, shoves the plaid suitcase inside, and clamps the padlock shut.

Frances is still holding the dust rag. She looks at it as though it could tell her what in the name of God is going on now.

There's a hush in the house, as though someone has an inoperable tumor or there's been a death. Marilla's hanging wet clothes on the wooden rack in the loft, on the stair railing, on hangers in the bathroom. When they dry, they'll have a faint smell of wood smoke. Hannah's underwear is so small it looks like a child's, Marilla thinks as she drapes a pair of lemon-yellow panties over a rung. She wonders where Hannah got those light, thin bones. The Pratts are all sturdy, they clomp along like cows in a field, and on her side they're built large, both men and women.

Tucker's out tramping around somewhere. Hannah is sitting on the floor next to the stove in the big room, her knees hunched under her chin, her knitting close to her eyes. Every once in a while she rips out a row or two. It reminds Marilla of a story she had to learn in high school about a woman who waited twenty years for her husband to come home from the war. She unraveled her weaving every night so she wouldn't have to marry another man. But who or what Hannah is waiting for, Marilla doesn't know. Mackerel sighs in her sleep, dreaming of moles and sparrows, Marilla imagines.

The wash basket empty, Marilla goes down into the kitchen and takes the mixing bowl from the top shelf. She opens a tin of flour, takes an egg out of the refrigerator. It's cold and smooth in her hand, silent, like the house. When she cracks it against the rim of the bowl and it slides down the side, she sees a speck of blood in it. A sign of spring, maybe.

Well, now that she thinks about it, her brother, Rolf, had

small bones. He was forever breaking them. He fell out of a willow tree one Fourth of July and they had to drive to Ellsworth to have the bones in his arm set. And it healed wrong and had to be broken on purpose and set again. The next year he broke his leg playing on an old iron merry-go-round they had in the schoolyard—the old school, not the one on Poplar Street. After Rolf hurt himself they broke it up with sledgehammers to haul it away to the dump, because it was too heavy to move in one piece. When she asked her father how they'd got it there in the first place, he said men used to be stronger then. Giants. Later on, in high school, Rolf broke the same leg again playing basketball. He shouldn't have been playing a game like that, but he always had to prove something. Marilla was taller than he was by then, bigger all over, and he hated that. It must have been from Rolf that Hannah got her fragile bones.

Marilla pours a cup of milk into the egg and beats it up with a fork. Rolf went into the navy after high school, did two hitches, kicked around the world some; the last she heard he was in California. He never called or wrote, and when Marilla wrote to tell him their mother had died, the envelope came back stamped MOVED, FORWARDING INSTRUCTION EXPIRED. She wrote to the postmaster of the town, explaining the circumstances, and she received a form letter with a check mark next to a paragraph stating that after a certain period of time has elapsed such records are destroyed. Somebody in the post office had taken the situation enough to heart to pencil a message at the bottom: Try the police.

She hadn't, though. If the police had him in their files, she didn't want to know about it. Anyway, not so long after that she left Lyle, and then she didn't really have an address herself. If any letters had come for her Lyle would have torn them up or burned them.

Mackerel rubs against her leg. She looks up from the mixing bowl and sees that it's snowing again.

The tide's on the ebb, halfway out, and the wind's churning up whitecaps. There's an ice floe on the water, large and square, like a platform or a raft. Hannah stands on the lip of land at the edge of the bluff, watching the floe adjust itself to shifts in current. Its maneuvers seem so delicate, its balance so controlled, it's almost as though somebody is steering it. She makes a small bet with herself that it won't be stranded on the mud flat, that it will make it out to the channel.

In the trees over her head a pack of ravens are screeching at one another. Territory? Sex? The sheer joy of argument? They flap from one tree to another, agitated by spring, it seems—or the hope of spring. Hannah's cold, though. She feels the chill seeping right through Tucker's heavy boots and the two layers of wool socks. It occurs to her that maybe it's she, Hannah, who's agitating the ravens by standing there. A huge one is weighing down a swamp maple branch, inspecting her. Maybe he's coveting the buttons on Tucker's pea coat, thinking about swooping down and snatching one to hide in his nest. He's so black, so big. Suddenly she opens her mouth and croaks at him to see what he'll do, and then she's startled and embarrassed, because she realizes there's somebody down on the beach below her.

He has on a brown uniform that has a greenish cast to it, and his face is ruddy, wind-whipped. He's wearing a pistol in a leather holster. Hannah doesn't know anything about guns, but it looks capable of blowing a very large hole in something. The ravens flap away as Hannah and the man stand staring at one another.

Then he begins to scramble up the bluff, grunting a little as he negotiates the slippery boulders and scraps of ice and exposed tree roots. She decides to stay where she is. She's not trespassing, poaching, or hunting out of season. She thrusts her hands into the pocket slits on the sides of the pea coat and waits. The brown leather of the holster is so shiny he must polish it. She imagines how he takes the pistol apart and oils it and reassembles it, loaded, ready to fire.

"You all right?" he asks when he reaches her.

"Yes," she says, surprised. This is not a challenge, after all. It's a rescue operation.

"I thought you were lost. You looked lost, just standing there."

"No, I live here."

He looks puzzled.

"I'm staying here for a while. With my mother."

He glances up at the house. "I don't know she had any kids."

He must be from away. There isn't a soul within miles who doesn't know all about Marilla's set-adrift daughter.

"Just the one. Just me."

"Been way at school, have you?"

She pauses. "That's right."

"Glad to be back?" He's looking at her intently, as though he really cares about the answer. As though it's not just idle curiosity or small talk.

"Yes, I am."

"Most of them don't come back. Or if they do, they're not too happy about it. Hell, I'm the same way myself," he says, taking a pack of cigarettes out of his pocket. "Smoke?"

"No."

"Grew up in The County and haven't been back home half a dozen times since I left." He puts a cigarette between his thick, rubbery lips and cups his big hand around it as he lights it. "Place called Smyrna Mills. Probably never go back again, now my mother's gone."

It's beginning to rain a little. There's nothing actually sinister about this man, this marine patrol officer. All he's after is illegal clamming. He's telling her about his mother in Smyrna *Mills,* for God's sake. But for some reason she feels a chill that has nothing to do with the weather. He's looking at her closely, wondering about her, storing away clues. These people are trained to be observant, to notice things that would go by an ordinary person. He's taking in Tucker's coat, her hair that's grown shaggy because it's been too long since she's had it cut. Maybe something in her eyes she herself doesn't know is there.

"Home for good, then?" he asks.

"I'm not sure," she says, backing away from him. "I'm freezing—I have to go in now."

"Nice talking to you," he calls after her.

When she's underneath Tucker, feeling him probe her, she realizes she forgot to notice what happened to the slab of ice in the tide.

Today is garbage day. Lyle slips out of bed without waking Frances and is out on the street by five A.M. You have to get to the cans before the truck rolls by, and as the days lengthen, that seems to be earlier and earlier.

The trouble with this town is that everybody's either a pack rat or a pinchpenny, or both: Nobody ever throws anything away they might possibly be able to sell or barter or that could, by some wild stretch of the imagination, come in handy someday. The summer people are different, of course, but they don't start flitting back into town until after mud season.

Still, you never know, and all Lyle has to lose is a couple hours sleep. It's true he might be spotted digging down into a garbage can, but it's not his fault Mid Flowers decided she had to live in Florida. Let people blame her if they want to blame somebody. He's only doing what he has to.

In the Caprice he cruises slowly down Poplar Street, keeping his eyes peeled for any clue that might announce a find. An unusually large heap of trash probably means somebody's either moving or else swamping out their attic or their cellar. What you can hope for is that the size of the job at some point overwhelms them, especially when they're old and there's no relatives close by, and that they'll lose heart and give the whole lot the heave. Last Tuesday, after Milford Potter went to the nursing home, Lyle found a carton of ancient kitchenware—egg beater, soap cage, masher, flatiron—just sitting there in the gutter, waiting for Lyle to pick up and haul away. You wouldn't believe it, but people pay money for those things.

The shed's getting kind of full, in fact. And worse, Frances is suspicious. She wanted to know why the padlock is kept locked now, instead of just hanging from the hasp to keep the door from sagging open.

"I heard in the office kids have been vandalizing outbuildings," he told her. "Dumping out cans of paint. Smashing Mason jars. Setting little fires."

"What kids?"

"I don't know. Just kids."

"I haven't heard anything like that."

"Maybe if you got out more, you'd hear things."

"Bev would have told me."

"Bev doesn't know everything."

"Well, I need my potting soil from the shed."

He carried the plastic sack of dirt inside for her and left it by the kitchen door, and he's noticed it hasn't been touched since. Also, she wanted to know where he went at the crack of dawn last Tuesday morning. He couldn't tell her he'd gone for a walk, that would have triggered another harangue about Monkey Bay Road. So he said he'd had a sudden craving for eggs and home fries at the Brass Lantern.

"I've never in my life known you to do such a thing."

"You haven't known me all your life."

"I have too. I remember when you were a little twerp in the fourth grade and you cried because a big boy took your milk money."

He remembers her from those days, too. Fat and bossy, with a heart like a lump of coal. But he only said, with dignity, "You haven't known how I felt about home fries."

That made her even more suspicious, unfortunately. He could see right into her head: She was sure that Marilla used to cook home fries every day of the week. The fact is, breakfast is the meal Marilla never fixes for anyone but herself. Or anyway, that's how she was on Poplar Street. "My mother made them for me," he said quickly.

"Well, why didn't you tell me, for heaven's sake?"

"I did. You forgot."

He felt bad about the guilty look he left her with, but at least he'd silenced her. She's silenced about the shed, too—for now—but Lyle knows he's soon going to have to find some other spot to stow his accumulation of junk.

On Flat Bay Road he finds an amber glass whiskey bottle lying in a scrap of snow. The bottle might look old, he thinks, if he soaked the label off and incinerated it for a while. A little farther on he spots a three-legged kitchen chair on top of a heap of trash by the drainage ditch. Under those chipped layers of paint the chair's solid maple, he guesses. He hunts around in the frozen dried weeds near the trash pile, but he can't find the fourth leg. How did it come to be detached and lost? he wonders. In a domestic dispute, maybe. Or under a very fat person. Without warning she crashed to the floor, and in the ensuing confusion the leg rolled under the stove or behind the refrigerator.

He looks up the slope at the house whose occupants have put out this load of culch. It's a rackety farmhouse, half covered in tar paper. The rest is unpainted board, weathered to a splintery gray. No TV antenna, which definitely means no refrigerator, either. He gives up any hope of recovering the leg and leaves the chair in the ditch. Tourists may be crazy, but probably not crazy enough to buy a three-legged chair, even if it is solid maple.

He doesn't stop at the heap in front of the trailer around the next curve, although something's sticking out of one of the cans, an old floor lamp minus the glass shade. Outside chance it's brass. Even if it's only iron, you could spray it with gold paint. But the trash pile is near enough to the trailer that whoever inhabits the place might hear him rattling around in the can, and besides, it's getting late. He wants to hit the dumpsters at the boat launch down the road before turning back.

The dumpsters turn out to be a disappointment, though. The only thing worth mentioning is a doll without a wig. Its eyes flicker open as he lifts it out. The grayish cloth body smells musty, and the rubber fingers of one hand are gone—chewed off, it looks like. By a dog, maybe. Probably cost more to fix up than he could ever sell it for. But he hates to have come this far down the road with so little to show for it, so he lays the doll on the backseat of the car and heads for home.

It's snowing. The hummocks and bogs in the woods are covered again, and the muddy places in the clearing. "Movie snow," Tucker says, pulling on his mustache as he gazes out the kitchen window. "They manufacture it in big machines and dump it on foolish actors playing young lovers."

Dreamily Hannah swabs a plate in slow circular motion, holds it flat under the tap, cradles it in the dish rack. He opens the door of the wood stove and pokes inside with a long iron bar. Then he shoves another log in, a big V-shaped piece of birch, almost the size of a man's lower torso. The door shuts with a clang.

She's looking inside a mug, wondering what she's supposed to use to get out the stain. Baking powder? Ammonia? Clorox? She can hear Tucker behind her, scraping chair legs toward the table. There's the ratchety sound of the match being struck.

"Why foolish?" she asks, after a while.

"What?"

"Why are the young lovers foolish?" She holds the slippery mug, undecided what to do with it.

"The *actors* are foolish."

"Oh."

"Or maybe not so foolish." His breath makes a whooshing sound as he inhales, as though he's vacuuming cigarette smoke. "At least they get paid big bucks to look like saps."

She lets the mug fill under the tap, dumps it over, hooks it to the side of the drainer. Worry about the stain another day.

"Is that what you want, Tucker? Big bucks?"

He thinks this over, smoking. "It's not in the cards for me. I used to buy lottery tickets until I figured out I'm not the type to win lotteries."

"Is that a type?"

"You bet your sweet ass it is."

The way he says it, not even thinking about what the words mean, excites her. She feels a little disoriented by the steady drifting-down of the snow, the warmth of the water. With concentration she scrubs the spider he fried his eggs in.

"What about you, Hannah? Do you want to be rich?"

When he speaks her name there's a slight hesitation between the two syllables, almost as though he's reluctant to let go of it.

"Once I did," she answers, putting the spider on top of the wood stove so it will dry out fast and not rust.

"What happened?"

"Oh, I don't know." She takes the towel with the green border from an arm of the rack and dries her hands. "I get bored easy. You have to stick at one thing to make it."

"Like your old man," he says, showing his small teeth when he smiles. "Look how well he did for himself."

"What you don't understand is how much I'm like him."

"Tell me," he says softly.

She stands by the stove, the damp towel in her hands. "He doesn't focus. He would have quit that insurance office a million times if there'd been anything else around here he could have done."

"Yeah?"

"He'd say the work didn't suit him, the way the forms were designed was stupid, Billy Flowers didn't appreciate him, the secretary spent too much time jabbering on the phone, the clients were a bunch of chicken-shit crooks and ignoramuses."

"Sounds about right."

"No, you don't get it. Maybe some of that was true and maybe it wasn't, but that's not the point. He made himself believe it, whether or no. He has no patience. Just like me."

"He stuck with it, though."

"Oh, well," she says, shrugging and hanging up the towel, "doing anything else would have meant leaving Stony Harbor."

"So?"

"There are some people who are glued to this place, like barnacles to ledge. If you tried to pry them away they'd . . . I don't know . . . die or something. That's the way he is."

"And Marilla," he says, looking out at the snow.

"Marilla even more than my father."

"You and me, though, we're different."

"Are we?"

"We don't need places. Or people, either."

She moves into the dim lean-to. Mackerel is asleep next to the knitting on the bed. Hearing Hannah's footsteps, the cat yawns and stretches her striped body toward Hannah to be petted. Cats don't know how lucky they are, she thinks. To ask for love and get it, just like that.

Marilla's sweeping the plank floorboards when Mittie bursts through the door. "Sorry I'm late," she says, flinging off her coat. "Harold was frigging with the carburator and dropped a screw or something and had to fish around in there with my happy-face magnet tied to a string."

"Did he get it?"

"He'd never let me drive off if he didn't. Might've wrecked the engine."

"Not to mention you."

"I doubt that garstly thought ever crossed his mind," she says, seizing a new video box from the rack. "*Reuben, Reuben.* What's this about?"

"It says on the box it's about suburban intellectuals."

"What did Millard go and order that for?"

Marilla doesn't bother to answer. She squats to poke the broom under the counter and unearths several bottle caps, a nickel, some cash-register tapes, and a dust ball.

"I remember we used to sing it in school. *Reuben, Reuben, dum diddly dum dum, what a great world this would be, if the men were all transported way beyond the Northern Sea.* Good idea."

"What would you have to complain about?" Marilla asks, pocketing the nickel.

"I'd think of something." From behind the counter Mittie watches Marilla sweeping the pile of dirt onto a glossy four-color poster that says PEPSI'S THE ONE. "Marilla, have you been putting on a little weight?"

"Maybe a pound or two," she says, wrapping the poster around the dirt.

"You're not up a stump, are you?"

"Are you kidding?"

"It could still happen, you know. My mother was pushing fifty when my sister Alva was born."

Marilla stuffs the crumpled poster into a trash bag. "Well, it's not going to happen to me, so you can forget that idea."

"Marilla . . . Is it him, or you?"

"Him or me what?"

"That can't . . . you know."

"I don't have any idea what you're talking about."

"It's him, isn't it? I've always thought so. You had Hannah, after all, even if it did take you forever to get around to it." She's yanking snarls out of her hair with a spiky plastic brush. "Well," she says offhandedly to the brush, "that's one good thing."

"What do you mean by that?"

"Nothing. You don't have to get mad."

"You know what drives me nuts? People walking in without knocking."

"What? This is a store. A public place."

"I'm not talking about the store, Mittie."

"I apologize. Put the broom down."

Marilla takes her parka from the nail and shrugs into it. "Norbert Oxberry's had *The Grey Fox* for a week. You'd better give him a call before the old goat starts claiming he brought it back and it's our records that are fouled up."

"Okay. Marilla, I'm sorry for butting in, only—"

"Never mind. You're probably right, I *have* put on some weight."

"Me too. In fact, I'm going to give up Snickers bars for Lent."

"Only two weeks of Lent left."

"Well," Mittie says, digging her hair out of the brush with her thumbnail, "not exactly for Lent. If you want to know the truth, it's more so Wayne will stop drinking so much."

"I don't see what one's got to do with the other."

"So God will notice I'm making this sacrifice and will help my boy in return."

"That's numb, Mittie. God doesn't make bargains like that."

"How do you know so much about God? I don't see you going to church on Sunday."

"You either."

"How else are we going to get our washing done?"

"All I'm saying is there's no use trying to bully God."

Mittie's looking at the brittle snarl of hair, which is perambulating along the counter as if it's taken on a life of its own. "I don't care. I have this feeling that if I hurt myself somehow, I can save him."

"In that case, you'd better give up something more important than Snickers bars."

"I wonder what's more important to me than Snickers bars," Mittie says meditatively.

"I hate to break this to you, Frances, but I think there's something wrong with Lyle." Bev shakes the crumbs from her fingers into the waxed-paper sandwich wrapper and taps her own skull. "Upstairs."

The vinyl pad sticks to her bottom as Frances readjusts herself on the bench in the breakfast nook. She's afraid to hear what's coming next, but she wants to give Bev the impression she's one step ahead of her. "A man's bound to be upset when he loses his job. The truth is, he's been better lately. More cheerful."

Bev's mouth had been open to bite into her cream-cheese-and-sardine sandwich, but instead she puts the sandwich down. "You know what they say about a depressed person who suddenly becomes cheerful, don't you?"

"Of course I do."

Bev's long experience as a teacher makes her alert to equivocation. Without pausing for breath she pounces. "All right, what do they say?"

"Why, that the person is coming out of the depression."

"No, dear. He's cheerful because he's made a decision to escape his misery and he's figured out how to do it."

"Lyle?"

"Well, you can't entirely rule it out, I suppose."

"Oh, my Lord. That's what the suitcase must be for."

"Suitcase?" Bev asks with her mouth half full. "What suitcase is that?"

"The other day he came home from the office with a suitcase in his hand. He hid it in the shed so I wouldn't see it. It was plaid, the cheap cloth kind that zips instead of buckles. Not a very nice one—I wouldn't put any clothes of mine in it. But men don't care about such things."

Bev looks confused. "What's a suitcase got to do with anything?"

"What you said about deciding to escape. He must be planning to escape with the suitcase."

"I'm afraid that wasn't the kind of escape I had in mind, Frances."

"Why are you being so mysterious, Bev? Are you deliberately trying to provoke me?"

"Calm down, Frances. How are you going to help Lyle if you work yourself into a worse state than he's in?"

Frances slams her coffee cup onto the saucer, and a chip

flies off the saucer rim. "Now see what you made me do."

"You are talking exactly like a second grader."

Frances gets up from the table and moves heavily to the bay window. Across an expanse of fresh snow she can see the shed, with the closed padlock hanging from the hasp. "What kind of escape, then?" she hears herself ask in a weak, high-pitched voice.

"Suicide," Bev says briskly.

Home fries with eggs and sausage flash before Frances's eyes. He wanted to taste home fries once more before—

"But we're getting off the track here," Bev continues. "I said there was something wrong with him. I did not say he's about to do himself in. Quite the contrary."

"But—"

"People contemplating suicide get rid of things. They give their gold watches and bowling trophies to their loved ones. They might take trips to the dump with their old love letters. They do not make trips to the dump to collect more junk than they already own and haul it away with them."

Under the snow near the shed are some lumps, unharvested cabbages. Frances watches a tree sparrow land on one of the lumps and then flit away. "Please do tell me what you're talking about," she says wearily.

Bev takes a deep breath, the way she does when she's about to explain the Pythagorean theorem or the causes of the French and Indian War. "Well, you know how I've been going from room to room, deciding what I want to take with me to North Carolina and what I'd just as soon leave behind—like that mahogany parlor suite I've always hated. But Mother would rise from the dead and smite me if I sold it or gave it to the Salvation Army."

"Yes," Frances says with a pang, both because of the thought of Bev's leaving and because she'd once looked forward to living with that furniture, especially the marble-topped occasional tables and the footstool with the Scottie dog done in needlepoint. She'd had no idea Bev hated it.

"Well, it's not going. Cost a fortune to move it, and Mother will have a hard time finding me in North Carolina."

Frances thinks about putting in a bid for it, but that wouldn't be appropriate right now, considering how worried she is about Lyle. And anyway, she's not sure she'd enjoy the tables and the Scottie dog without Bev. They'd only make her sad.

"So," Bev goes on, "one way and another I'm finding a good deal of rubbish to give the heave to, and I'm hauling it out to those dumpsters on Flat Bay Road, because you never know what the trash men will be so kind as to pick up and what they won't. Considering the taxes we pay—"

"Bev, not the parlor suite—you're not putting the parlor suite in the dumpster!"

"Of course not. Some fool will give me good money for it. But as I was saying, I drive out there early in the morning, before school. After school I'm too bushed. Yesterday around six thirty A.M. I was pulling into the spot where the dumpsters are, you know, where the clam diggers park their vehicles—but there was only one car there because the tide was in. And guess whose car it was."

"I don't want to guess, Bev."

"It was *your* car, Frances. And there was Lyle, big as life, hanging over the side of the dumpster. At first I thought he was being sick into it. I was so flabbergasted I just sat there, smack in the middle of the road. Anyone could have come along and rammed right into me. Then I realized he wasn't being sick at all, he was rooting around in there. And do you know what he came up with, finally?"

"No, Bev."

"A doll. A stark-naked bald old doll. I couldn't believe it. He looked at it for a while, turning it over and over in his hands. And then he put it in the back of the Caprice and started the engine. He had to drive *around* my car to get into the road, but he never even saw me. Now what do you think of that?"

Frances turns away from the window and stares at Bev. "I don't know what to think. What can be happening to him?"

"Beats me," Bev says, zipping up her galoshes. "I'm going to be late if I don't get a move on."

Curlers then looked like little bones, the thighbones of small animals, squirrels maybe, or rats. Marilla remembers watching her mother wind hair around them, secure them with rubber bands hooked from end to end. Then she'd saturate the tight bundles with solutions and wrap the whole thing in a triangle cut from a shower curtain, which had black swans on it.

She'd have a cigarette between her lips while she worked, and her fingernails were long and pointed and painted maroon. For years maroon fingernails were Louise Geary's signature. When the manufacturer discontinued that particular shade, Lou grieved.

One day Marilla said, "I hate those people, Mumma. Can't you keep them out front?"

"Sometimes they need to use the bathroom, Marilla. Or the phone."

"Tell them to do those things in their own houses."

"They have emergencies, Marilla."

"They're nosy, that's all. They want to stick their nose into our business."

"Do you have such private business, then?"

"Yes, Mumma, I do."

"Well, you oughtn't to. You're not old enough to have secrets."

And that was the end of it. Her mother let those women

wander all over the house. They'd flush the toilet wrong and let it run and run. They'd burst in on Marilla doing her homework in the kitchen and never even apologize. Their heads looked varnished, the color of brass. They thought her mother had turned them into queens.

"They're our bread and butter, Marilla," Louise said, but she liked her work too much to suit Marilla.

Louise had been patient with her husband's long illness, but she never understood it. She was tough and she thought it was some defect in his character that he allowed the disease to overwhelm him. Then, when she herself was dying, she didn't understand that, either. She battled it inch by inch, but she knew she was losing, and that made her bitter.

She had a voice deep as a man's, from the smoking. Sometimes when she answered the phone people thought it was Rolf or that they had the wrong number. And she was tall and sturdy, like Marilla, but there was something wiry about her, too—in the sense that wire has tensile strength, it resists being torn apart, it fights back.

Often Marilla wishes that quality had been passed on to her, but in the end, Lou Geary's strength didn't make any difference to her, she suffered all the same. Maybe more.

Hannah's underpants are silky skimpy things the colors of Popsicles: lemon, lime, grape, orange, raspberry. God, Tucker loves those little scraps of cloth.

She's muscular in bed. She's apt to sink her teeth into his shoulder or bruise his ass with her heel. Her hair goes limp with sweat and sticks to her neck. He buried himself in Marilla, there's no question of that with Hannah.

Sometimes when he watches her tapping her foot restlessly against a chair rung, or yanking out a row of her knitting, he sees himself in her and wonders if he isn't in some magical way her father. He imagines one of his tiny fish hiding out inside Marilla for years, lying in wait in some inner fold of tissue, one day darting out and piercing an egg. He does feel something of incest in what they're doing. It's also like a delicious kind of whacking off, Hannah fucking Hannah and him fucking his own self.

She says she's like her father, but that's crazy. It's Tucker she's like.

He thinks about taking her away with him.

His hand on her ass, he looks at the green striped rag Marilla tied around the stovepipe to keep it from leaking. They were talking about Hannah that day. He had a hunch the girl was going to make mischief. Could be that Marilla did, too. He remembers how tense she was, tying the knot in the rag, talking about how Hannah was maybe going to stay in town, maybe going to find herself a man. He laughs, realizing that *he's* it, the bug caught in the spider's net, the victim too stupid to struggle, even.

"What's so funny?" Hannah asks.

She's let the hair grow in between her eyebrows, in her armpits. She smells salty, from the sweat.

"Nothing's funny."

"You're not going to tell me, are you?" She moves out from under his hand, props herself up on an elbow. Over her head, nails poke out of the ceiling.

"I tell you everything there is to tell."

"Yes, like you told me those plants downstairs are tomato seedlings."

"Don't you believe me?"

She traces a circle around his navel with her thumbnail, hardly touching his skin. "No."

"What do you think they are?"

"Grass. Pot. Dope."

"I guess you're not as dumb as I thought."

"How come you grow it but you don't smoke it?"

"Does Mr. Tiffany wear a diamond tiara?"

"That's no answer."

"I'm in the business. I sell it."

"You could still smoke it."

He shrugs. "Don't have the taste for it anymore."

The circle around his navel is tighter, and she's pressing down harder. It hurts, but it arouses him, too.

"So why did you lie to me?"

"Cut it out, Hannah."

"Why should I?"

"I don't like it."

She drops her head to his chest, listens to his heart pulsing in his ribcage. "So why did you lie?"

"To protect you, I guess."

He feels her cheek, damp against his skin. "How would lying to me protect me?" Her words seem to move to his ears through his bones rather than through the air.

"In case some busybody starts asking awkward questions, you wouldn't get involved."

"Or be so likely to give you away."

"All right. That, too."

He listens to the couch springs squeal, her bare feet thud on the rug, the jeans zipper closing.

"Who might be asking questions, Tucker?"

"Any number of people."

He opens his eyes and sees her at the window, looking out at the bay. "The marine patrol officer?"

"It's possible."

"He seems to hang around here an awful lot."

"Maybe he's in love with Marilla. Maybe they're having an affair."

"That's disgusting, Tucker."

"Is it?"

She turns from the window and looks at him. "What could he do to you?"

"Oh, make life somewhat unpleasant for a while."

"That's all?"

"That's enough. I don't particularly like to be messed with."

"Aren't you scared?"

Her shoulders are narrow. Her tangled hair, dry now, almost reaches the ribbing of her sweatshirt. She looks like a child.

"Would you like to know what really scares me, Hannah?"

"Tell me."

"You know where Caribou is?"

"Up by the border somewhere."

"There's a monitoring station up to Caribou. It measures the ozone in the stratosphere. You've heard of ozone?"

She's looking puzzled, her brows pulled together. "Sure. I guess so."

"This month, the month of March, the ozone level over Caribou dropped eight percent. Eight percent, Hannah."

"You're scared about the *stratosphere,* Tucker?"

"Less ozone up there, and ultraviolet rays sneak through. They kill the algae in the bay. Everything that feeds on the algae dies, and the feeders that feed on them die."

"Henny Penny, the sky is falling."

"No algae, nothing to consume CO_2. CO_2 warms things up and the ice caps melt. The water in the bay rises. One fine day the tide swirls around the house and sucks it down into the sea."

Hannah winds a hank of hair around her finger and laughs. "I can tell when my leg is being pulled. Like with the granny in the canoe."

"It's all interlocked, Hannah. Everything's interlocked."

* * *

Lyle said that if she didn't want to do it, then she must not want to marry him, either. Frances could see the logic in that, or at least she had it drummed into her, he said it so many times. Just because his divorce wasn't final yet didn't mean he didn't have needs, the same as other men.

He left Hannah at his sister's house in Unityville and picked Frances up at her apartment. At that time she was living in a furnished studio over the Sand-Witch, right in town, and when she came down with her little blue vinyl overnight case and got into his Malibu, she thought everyone in Stony Harbor must know what she was going to do.

He was wearing a new hat, a suede sort of cowboy hat. When he took it off and put it on the bed in the motel room, he had a red band across his forehead. Inside the hat, oil had leeched into the suede.

The motel room smelled of cigar smoke, and the metal shower stall was scabby with rust. He emptied his pockets, hung up his jacket, and went into the bathroom. He'd left a set of keys, his wallet, some change, and three foil packets on the bedside table. She thought the packets were Handi Wipes, and she tore one open so she could clean the fingerprints from the glass dresser top, but it wasn't what she expected. Though she'd never seen one, she guessed right away what it was for.

She felt ridiculous to have made such a mistake, and at first she thought of hiding it, in one of the dresser drawers or on the shelf above the clothes rack, but she realized he'd know how many he'd brought with him. He planned to do it three times. So she crammed the thing back in the packet and turned over the edge as neatly as she could. Maybe in the dark he wouldn't notice.

The next morning, when Lyle was paying the motel bill, she saw a toy bunny in the gift shop adjoining the office. It was made of real rabbit fur and had little pink glass eyes. She snatched it off the shelf and asked him to add it to the bill because she wanted to bring something back to Hannah. He argued that Hannah was nearly thirteen, too old for stuffed animals, and she'd never been one to play with that kind of thing anyway, but Frances explained that teenage girls like to display them on their beds. She held it on her lap all the way home.

The rabbit was one of the things Frances cleared out of the back of Hannah's closet after Hannah left home. She'd never had it on her bed, not even for one day. Well, the girl has a cold heart, just like her mother. Poor Lyle, now he's pulling dolls out of dumpsters. He does seem to have had more than his share of bad luck.

Hannah came into the kitchen and found her father making a pencil mark on a cupboard door. He was kneeling on the counter, various tools around him. She poured dry cereal into a bowl before she asked him what he was doing.

"Installing a hasp," he said.

"What's a hasp?"

"You put a padlock through it."

She got a carton of milk out of the refrigerator and dribbled some over the cereal. "Why?"

"Why what?" he said, picking up the hand drill.

"Why are you doing it?"

"Frances asked me to."

Standing there, Hannah spooned cereal into her mouth. She watched the paint flake as the drill pierced it and then sawdust sprinkled onto the tools.

"What does she want to lock up?"

"Dammit," her father said, as the screw jumped out of his hand, bounced off the counter, and disappeared into the spatter pattern on the linoleum. "Find the screw for me, sweetheart. You have young eyes."

She could feel the chill of the linoleum through thin seersucker as she groped on her knees for the screw. The pajamas were tight in the crotch, tight all over. She'd grown since last summer. Last summer, while she was sleeping, he'd unbuttoned these pajama tops and fingered her nipples.

"What's going on here?" Frances asked, coming into the kitchen. She was carrying a bundle of dirty clothes from the hamper, clothes belonging to the three of them, all tangled together. She dumped them at the top of the cellar stairs and peered through her eyeglasses at Hannah crouched on the linoleum.

"He lost a screw."

Frances went to the stove to pour herself coffee out of the Silex. Her legs were at Hannah's eye level. Below the chenille and the eyelet-edged ruffle of her nightgown, her shins were thin as rolling pins, shiny, mottled yellow and purple. They disappeared into fuzzy, boat-shaped slippers.

Hannah knew better than to pursue the question of the padlock, but she did it anyway. "What are you going to lock up?" Hannah asked, rocking back onto her heels. Her father was squatting on the counter, waiting for her to locate the screw.

Frances settled herself into the breakfast nook with her coffee. "Somebody's been coming down at night and helping herself to snacks," Frances said.

Hannah spotted the screw on a blotch of green, but didn't say anything.

"I'm not going to mention any names. She knows who she is."

"If you're talking about me, it's not true," Hannah said. She looked up at her father, but he'd picked up the pencil and was marking the door frame. "I don't come down at night. I don't eat snacks."

"Well, somebody's been into my candy, and I don't think we have any little mousies in the house, do we, Lyle?"

"It's a lie," Hannah said.

The odd thing was that she felt riddled with shame, even though she hadn't taken the candy. But she might have, just the way she'd stolen money out of her father's pocket. Maybe Frances had her number and was acting to prevent something Hannah was capable of doing in the future. Still, she said it again, with icy calm. "It's a lie."

"I think you'd better be careful who you call a liar," Frances said. "Hadn't she, Lyle?"

"Haven't you found that screw yet? The cheapskate bastards don't put any extras in the package."

Hannah scooped up the screw and dropped it into her father's palm.

"Lyle, you're not going to let her get away with that, are you?"

Hannah said, "You're the one the candy should be locked away from. You shouldn't eat candy because you're already too fat."

Her father yanked her toward him by her elbow and slapped her hard on the side of her jaw. The screw went flying, and the drill crashed into the sink. They punished her by making her spend that whole day and the next in her room. She had plenty of time to think. She figured out it was Frances coming down in the middle of the night to eat her own candy, and she had to protect herself from herself by blaming the sin on Hannah. Maybe she knew what she was doing, maybe she didn't.

When Hannah found out that her father had charge of the padlock key, not Frances, she knew she was right.

* * *

The time has come to transplant the seedlings into individual pots and turn on the Gro-Luxes, but Tucker puts it off, and every day the plants in their flat become spindlier and their roots more intertwined. He doesn't have much heart for the job, because something tells him he won't be around to see the crop mature.

There's a heaviness in the house; it's as though the fog outside has seeped through cracks in the wallboards and weighted everything down. He feels like stones are tied to his ankles. He'll have to get out, or suffocate.

It's terrible, the three of them living together. He doesn't think Marilla knows what's been going on—why wouldn't she say something? Why wouldn't she damn him to hell and her daughter, too? But she's not her normal self, either. At night in the loft, when she turns over in her sleep, she seems to have to struggle to do it, as though her body is under pressure. She sleeps more deeply.

From the bed he watches her getting dressed, getting ready to go to work. She fits her heavy breasts into the cotton bra, reaches behind her to hook it in back. She moves slowly, ponderously, like a bulldozer.

"What did you dream about?" he asks.

She turns and gives him an odd look, as though he's never asked the question before. Maybe he hasn't.

"I never dream anymore."

"Anymore since when?"

"I don't remember," she says, shrugging.

Lyle told Billy he couldn't work this afternoon. No excuses, he's beyond that. What's Billy going to do, fire him? Anyway, there's not much to do around the office now, just sit at his desk amid the taped cartons and drink instant coffee and listen to talk that's like flies buzzing on a ceiling, like the hum of a distant highway.

He's been waiting impatiently for this day, the third Monday in the month, when Frances goes to her club meeting. At half past one he rounds the side of the house and sees, to his frustration, the Caprice still parked in the driveway. It's not like her to skip the club meetings, and he worries that maybe the arthritis has kept her from going, or the fear that Mid Flowers in Florida will be the central topic of the afternoon. Cautiously he opens the kitchen door and calls her name. But there's no sound except for the furnace kicking on in response to the blast of chill air from the open door, and then he remembers Frances mentioning that one of the other members was going to pick her up, something about a tray of cupcakes. He shuts the door again and slogs out through the mud to the shed. The glacier of drifted snow there is retreating. He sees the yellowed tops of cabbages, the spine of the stone wall, the cross plank of his sawhorse.

He has two hours, maybe two and a half if the girls linger to gab, but he can't count on that. He unlocks the padlock and swings the shed door wide open, forcing it over a crust of ice. He needs the wheelbarrow, but there's so much junk in the shed that it takes him a while to shift things enough so he can extricate it. He scrapes his knuckles on the underbody of a Royal portable, which has long ago been separated from its case, and a splinter from the wheelbarrow handle jabs into his palm. When he has loaded the wheelbarrow as full as is practical, he trundles it toward the house. It's slow going, through the bog, and an alligator handbag bounces off the top of the heap and lands in the mud. He'll be able to wipe it off, though; luckily it's simulated leather, not the real thing.

It's tricky getting everything into the house, because he doesn't want to take time to pull on or pry off his rubbers every time he crosses the threshold, and Frances would surely notice an accumulation of mud in the rag rug by the kitchen door. So he kicks it out of the way and resolves to scrub the linoleum under it when he's done. Two more wheelbarrow trips and he's ready to haul the whole caboodle to the attic.

But his heart is beating uncomfortably with the exertion and with the possibility that Frances might come home early with a sick headache or some other complaint. He pours himself some water out of the glass jar in the refrigerator and makes himself sip it, slowly, until his pulse is under control. He thinks about taking his blood pressure and then rejects the idea. He can't stop now, with the kitchen floor piled high with rubbish: Even if his BP is out of sight, he'd just as soon not know about it.

He unzips the moldy old suitcase and begins to cram whatever will fit into it. The battered unabridged Funk and Wagnalls dictionary and the stone doorstop painted to look like a sleeping cat make it weigh half a ton, never mind all the other rubbish he wedges in there, but at least he'll have to make fewer trips upstairs. He's glad he had the foresight to filch the suitcase from the cellar under the insurance building way back when he first got his idea. Billy was up to something with that suitcase around fifteen years ago, but then whatever it was came to an end, and Billy stowed the suitcase in the cellar and forgot about it. At the time Lyle had felt sorry for Mid, little knowing that the same thing was going to happen to him, and worse, and that one day Mid would triumph at everybody's expense, including his own. Thinking about the worm turning that way gives him a perverse sort of pleasure, and the strength to lug the suitcase up the two flights with only a brief pause on the landing.

They don't heat the attic stairway, or the attic, and as he opens the top door the cold, close, dusty air pinches his nostrils. It's dim under the rafters, and the windows at the gable ends are covered with cobwebs. He sits on the sheet-covered couch to rest a minute before unpacking the suitcase. Gradually he finds his eyes adjusting to the gloom.

Lyle hasn't been up here since he and Bramley Johnson, who he hired for ten dollars, moved all of Marilla's furniture up here the week before he and Frances were married. When she said she wanted to get rid of it he'd thought she must mean burn it. He got a bonfire permit from the town office and bought a quart of charcoal lighter to douse the upholstery with, and he and Bramley were just struggling out the kitchen door with the old brown couch when Frances dropped by to see how they were coming with the move, and yelled bloody murder, and made them haul the couch back through the kitchen and up to the attic, and all the other furniture with it. She was shocked he was planning to burn the stuff, and he was shocked she wanted to save it. You might call that their first quarrel, with half-witted old Bram Johnson standing there on the back stoop grinning like a maniac.

That couch they had in the trailer on Seal Neck Road, he and Marilla. He lifts the sheet, and puts his nose down close to the coarse wool material, and imagines it still smells the way the trailer smelled, of kerosene, and cooking oil, and the soap she used. He remembers making love to her on the couch soon after Hannah was born, and they had to snatch a few moments between feeds. He remembers the milk in her breasts, how swollen they were, how the milk would leak out on its own when she was in his arms. He wishes to hell Frances hadn't come by that day and he'd burned it all.

He doesn't bother to unzip the suitcase and empty out its contents. He knows now he couldn't possibly stand on his front lawn and bargain with tourists over Marilla's things, or Hannah's, or even the sticks and oddments belonging to strangers. They're too private, it would be too painful. He's amazed he ever thought he could make a living that way.

He lugs the suitcase down the two flights and loads it, as well as all the accumulated trash from the shed, into the car. When he returns from his trip to the dumpster he sees that the wheelbarrow has made six slithery ruts, like the trails of snakes, in the mud. Carefully he smears them over with his rubber. He's just replacing the rag rug over the clean linoleum by the kitchen door when Frances unlocks the front door and cries, "Halloo, I'm home."

Tucker looks out the window at Hannah's little yellow Pinto parked by the alder thicket. The alders have catkins, like punctuation marks. She's sitting at the table, working on the thick gray sleeve, her needles clacking one against the other.

"Let's get in the car and go," he says suddenly.

She looks up, the stitch halfway between needles. "Go where?"

"Boston. Anywhere."

She slips the stitch onto the needle and lays the knitting on the dull metal tabletop. "What are you saying, Tucker?"

"Not for a lark. For good."

She's tugging at a hank of her hair. Outside, herring gulls are yowling and squawking, but you can't see them, because everything beyond the alder thicket is obscured by fog.

"What about my mother?"

"It's insane, the way things are. Three wasps in a bottle."

"She doesn't know, I'm sure she doesn't."

Smoking a cigarette, he leans against the cold iron wood stove. He hasn't bothered to light it because it's fifty degrees out.

"What makes you so sure?" he says. "You don't understand one thing about Marilla."

"And who's to blame for that?' It wasn't *me* left *her*."

Ash drops onto the plywood floor. "We'd better not start talking about blame, Hannah."

"We could stop," she says after a while.

"That's what I told you we *couldn't* do. Remember, Hannah?"

"I don't understand why."

"Because you like it too much," he says, coughing.

"And so do you."

The filter sticks to his lip, and when he takes the butt out of his mouth to toss it into the stove he finds he's torn the skin. He tastes blood on his tongue. "We have to get out of here," he says. "Now. Today."

"Shouldn't we think it over?"

"Put your coat on and get in the car. I'll be there in a minute."

"We have to leave her a note, at least."

"I'll take care of it."

"Tucker—"

"I said I'll take care of it."

She abandons the knitting and walks to the mud room, unsteadily, as though she'd been awakened in the night by an emergency telephone call. He opens the cellar door and hurries down the plank steps. Into a plastic shopping bag he packs six Mason jars full of weed, all he has left of last year's crop. He extracts a roll of bills from their hiding place in a clay sewer pipe and stuffs the money into the rear pocket of his jeans.

When he shuts the back door behind him he sees her sitting in the car, her uncombed hair on the collar of her schoolgirl coat, and he feels a wild sense of release, like a cork bursting out of a popgun. He runs to the car, the plastic bag cradled against his pea coat.

"It won't start," she says dully, as he opens the door on the passenger side.

"What?"

"The battery's dead."

"Shit," he says. "The jumpers are in the truck."

"We'll have to wait until she comes back."

"Are you nuts? Turn the ignition on and put her in second. I'll push from behind, and when she gets going good down the drive, pop the clutch. Get it?" He drops the bag on the seat, hearing the jars clink into one another, and slams the door.

Damn the mud, anyway. The car's a tinny enough little heap, but it takes nearly all his strength to shove it out of the bog it's parked in and onto the driveway. Stones in the driveway have been scooped up by the snowplow and are lying exposed in the muck and gravel. No problem for the pickup, it sails right over them, but they scrape the underbelly of the Pinto as he shoulders it inch by inch through what seems like wet tar. He can feel the wad of bills pressing against his butt. He pauses for breath, and Hannah winds down her window.

"We're never going to make it," she says.

"Yes we are. Easy as pie, once we get her on the downward slope."

"It's too muddy to go fast enough."

"She'll go, take my word for it."

"You'll have a heart attack."

"Shut up and steer!" he yells, leaning his shoulder against the car frame. The metal's so thin he can almost feel it buckle.

The driveway rises gently as it moves away from the swampy spot near the alders—it seems like goddamn Mount Katahdin—but he knows there's a sudden drop near the telephone pole about twenty yards ahead, and after that it's downhill almost the whole way to Monkey Bay Road.

Moisture begins to trickle down the back of his neck. His sock's working down into his boot and the leather's rubbing up a blister, probably going to end up with blood poisoning, but he doesn't want to stop and lose momentum. Overhead, somewhere in the fog, gulls are screeching.

When at last he reaches the top of the rise he takes a deep breath and gives the Pinto a tremendous running shove. He sees Hannah's head wobble as the car hits a rock and veers off it, and then the car's moving fast enough so he doesn't have to push anymore.

He stands there, gripping the stitch in his side, watching the car wind down a curve and disappear into the fog. Pray to God she doesn't stall it waiting for him at the bottom, he thinks, and then he hears a hollow *thunk,* and he knows they're not even going to make it that far.

April

The moving van kicks a scattershot of gravel onto the spiky dead grass as it pulls away. Lyle and Billy's yellow dog, Hardy, watch Billy bend over and rake the pebbles out of the grass with his fingers.

"It doesn't matter now, does it, Billy? If there's crap on the lawn?"

Come to think of it, when did it ever matter? Did anybody charging in to file a claim ever pause to admire the landscaping?

"Some ladies came by yesterday," Billy says, rattling the pebbles in his hand like dice. "They're looking for a place to start up an art gallery."

"Oh," Lyle says. The van farts a black cloud as it waits to turn onto Main Street.

"I'll tell you, I wouldn't mind getting this building off my hands. Two mortgages are going to kill me."

The truck makes the turn, finally, and heads up Route 1 in the direction of Machias.

"So what are your plans?" Billy asks.

Plans. The word has a formal, orderly sound to it, like an architect's drawings or navigational charts, that is ridiculously at odds with the swirl of thoughts careening around in his head. When he speaks it hurts to move his jaw. "I haven't quite worked it out."

"What was that?"

"I'm still working on it," Lyle yells, way too loud this time.

"Well, all the best," Billy says, tossing the pebbles into the road and pumping Lyle's hand. "You got my address in Florida?"

"Roz gave it to me."

"Good. Make sure you remind Fran to send us a Christmas card." He whistles to Hardy, who is nosing something in the weeds behind the state liquor store, and rambles off.

Lyle feels grit in his hand. There's nothing more to do here, he thinks, as he walks slowly up Water Street. This part of his life is over.

Thinking about his life, he pictures it as some kind of plant that got amputated. Stepped on by a cow, maybe, or broken off in a hailstorm. It didn't die, it sent out other shoots when the main one got lopped off, but they grew out at irregular, awkward angles. His life doesn't have a shape, he thinks as he crosses Main Street. Now it can't ever have one.

He thinks about the amputator, idly working the tides in Monkey Bay, living a subsistence sort of life, taking Marilla the way he might pluck a mussel out of a tidal pool and crack it open on a rock, giving no more thought to it than a gull would, but with less need.

Lyle's rubbers squelch on muddy Cottage Street. That kind of life can be amputated, too, it occurs to him. Why not? Only the sea goes on forever.

They've climbed down the bluff and are standing on wet, matted cordgrass, looking across the mud flat. It's dead low tide, misty, overcast. Inside the house Marilla is running the vac. The hum of the machine is still in Hannah's ears.

"You didn't leave a note for her," she says, grabbing his wrist. She takes the cigarette from between his fingers and drags on it. "You promised you would."

"How do you know I didn't?"

"I looked everywhere for it," she says, coughing.

He takes the cigarette away from her. "So you could read the tender words I left her with?"

Hannah feels sick and aroused at the same time. "So I could get rid of it before she came home."

"I left it in the loft. On our bed."

"Liar."

"Under the pillow."

"I looked there, too."

There are clumps of sea lettuce on the cordgrass, like green scum. There's rockweed, too, and open clam and mussel shells, abandoned by the tide.

"Were you just going to leave her with nothing? Thinking we'd been kidnapped?"

"She wouldn't have thought that," Tucker says, throwing the butt onto a grassy hummock. "She'd have been able to figure out what happened. Why rub it in?"

The cigarette has left a sour taste in her mouth. "She'd have blamed it on me."

"Well?"

"It wasn't my idea to get the hell out without so much as a word."

For no reason that she can see, he laughs. Idly he steps on a mussel shell, and it makes a soft crackling sound under his boot.

"You know something, Tucker? I've hated you for years."

"That right? You pick peculiar ways of showing it."

"I'd really like to hurt you."

"It's yourself you're liable to hurt the most."

She can feel the nausea rising. "I know that now."

A fighter jet streaks over their heads, deafening them. They're right under a training path, the pilots practicing flying low over varied and difficult terrain.

When the racket dies down, Hannah says, "She hasn't said anything about the car."

"Maybe she hasn't noticed it's gone."

"Are you crazy? There's two ruts like trenches where you pushed it out of the mud."

"You'll have to think of something to tell her, then, won't you?"

"I'm not good at lying."

Grinning, he says, "Tell her you were just going out for cigarettes."

"Tucker, what did they say at Pilcher's?"

"Nine fifty for the body work. Then there's the busted gear box, plus a few other odds and ends."

"Jesus. I don't have anywhere near that kind of money."

"Oh, I forgot. Twenty for the towing."

"It's not even worth that much."

"So collect the insurance and get yourself another heap. You do have insurance, don't you?"

"Not collision."

"Figures."

"I didn't think I'd be unlucky enough to go whomping into a tree."

"You should have asked your old man's advice. He could tell you people go whomping into trees when they least expect to."

"Oh, shit, Tucker."

"Maybe you could get the money out of him."

The tide's beginning to creep in. The water's a narrow, rippling, dull-gray band on the far edge of the mud flat. She shakes her head. "I can't ask him."

"Because you're here?"

She feels the silver from her father's trouser pocket cutting into her palm. "No. Something else."

Tucker doesn't question her further. He shakes a cigarette out of the pack and holds it, unlit. The wind has picked up a little, bringing with it the smell of salt and rotting sea animals.

"Tucker, I'm scared."

Through the stained pigskin she feels his hand tightening on her arm. "What are you scared of?"

"I don't know. Whatever's coming. I feel like I'm standing right on the edge of something, about to fall off."

"It's only mud you'd fall into," he says gently, rubbing the pigskin. When he's kissing her they hear a rifle shot. Though the sound is far away, deep in the woods, she pulls herself out of his arms. "What can you hunt for in April?" she asks.

"Crows. That's all, only crows."

Marilla unplugs the vac and sees Hannah standing in the doorway, holding the knitting.

"I thought you'd gone out," Marilla says, beginning to wind up the cord.

"I went for a walk."

"Looks raw out."

"Last night I finished the sleeve," Hannah says. "I stayed up half the night to do it."

"Have you decided who the sweater's for, then?"

"I just made the sleeve extra long, so it will fit anybody."

"Well, that's one way."

"Will you cast off for me?"

Marilla sits on the couch and takes the knitting in her hands. The wool feels coarse and prickly. Whoever wears the sweater had better have tough skin. "You know, you ought to learn how to do this yourself."

"I'm too lazy."

"What will you do when I'm not around?" she goes on, and then could bite her tongue, realizing what she's said.

But Hannah, standing at the round window, doesn't seem to have heard. She's twisting a strand of her dark hair in her fingers. Finally she asks, "Remember the day we saw the fox?"

"I remember."

"I saw another one, on my walk."

"Did you? Where?"

"You know where Dummer Stream goes under the road in a culvert?"

"Sure."

"In the grassy meadow there. But he wasn't red—he was a beautiful golden yellow color, with a gray tail."

"Yellow?"

"He was trotting along, very daintily, and then he saw me. He stopped and stared at me—we stared at each other—for fifteen seconds or so, and then he ran off into the woods."

"It can't have been a fox. Foxes are always red or black."

Hannah turns away from the window. "You don't believe me, do you?"

"I just don't think it could have been a fox."

"What, then?"

"Coyote, maybe."

"He looked exactly like a fox. Same size, same pointy muzzle, same tail. Except for the color."

Marilla lays the sleeve and the pair of needles beside her on the couch.

"Coyotes are big and rough-looking and they sort of slouch," Hannah says. "And their fur isn't bright like that, even if it is yellowish."

"All right."

"He has to have been a fox."

"Does it matter so much, Hannah?"

"I suppose not," she says, shrugging. She comes away from

the window and sits on the leather hassock that one of Tucker's friends from Boston brought once. It came empty—made in some Arab country—and the two of them stuffed it full of balled-up newspaper. Now one of the seams is splitting and the dye is flaking off the leather.

"I had an accident," Hannah says.

"What kind of accident?"

"I was going to town to get my hair cut, I couldn't stand it another minute. The battery was dead, so I asked Tucker to push from behind. The engine started up all right, but something happened, I was going too fast, and I hit a rock or a patch of ice, and I lost control. The car went off the road and bumped into a tree."

"But you weren't hurt."

"Shaken up a little, that's all."

Hannah's poking her finger into the split seam. She digs out a scrap of yellowed newspaper and then stuffs it in again.

"I saw the car was gone."

"They came up from Pilcher's and towed it."

"So you never got your haircut."

"No."

"I could run you into town this afternoon."

"No, that's okay." Hannah's head is down, she's still worrying that seam. "What did you think when you saw the car was gone?"

"I thought maybe you'd gone to Boston."

"Would you have minded?"

"Yes, I'd have minded."

Frances folds yesterday's newspaper, mostly unread, and crams it into the trash bin. Her slippers stick to grease on the linoleum as she moves between cupboard and stove, getting herself a cup of coffee, but she doesn't have the energy to do anything about it. Overhead, Lyle is walking about in the bedroom. She can't imagine what he's doing. It's not pacing, not so regular and determined as that, but rather a few tentative steps in one direction, and then a pause during which she thinks he's finally settled himself, and then another few steps off in some other direction. Endlessly fiddling, accomplishing nothing. It's driving her mad. Soon he'll be down for coffee, smiling foolishly, wanting her to talk to him and keep him company. She just doesn't have the heart for it anymore, she thinks, dropping onto the padded bench in the breakfast nook. If only her joints didn't ache so. If only the sun would shine. If only she could have the house to herself again.

In the chucked newspaper is a story about teacher certification. Oh, for months now there have been articles about bills in the state legislature designed to put an end to automatic recertification. Or it could be that the system has been changed by Maine Teachers Association rules voted in at the last convention. Or by executive order, even. For a long time Frances barely paid any attention to these stories, assuming they had nothing to do with her, or Bev either, and so she knows no details. Now she's afraid to read them. Her eyes go out of focus when she comes across the word "certification," and quickly she turns the page.

It's supposed to be spring. The snow is mostly gone; there's just a pitted crust behind the shed, where the sun never reaches. When you're out there you can hear it melting, trickling down into the sodden moss.

But she feels cold, cold right down to her bones. Even the coffee doesn't warm her, and the taste is like tarnish.

What's happening can't be happening. They made a solemn bargain, she and Lyle. She can almost feel the girdle pressing in on her organs again, squeezing the life out of her, almost smell the chalk dust and the panic of facing a classroom on a Monday morning.

How was she to guess he'd lose his wits and then be left in the salt air to rust, like a broken-down car?

She doesn't blame Mid anymore. With a horrible clarity she sees that Mid was just the excuse Billy used for closing up shop and moving to Florida. It was the only way he could get rid of Lyle, and the chaos Lyle created, without actually firing him. Really, you have to be grateful for the sacrifice he made. Indebted, even.

She sees, also, that it was Hannah coming back and then going to stay with Marilla, a deliberate slap, that pushed everything over the edge. The doll that Lyle dug out of the dumpster proves it. In some weird, terrifying way he was trying to recover his child.

Frances wishes she could shake that girl till her teeth rattle, really teach her a lesson. So silent, so secretive she always was, just like her mother. Scorning every kindness, every effort Frances made to be a mother to her, just biding her time until she could stab Frances in the back.

She stares out the window at the shed. It looks so innocent and ordinary, its tar-paper roof nailed down tight against the wind, its door tidily shut and padlocked. She knows the Hannah doll is in there, though. He never cared for Frances the way he cared for those two. She might as well face it. They both left him, and Frances is stuck here, stuck with the mess they created.

She hears his footstep on the stairs. He'll expect her to heat his coffee for him, serve his milk in the little pitcher with the blue cornflowers. She feels like wringing his neck.

She was wearing a red slicker and her thick hair was woven into a single braid. On the end of the braid was an ornament made of two clear plastic balls somehow twisted together. No, the balls weren't clear, they had shifting rainbow colors inside, and gold flecks. Lyle didn't remember seeing the ornament before, but he didn't ask her where she'd got it. She'd say impatiently, "Don't you remember when I stayed at Aunt Trudy's and her friend from Unityville gave it to me?" or some other explanation like that. He didn't like to question her too closely.

The dog was scrambling around on the backseat, digging its nails into the upholstery. It was a damp day, and the dog smelled like the inside of a shoe. Lyle was glad to be getting rid of the wretched animal, but at the same time it felt like a defeat. He couldn't tell whether Hannah cared or not. She just stared out the window, snapping and unsnapping the hooks on the red slicker.

He'd been going into her room at night. He couldn't stop himself, no matter how hard he tried. Something pulled him there like a wire. He thought it was safe, because she was such a heavy sleeper. And anyway, she was his. Where was the harm? He wasn't going to hurt her, he wasn't that sort of man.

One night after he went back into his own room he heard her crying. She sounded choked, as if she had her fist jammed into her mouth. He was terrified she was going to get on her bicycle and ride to Monkey Bay, even though she'd promised him, cross her heart hope to die, that she'd stay with him forever.

The next day he heard about the dog that had been thrown out on the road and he went to Pilcher's garage, where it was hanging around, begging scraps, and brought it home. Hannah'd always wanted a dog, but Marilla wouldn't let her. He'd prove to her he loved her more than Marilla did.

But from the beginning the dog had been a disaster. It must have figured that because it had been rescued and named Lucky, it could crap wherever it took a notion to. Finally he lost his patience and said the dog would have to go. He was planning on giving her his word that if the Animal Rescue

League couldn't find a home for Lucky they'd take him back, but he didn't need to. Before he had a chance to make the promise, Hannah attached the leash to the dog's collar and led him out to the car. The dog was so dumb his feet were going in four different directions and she had to drag him.

On the way home from the shelter he said suddenly, "Sometimes when you hurt somebody it's because you love them so much you can't help it." She glanced over at him, but her face was blank, as though she had no idea what he was talking about. Maybe he'd only imagined he heard her crying that night, maybe it was the wind.

There's been a string of chill, drizzly days. Nothing out of the ordinary for April, but the unsettling thing is the wind, which never lets up. It whines in the spruces like some kind of relentless machine. Marilla longs to be outside digging up the potato bed, cultivating the soil to plant peas and radishes, but the soil is still too soggy. It smells sour with rot. She buys a bag of lime to sweeten it, and when she tears open a corner of the bag, the wind whips the lime into her eyes. No help for it, she'll just have to be patient.

She's putting on weight, just as Mittie said, it's like pads of hard rubber on her hips and thighs. When she happens to touch herself, pulling on her dungarees or turning over in bed, she's surprised by the extra flesh, as though it's part of somebody else. She has to suck in her breath to get her pants buttoned, and then the flesh laps over the waistband. She's always been big, but never fat. Fat women puzzled her, how they could eat what it would take to fuel all that lard without making themselves sick. Now she understands about being that hungry. Can it be change of life already?

After work Marilla turns the truck down Torry Point Road. Pilcher's is three-quarters of a mile down the road, a lot full of derelict vehicles surrounding a concrete-block garage with a corrugated roof. Out front, under a homemade sign (PILCHER BROS) made out of light bulbs screwed through holes in a huge sheet of plywood, she spots the little yellow car. One fender looks like somebody took a maul to it. She sits in the idling pickup, the wipers whapping back and forth, and wonders what it is about Hannah's story that doesn't ring quite true.

After a while Howell Pilcher comes limping out of the office end of the garage. He's the only brother left: One got shot by his girlfriend's husband and eventually died of the wound, and the other drove a Chrysler convertible into the Singing Bridge one Saturday night. Howell's left leg has been shorter than the right since the Korean War.

"Help you?" Howell asks, pushing his Agway cap far enough back on his head so he can see who's in the truck.

"I was looking at that Pinto."

"Don't know as she's for sale."

"Banged up pretty good."

He looks over at the yellow car, which seems to crouch dismally in the drizzle, like a wet cat on a stoop.

"Guess I can fix her."

"Must have been going at a good clip when it hit whatever it hit."

Howell limps a little closer to the window. She's sure that by now he's made the series of connections between Marilla, the pickup, the pickup's owner, the Pinto, and the Pinto's owner—but if she's going to play dumb, he's figuring, he might as well do the same. "Tree," he says.

"Hit it pretty hard, did it?"

"Don't take much of an impact to put them tin cans out of commission."

The rain's coming down harder, and Howell has to hold on to the cap to keep it from flipping off his head. "Owner might be better off with something solid," Marilla says. "Like a pickup."

Howell runs his eyes over the side of the pickup, taking in the rusty lacework at the bottom of the door, the dent in the roof where a stone bouncing off a load of fill in a dump truck once landed. "Lookin' to make a trade?"

"Oh, nobody'd be interested in this pile of nuts and bolts. Too many miles on her."

Howell smiles craftily. "At least she's runnin', which is more'n you can say for the Pinto."

Marilla smiles too, and cranks up the window. Halfway up Monkey Bay Road she realizes what was odd about Hannah's story, nothing to do with the Pinto after all. She'd never have let that woman in town cut her hair. Butcher it, probably.

Tucker turns something over with the toe of his boot. It's a mouse, a fringe of black blood on its neck. The mouth gapes open, revealing tiny sharp teeth. "Mack's been busy," he says.

She sits on a boulder, her hands shoved into the pockets of the old pigskin jacket. The water's lapping the drenched cordgrass at the foot of the bluff. "Why doesn't she bring them home, like other cats?"

"Maybe she doesn't give a shit about our opinion."

"Thank God for the sun," Hannah says. The light is glinting on the bay like a million small-scale explosions, each over in a split second. "I thought I was going to go nuts in all the wind and drizzle."

He lays his hand on her head. "Marilla doesn't look good," he says. "She looks washed out."

Hannah sucks in her breath. "Do you think she knows?"

Her hair feels thick and coarse in his fingers, different from her mother's. There's a scrap of dead leaf caught in it, a cluster of pine needles. He slips his hand inside her collar and rubs her neck. It's slightly rough, scarred. She shivers at the cold touch.

"Tucker, does she know?"

"She knows, but she hasn't guessed yet."

"What's that supposed to mean?"

"You ought to be able to figure it out," he says, moving away from her and groping for cigarettes.

"We'd better get going before she does guess. Or I have to get my hair chopped off by some lunatic."

"What?"

"Tucker, let's get out of here. Please."

"There's the little matter of the car."

"We could hitch."

The match flame trembles in the breeze off the water. "I'm getting kind of long in the tooth for hitching."

"You are not."

"I am if I say I am."

"Are you telling me you've changed your mind?"

He's smoked half the cigarette, in long, slow drags, before he answers. "Not exactly."

"Well, what exactly?" She jumps up from the rock and puts her hand on his arm. He can feel her nails through the flannel. "So she looks pale, so what? I happen to know she has the curse."

"Why did you run the car into a tree?"

"I didn't do it on purpose, for Christ's sake."

"No?"

They stare at each other for a long moment, and then she drops her eyes. "I don't know."

"Listen, Hannah. Down cellar there's some money rolled up in a rubber band. It's inside a sewer pipe, clay, elbow-shaped. There's dirt plugging up the ends—you'd have to dig it out to get at the bills."

"So we don't have to hitch, after all—is that what you're saying?"

"You can do what you want with the information."

"You're putting the whole burden on me. That isn't fair."

"What is fair, Hannah?"

"You're not coming with me, are you?"

Her face is flushed. For almost the first time he can see her mother in her.

"You wouldn't touch me the way you do if you didn't care about me," she says.

"I didn't say I don't care."

"Tucker, I understand now why she did what she did. I don't blame her anymore."

"What's that got to do with anything?"

"I wouldn't be taking you away with me to hurt her, if that's what you think. If that's why you're dragging your feet now."

What he should say is: *Here's what I'm doing for you, Hannah, letting you go. Letting you get away clean.* But what he does say is, "You and your mother, you've both got a screw loose." He gives the dead mouse a kick and heads up to the house.

It's like heartburn, like seasickness. It has its own smell—that of ashes doused with water, the inside of a chimney on a damp day or a house after it's burned. He can describe it but not put a name to it, this feeling he has. It's gnawing away at him. There won't be anything left of him if he doesn't find a way to get rid of it.

From the bedroom window Lyle watches a bunch of starlings land on a telephone wire. He thinks about the slingshot he made once. He skinned the forked stick with a penknife, rubbed it until it was smooth as ivory. He collected a pocketful of small gray stones from the little cove over by the cannery. He tried to hit starlings, nuisance birds, but they always flapped away before the stone could reach them. He got a toad, though. It was squatting on a rock back of the house. He remembers the numb way it blinked at him as he was taking aim.

The toad wasn't the only thing he ever killed. He drowned a pair of kittens in a pail, scrawny blind creatures. His mother had the cat fixed afterward. He smashed a porcupine with the Malibu, deliberately squashed it, rather than driving around it. They think they own the road, porcupines, they think nothing can ever hurt them. There was that shepherd always running loose on Seal Neck Road. Marilla was afraid to put Hannah outside in her carriage. He slit open a piece of liver, sealed Rat-tane inside it.

The odor of Bev's sandwich somehow reaches him, fumes of luncheon meat exploding out of waxed paper. He hears their voices buzzing like hornets. He knows they're talking about him. He'll raise the flag the day that woman is gone to Florida or wherever it is she's going.

She told Tucker she doesn't dream anymore, but this morning she wakes up queasy with guilt. something about socks, a mess of them on the floor. They're black, child-sized, full of holes, stiff with grime because she's neglected to wash them. Hannah's socks.

Tucker's still asleep, gently snoring, his mouth partway open, a fleck of spittle on his mustache. For a moment Marilla watches his shoulder rise and fall as he breathes. She knows something is wrong. Yesterday she was down cellar after potatoes and saw that the light was out over his seedlings. She followed the cord to the outlet and found it unplugged. She pressed her fingers into the compost in the flat. It was dry and crumbling. The plants seemed barely alive, but she thought she'd better not water them.

By April the plants are always in their big pots under the Gro-Luxes. Maybe he's decided to give up his trade for the time being because he's worried about the marine patrol officer hanging around. For some reason she thinks of Monkey Gibben. But it wasn't revenuers that killed him.

Half the clothes she owns she can't get into anymore. She puts on a pair of jersey slacks that have an elastic waistband and sees in the mirror that she does look pregnant. Her breasts feel heavy, like clumps of sodden earth.

Down in the kitchen she lets the cat in, shakes Friskies into her bowl, measures coffee into the percolator basket. It's another overcast day. The blue curtain on the lean-to door hangs limply, not quite pulled all the way across. In the gap Marilla catches a glimpse of a rumpled sheet, a striped anklet. The socks from the dream come back into her mind, and now another detail, that in the dream Hannah's bed was a rough wood box by the door of the trailer and she had to curl up to fit in it. Marilla doesn't believe in dreams, that you can read them like tea leaves. But she feels the remorse plain enough and knows what that means.

Her stomach rumbles with hunger, but she's not going to eat. Fasting is the only way she can think of to deal with the pain she's feeling. She drinks the coffee black and after a few mouthfuls empties the cup into the sink.

Hannah's knitting is on the table. She left off in the middle of a row, the two needles crossed, the coarse gray yarn coming unwound from the ball and dribbling through crumbs and ash. Absentmindedly Marilla rewinds the yarn and takes a stitch or two and then finishes the row. She sees that her stitches are looser by comparison. She can actually feel the tautness in the interlocked wool, it's almost as though the sleeve might spring apart of its own tension.

She hears the cloth curtain yanked across the wire, looks up from the sleeve to see Hannah's flushed face and tangle of dark hair. Her legs and arms are naked, she's wearing bikini panties the color of grape juice and one of Tucker's undershirts.

"Mumma, what are you doing?"

Hannah hasn't used that word for years, but Marilla knows there's no significance in it now. She's foggy with sleep—surprised, maybe, out of some disturbed dream of her own.

"Just finishing the row for you," she says calmly. "You left it in the middle of a row."

"I couldn't sleep. I thought working on it would relax me, but it didn't. So I went out walking."

Marilla lays the sleeve on the table.

"It was so dark. No stars, and the moon just a fuzzy blur. I don't know why I didn't stumble into a hole and break my neck."

"You were lucky."

Hannah looks at the sleeve. "You'd better finish the whole thing."

"What, the sweater?"

"I'm going to leave today."

"But we haven't—"

"Don't want to push my luck," she says, laughing harshly.

"What about the car?"

"I've decided to junk it. I'll hitch to Bangor, take the bus from there."

"I wish you wouldn't go yet."

Hannah's shivering, clutching her own arms. "I have to."

"Well, take the knitting with you. You'll find somebody to give it to."

"No, it's ugly. Only fit for Maine."

"Oh, Hannah."

"I'm sorry."

"Let me drive you to Bangor. I can get Mittie to switch hours with me."

She shakes her head, and Marilla knows there's no use arguing with her. She looks so thin. They're forecasting flurries for Washington County. She came in snow, she'll leave in snow.

Somebody's tried to bleach it out, the ink stain, but it's still there, deep down in the grain of the oak. Frances could have told them they'd never get it out. Some days it was a skull, other days it was a mouth open in a howl. She used to keep her jar of sharpened pencils over it, but the jar always got moved. Grimy hands shoving papers onto her desk, meddling with her things the moment her back is turned.

She listens to the clock ticking. Odd how long a second actually is, when you're keeping your mind on it. It's as though the mechanism in the clock has to force itself to hold back. You'd think all that stress and strain would wreck it, eventually. Wear out the crucial parts that probably can't be replaced anymore. Yet she's certain it's the same clock. She recognizes the stainless-steel case. It's like a great, secretive moon.

They've painted the cinder-block walls. They're bright yellow now, but you can see where cellophane tape has been applied and then torn off, lifting the newer paint. The old pale green that she remembers speckles the wall like a rash. The asphalt tile on the floor is the same dull gray with swirls of cream, designed to hide dirt. Some of the tiles have curled edges on account of floods. They built where the water table is so high you don't dare flush the toilets in the spring. It was the cheapest land they could get. It's really a swamp, is what it is.

Some people say the school is sinking. They hired a firm of engineers to make a report and there was a big argument in Town Meeting, one faction accusing the other of mismanagement and worse. Selectmen lurking in the foundation bushes with measuring sticks and levels and plumb lines. The dispute has died down now, though. Even if the school really is disappearing into the muck, it will take a very long time for it to happen. Generations, possibly. Eons.

In a distant office a telephone begins to ring. Nobody to answer it, because it's school vacation week. Bev is in North Carolina getting utilities hooked up and interviewing wallpaper hangers.

Frances looks down at her feet. She sees that she has come to school in bedroom slippers.

A woman is standing on a concrete-block stoop in front of a trailer, a bowl in her hands. She just waits there, patiently, as the pickup rumbles by her, and though Hannah turns around to look, she never finds out if the woman is let in or not.

"Who lives in that trailer?" she asks.

"Phil Erridge's widow. She has cancer, I'm told."

The woman with the bowl could be me, Hannah thinks. Wanting to say: *Here, take this, it's all I have to give you,* and the sick person doesn't hear me knock or maybe isn't even home.

"Grass is greening up," Marilla says.

"Yes."

"Or the clover, anyway. Clover comes first. That and the wild onions."

But Hannah couldn't say, *It's all I have to give you,* because that would be telling too much. All she could do is thrust the bowl into her hands and take off, running.

"Do you have money?" Marilla asks.

"Enough."

"I'll get Tucker to sell the Pinto for parts. So be sure to

send me your address, when you have one, so I can mail you the money."

"No, you keep it."

Marilla shifts down into second gear before going over a frost heave. "Why should I? It's yours."

"For my board."

Marilla takes this as a rebuke, Hannah sees, and is silent. It goes all the way back to the day Hannah said to her into the telephone, "No, I can't go live with you. That's not my home where you are, *that's not my home.*"

She just can't stop hurting her, even when she wants to.

"But I will send you my address."

Marilla nods.

"It may be a while, so don't worry. I know people near Boston I can stay with while I'm figuring out what to do next. I'll be fine."

A scattering of raindrops falls on the windshield. Hannah's thinking about her father now, wondering if he'd really have been so bad off if she *had* gone to live in Monkey Bay. She thought she was staying to keep him from crumbling, but it could be she was fooling herself. Maybe, as far as he was concerned, she and the sad skinny girl on the Gilley Road and Frances and even Marilla were all interchangeable. Maybe that's all love is, after all—dependency. And sacrifice is nothing but a big ego trip.

It's raining harder, drumming on the roof of the pickup, and fat snowflakes are mixed in with the rain. When they reach the end of Monkey Bay Road Marilla says, "I can't just let you out in this. You'll be soaked to the skin."

"No, it won't take me long to get a ride."

On the opposite side of Route 1 is an A-frame shack that used to be a bait shop but is now boarded up. Marilla parks the pickup in the gravelly clearing in front of the shack. You can't actually call it a clearing anymore, since weeds and pine seedlings have sprung up between the pebbles. The wipers clack, scraping the windshield, as Hannah gathers up her overnight bag, gloves, paper bag of sandwiches. There's really nothing to say now. Hannah feels empty of words, and even thoughts are all leading to dead ends. She leans over to kiss Marilla's cheek and realizes there are tears there. " 'Bye, Mumma," she says, and climbs down out of the pickup.

She was right, she's hardly wet at all before a van heading west skids to a stop and takes her aboard.

Tucker lifts the clay sewer pipe and sees that dirt still packs both ends. Stubborn silly brat, too good for his money. To hell with her, then, and her wrecked cars and half-baked unfinished projects. She'll never settle. She'll always be restless and unsatisfied. It's not what he wishes for her but what he knows, as well as he knows himself.

For the first time in his life Tucker feels what Lyle must have felt when Marilla left: a dull, aching misery, a wound in the chest so enormous it stretches from gullet to belly, from armpit to armpit. What Hannah must have felt then, too. He smiles. She got even all right, but not the way he expected.

He sits in his chenille-covered chair, the sewer pipe in his hands, his feet up on the rackety table. The money was part of the sacrifice he was making, sending her away alone. Now that she's left it behind, he sees there was something hollow in the sacrifice, because they couldn't have made it work, anyway. They'd have started to squabble, pick on one another. She'd get on his nerves with her hair twisting and foot tapping. He'd have to work at some idiot job or other to pay the rent. She'd notice how old he is. She'd take a pair of tweezers to her eyebrows. Sooner or later she'd fall in love with somebody else. And at bottom it would all be because she didn't really need him.

She wouldn't even let him have the pleasure of being flat broke, damn her.

So how do you stitch up a hole that big? There isn't the flesh, the skin to cover it. Physically he feels his armpits pinch, his shoulders pull together. Jesus, it might gape that way his whole life.

Upstairs the telephone begins to ring. Somebody from the Cancer Society, he imagines, wanting Marilla to go soliciting, or some jerk trying to sell vinyl siding. Or a kid who has dialed the wrong number but would be too stunned or dim-witted to hang up if he answered—would grip the receiver numbly listening to him yell, "Hello? Hello?"

After fourteen or fifteen rings there's silence. The silence is much deeper than before. Down here you can't hear much of what goes on in the world: rain or crows or the cat mewing to be let out or fighter jets or Jehovah's Witnesses pounding on the kitchen door. It's what he's always liked about the cellar. Nobody quite sure if he's here or not, and him not always sure what's out there. Not caring, either. But now it makes him feel strange, the aloneness. Frightened, almost, to be cut off this way.

He wishes Marilla was home. He'd sit at the table, smoking, watching her move from cupboard to counter. He'd listen to the scrape of the sifter, watch flour sprinkling into a bowl like snow.

He stows the sewer pipe in a cobwebby nook behind a stack of newspapers and starts upstairs. Twenty past eleven, he sees by the windup clock in the big room, too early for lunch. The phone begins to ring again and he thinks he'll ignore it, let the Cancer Society lady go hang, but then he picks up the receiver.

"Where the hell were you?" she says. The line is crackling with static.

"Down cellar."

"I let it ring and ring. You didn't break your neck to get to it."

"In this house it's always a wrong number."

"God, you can be such a prick."

"I love you, too."

She hesitates, and he can hear people at other pay phones shouting their own messages. "Do you?"

He clears his throat, coughs, doesn't say anything.

"What? I can't hear you."

"Put your finger in your ear."

"Listen, Tucker, the bus is leaving any minute. I want you to tell me I'm doing the right thing. Tucker?"

He says into the static, "Sure, Hannah. You're doing the right thing."

Lyle sits on an outcropping of ledge, the thirty-thirty Winchester across his knees. The stock is smooth, slightly oily, a reddish-gold color. The rifle is loaded. When he bought the bullets in Ellsworth the clerk asked him what he had in mind shooting and he said, "Vermin." He had the answer all prepared. Without cracking a smile the clerk said, "It's always open season on rats."

Lyle watches a bug scuttle up a birch trunk. The tree hasn't leafed out yet, but the buds look full, ready to burst. Drops of rainwater fall on him when the wind agitates the branches. Crows yell raucously to one another, *yawk—yawk,* and a lame-brained chickadee whistles the same thin call over and over, *peewee, peewee, peewee.* It's getting on his nerves. He lifts the rifle and takes aim at the chickadee, but doesn't fire. He doesn't want to alert anybody.

He's waiting. It seems like he's spent a good part of his life waiting, so he can wait a little more.

The tide's halfway out or halfway in, he doesn't know which

way it's running. The rock he's sitting on is not very far from the edge of the bluff. Through the woods he can see the house, and a patch of garden where somebody's been turning the soil over. There are two big compost boxes made of rough board and a desolate sandy spot with a few cinder blocks and crabgrass. He has an idea that's where the chicken house was supposed to be. He remembers the late-afternoon sun in his eyes as they talked about different breeds of chickens. He remembers the bitter taste of the beer, a cheap brand, tinny from the can. The chicken house must have been a failure. Either it never got all the way built or it was abandoned and torn down, the wood used for other things. It pleases Lyle to think of that failure.

The house is no great shakes, either. It's like a collection of jerry-built hutches and sheds stuck together any which way. Again he raises the weapon and carefully sights a round porthole, a gutter pipe, a slab of granite on top of a chimney, a rusty streak on the weathered shingle, a cat sitting on a railing. He feels the weight of the rifle in the tenseness of his shoulder muscles. His finger on the trigger has become numb and tingly. He lowers the gun and flexes his hand to restore circulation, but the pain is spreading to his elbow. Like the poison of a snakebite, he thinks. He knows it's all in his head, but so what? If he can't pull the trigger when he needs to, he can't pull it, the reason makes no difference.

But the blood returns to his finger and the pain in his arm eases. Tension, that's all. The wait could be long, and he'd better relax. It would be safer not to think, to turn himself into something hollow. Like one of those wrinkles down on the beach. He closes his eyes and thinks about the shell, the long chalky corridor, twisting ever inward. For a long time he sits that way, his hand stroking the rifle stock, waiting.

When he opens his eyes he sees that the tide is all the way

out. The mud flat is a dull metallic color, speckled with rocks and clumps of seaweed. There's a clam digger out there, no bigger than a flea. His target, maybe.

And then he's aware of somebody else, much closer, coming at him from behind. He jumps up from the ledge, stumbling, clutching the gun.

"Morning," the man says. He's wearing a mud-brown uniform and his thick-fingered, hairy hand is on the handle of the pistol. His red face looks like it's been sandpapered.

"Morning."

The officer looks the Winchester over carefully. "Hunting?"

"That's right."

"What you looking to bag?" he says slowly.

"Crow."

"Got your mouth set for crow pie, I guess."

Lyle doesn't say anything. The officer moves a liittle closer, his heavy boots squelching on moss. "I don't suppose you have your hunting license on you."

"It's home," Lyle blurts out. "In my bureau."

"I figured. Well, the way I hear it, crows cook up kinda stringy. Tougher'n old galoshes, matter of fact. Hard to swallow." He smiles. "A man could die that way. Choke to death, eating crow."

Lyle thinks his heart is in danger of exploding.

"Take my advice and forget about crows. Go pick yourself out a nice chicken over to Shop'n Save. You won't even have to pluck it. Save everybody a whole lot of trouble."

On his way through the woods to the place he hid his car, Lyle thinks about blowing his own head off. But he feels too ridiculous. People would only laugh, thinking he did it by mistake. He slings his father's rifle onto a pile of rotting leaves and doesn't even bother to bury it.

May

She's hanging a pair of Lyle's boxer shorts on the line when the thought hits her. She's so startled by the logic and justice of it that for a long moment Frances stands with the clothespin pinched open, the wet, half-hung shorts dangling from their elastic. They made a bargain, she and Lyle. He'd take care of her so she wouldn't have to teach, and she'd never leave him. But what if one of them breaks it? Then the other one is no longer bound to it, are they? She's off the hook, as easy as that.

He had no business making such a promise in the first place. She should have paid attention to the queasiness in her stomach, the premonition that she was getting into something she'd be sorry for. If she had, she'd be packing to go to North Carolina right now, instead of hanging Lyle's laundry in this wet, miserable weather.

But it's not too late. Let him hang it himself.

She leaves the shorts dangling and the basket right where it sits, on a crumbling cinder block, and goes inside to telephone. It's 8:42 on a Monday morning; Bev will have launched into her first-period social studies class. "You'll have to get her out of class," she tells the assistant principal's secretary, who answers the phone. "This is an emergency."

"What kind of emergency?"

"Never mind what kind," Frances says coolly. She feels in control now. Listening to the receiver go *thud* on the desk blotter, she sees the stack of machine-readable achievement tests beside it, the heavy-duty stapler attached by a chain to the desk leg, the brass bowl of paper clips, the philodendron struggling to survive in air thick with cigarette smoke.

"What is it?" Bev cries into her ear. "What's the emergency? Did somebody die?"

"No, nobody died. The mahogany parlor suite," Frances says. "You haven't sold it yet, have you?"

"I can't believe you dragged me out of class to ask me that. Have you lost your mind?"

"The little tables with the marble tops. At least we could have those."

"What are you talking about, Frances?"

"And the footstool with the Scottie dog. I'll pay the moving costs. I'll make him give me the money. It's the least he can do, after everything he's put me through."

"Frances, back up a minute. I'm having trouble following you."

"But it's so simple. I can't understand why I didn't think of it before. He broke the agreement, so it's finished, over with, kaput."

"What agreement?"

"Listen, Bev, I can't talk anymore right now. I have to go pack."

"Frances, are you saying you're going to North Carolina?"

"Just like we've always planned."

"You mean you're leaving him?"

"That's what it amounts to, I suppose. But it's his own fault. He can't really blame me, any more than I blame Mid or Billy."

"Frances, school's not out for six more weeks. That will give you time to think things over."

"I'm fed up with thinking. I'm going now. Today."

"But the place is full of wallpaper hangers."

"Bev, you still want me, don't you? You haven't changed your mind?"

"Of course I haven't. But—"

"Then I don't give two hoots about wallpaper hangers."

"Frances, I'm beginning to hear a rumbling down at the other end of the hall."

"When I've finished packing, I'll go over to your house. You can drive me to the airport when you get home from school."

Frances hangs up before Bev can say anything more. She's in a hurry. Don't think she doesn't remember the smashed picture frames behind the shed, they've been in the back of her mind for years. She has to get out of here fast, if she's going at all.

Before they were married Lyle took her to meet his old grandmother over to Dudbridge. She lived by herself in a farmhouse on the Flag Road. It was winter, and the river was clogged with ice. The house seemed to be in the middle of an orchard. Marilla remembers the dark, gnarled, interwoven branches tugging at her coat as she and Lyle plodded through unshoveled snow.

For an old woman she had a surprising amount of meat on her bones. She must eat well, Marilla thought. She wasn't gray, exactly, her dark hair had just gone dull with age. It was oily, and sparse, and you could see the dead-white scalp.

Marilla and Lyle were crowded together on a narrow, stiff-backed sofa. He took her hand and hung onto it. His palm was hot and damp. She felt uncomfortable sitting there in front of the old woman with their hands clamped together that way, as if he was holding some more intimate part of her, like a kidney or heart. She tried to take her hand back, but he only hung on harder.

There was a dog, a smelly, shaggy little female. She presented her belly, rubbed her haunches on the carpet, touched Marilla's ankle with her wet nose. The wood stove hissed and smoked, burning green wood. The windows rattled, loose in their frames.

Suddenly the old woman thrust a snapshot at her. It was black-and-white, creased in the middle, Lyle toddling across a lawn. He was fat, blond, curly haired, his expression pinched, as if his mother had left him alone with the stranger who took the photograph. "Who took it?" Marilla asked, but the old woman didn't know and wasn't interested in the question. She snatched the snapshot away, thinking, perhaps, that Marilla was hoping to keep it.

"I don't guess you want to see my old nigger today." The old woman gave Lyle a sly smile, flirting with him.

"But I do, Granny."

"What was that you said? You're bored with him? You're too grown up now?"

"Show Marilla," Lyle shouted, though it was plain the old woman wasn't deaf. "Let Marilla see."

"Say pretty please."

"Pretty please," Lyle said.

"Oh, I knew you'd decide you wanted to see my old nigger," she said. "I knew you'd want him, even if you are a big boy now."

She rummaged in a drawer in a cupboard and brought out a sealed glass vial filled with brownish liquid. When she held it under Marilla's nose, Marilla could see a small black figure inside, like a shriveled baby or a naked old man. Lyle dropped her hand and took the vial.

"Go on, make him dance," the old woman said, egging him

on. He cupped his hands around the bulb at the end of the vial, and the liquid began to boil, and the little figure rose up in the bubbles and twitched, jiggled, jitterbugged. Lyle stared, fascinated. "My father brought that back from the Chicago World's Fair in 1893," she told Marilla. "My father was an adventuresome man."

The old woman died of a stroke when Marilla was pregnant with Hannah. After the funeral Lyle searched all the cupboard drawers, because she'd always promised the dancing nigger to him. He never found it, though. He suspected one of his sisters got there before him, but they denied it, and he wasn't able to prove anything. Secretly, Marilla was glad. It gave her the creeps, the nervous little figure in the bottle.

Lyle looks at the laundry basket lying on its side next to the cinder block. Some of the clothes have spilled out. They've partly dried, stiff and desiccated, the wrinkles pressed into the material. The ones underneath are still damp. Clothespins are sprinkled randomly in the grass, half hidden, like Easter eggs. Only one piece of clothing clings, tenuously, to the line.

He turns the basket upright, piles the clothes inside, gathers as many clothespins as he can find into their burlap sack. He feels sick with foreboding.

As though taking an inventory, his eyes focus on various details in the yard: the tight buds on the forsythia, the cabbage stalks, the pussy willows sprung into caterpillars, the clamped lock on the shed, the low wall of pumple stones, the plastic trash bin with its lid firmly in place. All is as it ever was.

It is four thirty in the afternoon. The temperature is fifty-seven degrees Fahrenheit. The wind is out of the southwest. The sky is cloudless. Nothing is between him and . . . what? Outer space? The heavens? The void?

He unpins the pair of boxer shorts, folds it, and takes it with him into the house. Inside, there's a faintly sour smell, fumes from the septic field backing into the sink. That happens on windy days, Lyle has never understood why. She hasn't plugged the drain. No food has been cooked for a while. The tea kettle is cold. When he lifts it from the burner something gritty rattles inside—metallic deposits, left by gallons and gallons of water, years' worth of water, boiled away, evaporated.

He turns on the exhaust fan over the stove and then, on second thought, switches it off again.

Next to the telephone in the living room he sees a clothespin. There is a connection, he is sure. He sits in a chair across the room and stares at the telephone. Either it rang and she answered it, or she made a call. For a long time he thinks about this. He pictures her reaching up to the clothesline. She is wearing bedroom slippers and a cotton housedress, the material straining at her armpits. Her fingers pinch the clothespin clumsily, painfully. She manages to attach the shorts to the line with one clothespin. She reaches for another in the burlap sack, and grasps it, and then—

But wait. She wouldn't be able to hear it ring. A hundred times over the years he called her from the office and there was no answer, and later he asked, "Where were you? Where did you go?" and she always said, "Why, I was here all the time. I must have been hanging out the wash when you called." Or watering the vegetables. Or putting wrapped fish bones in the trash bin. Or sitting in a lawn chair having a glass of iced tea with Bev.

All right, she made a call, then. Something came into her mind that prompted her to stop dead in the middle of hanging his shorts, to abandon the wet laundry and come charging into the house, her slippers flopping on the linoleum.

It's now quarter to five. For a long time he doesn't move from the chair. He listens to the clock ticking. Somewhere a child yells, a dog barks. There's a low buzz of voices as people pass, walking in the road. Maybe he even dozes a little, because when he looks at the clock again it's nearly six. He knows she's not coming back to fix supper. He knows if he went upstairs and looked in her dresser drawers they would be empty.

With an effort of will he rises out of the chair and dials Bev's number. He's not really surprised when there's no answer.

Marilla has planted one short row of dwarf gray sugar peas. She lifts a clump of rockweed to see if they've started to come up. The rockweed is dried crisp on top, but the bunches of pustules underneath are still wet, swollen, stinking like dead fish. No peas yet. It's been almost two weeks. She hopes the seeds haven't rotted in the damp soil. All that rain in April, Marilla thought it was never going to end.

She pulls on her cotton work gloves and thrusts the shovel into the soil in the next plot. It turns over easily, but there are stones, always more stones, to pick out of the soil and fling into the woods. It's as though something is sending them up from deep inside the earth, or that they have to come to the surface to breathe, like seals or cormorants.

She dumps a couple of buckets of compost on top of the turned soil, and then a dose of lime, and begins to work them in. She's sweating now; the sun is hot in the sky. Suddenly there's something hard and painful in her sneaker. She pauses, and wipes her forehead with her sleeve, and leaves the shovel upright in the plot. The clover feels cool and damp underneath her as she removes shoe and sock. It's a pebble, a white chip of quartz. There's a red indentation below her ankle, near her heel.

Tucker comes around the corner of the house, smoking. He squints in the sunlight, and she realizes there's something different about him. He's shaved off his mustache. As he comes nearer she sees that the place on his upper lip looks pale, naked, compared with the rest of his skin. He's wearing a blue shirt full of creases; he must have filched it out of the ironing basket.

He sits next to her on the clover and looks at the red mark on her foot. He takes one more drag on the cigarette and tosses it away. She opens her hand and shows him the pebble. The cigarette is still lit, smoldering in the clover and dandelions. The smoke curls, wavers in the wind, twists like a corkscrew.

She pulls on her sock and then her sneaker, and ties the lace. Herring gulls are screaming, down over the mud flat. It's low tide, and three or four clam diggers are way out, hunched over the mud.

In the woods, there's a powerful of smell of wet humus, mushrooms, fir and spruce needles, moss. The air here must be twenty degrees cooler. A red squirrel rattles its teeth like a toy machine gun. Tucker is behind her, dead branches crackling under his shoes.

A hairy greenish fungus drips from these trees on the edge of the bluff. It's called old-man's beard. It grows on trees that are dying, their roots too wet, the water table too high. Some of the trees have listed, their exposed roots wrenched out of the thin soil that covers ledge and clay. But they can't fall all the way down because there are too many other trees around them, and their dead branches hook onto the dead branches of those other trees. Spruce and fir seedlings grow in the pockets of light where trees have tried to fall.

She sits on an outcropping of ledge. This is smooth, flat rock, a gray color that is the same as her eyes. She can hear songbirds of some kind, but they stay hidden deep in the woods. He is unbuttoning her shirt. His fingers are cool and dry. He's licking her neck, which is salty from sweat. His hands are on her breast as though he's weighing a heavy piece of fruit.

The fir needles smell sweet as candy, so sweet she's dizzy. She lies back on the granite. He's sucking her nipple, his face buried in her flesh. It's strange not to feel the bristle of hair on his lip.

In the bedroom there's a sweet, musty smell Lyle hasn't noticed before. It's like the way his mother's coat smelled after she died, the cloth still impregnated with her perfume, but with other things, too—her body odor, dust, mildew.

The lamp on Frances's dresser was designed to look like an oil lamp, with pink roses on the milky glass base. He remembers how pleased she was when it arrived—her "pride and joy," she called it. It doesn't give much light. You can't knot a tie by it or find a popped collar button.

His mother didn't leave a note, either, and the doctor wrote "cardiac arrest" on the death certificate. Women are smart. They say things like, "Those of you who failed the test, I don't have to tell you, you know who you are." They understand that the guilt you create for yourself is more painful, more grinding, than any blow they could deliver.

In the wastebasket is a tangle of nylons with runs in them, an empty foot-powder can, an artificial flower off an old dress, a comb with broken teeth, the hankie with the stain from the time she got a bloody nose in the Bangor Mall.

The dresser drawers, of course, are bare. And so is her Leatherette jewelry box, except for the pieces he gave her. When he opens the top of the box, a musical mechanism inside plays "After the Ball." Her pearl friendship ring shines dimly in the glow from the lamp, also her wedding ring. She must have forced them over her swollen knuckles, with soap maybe.

He doesn't know what time it is. His watch has stopped, and for some reason she unplugged the clock radio on the bedside table. Maybe she thought of taking it with her and then changed her mind. He remembers going into Wes Bunker's hardware store in Ellsworth and picking it out for her. He had to choose between a cream case and a maroon case. It took him a long time to decide. He'd given one just like it to Billy for Christmas, in maroon, and Billy made a big deal out of it. Frances liked hers, too, or she said she did, but he might just as well never have bothered. Maybe she'd have liked the cream better.

He gets between the bedspread and the blanket and closes his eyes, but doesn't sleep. He thinks about the wet clothes in the wash basket. He thinks about an empty sleeping-pill bottle rolled under a dresser. He thinks about the card the midget gave him to keep, even though he didn't deserve it. His eyes burn, his head aches.

A bird begins to sing, and he knows the sun must be about to come up again.

Marilla's cutting chicken meat off the bones, mincing up the scraps for the cat. Rock-and-roll tunes from the late fifties are on that rinky-dink nostalgia station out of Machias. Elvis. The signal flutters around the band. Songs from their youth. Songs from before Hannah was even thought of. The cat winds around Marilla's legs, knowing she's going to get hers.

He opens the table drawer to look for matches and sees the two woolen sleeves there, rolled around the needles. Marilla half turns from the counter, catches him looking at the knitting. Her gray eyes are dark, almost black. "She asked me to finish it for her," she says.

"Are you going to?"

"I feel like if I do, she'll have nothing to come back for."

He shuts the drawer.

"I finished the second sleeve so it wouldn't ravel. That's all."

There are book matches, cadged from the bank, in a jar on the windowsill. STONY HARBOR BANKING AND TRUST COMPANY, they say in spidery lettering. He strikes a match and sees, from the way the flame wavers, that his hand is shaking. He misses her, damn it. The dull ache in his chest doesn't go away.

He switches off the radio.

Marilla puts the dish of scraps down for the cat. She's not a graceful woman, he thinks, watching her. She moves awkwardly, her footstep is heavy on the plywood, she has too much weight on her hips and belly. She holds a knife in a dangerous way, it's a wonder she's not always slicing into herself.

"I got a letter," she says, beginning to wrap the bones in newspaper.

"Today?"

"I went into town after work. It was in the box."

Tucker sits at the table smoking, waiting for her to continue.

"Lyle happened to be standing there, in front of the boxes."

"Lyle?"

"He looked strange."

"How do you mean, 'strange'?"

"I don't know—sick or something."

He doesn't give a shit about Lyle, he'd as soon Lyle was at the bottom of the sea. He wants to know what's in the letter. But he can't ask. He moves the glass ashtray toward him, scraping it over the zinc.

"I think he recognized her handwriting on the envelope."

"What did he say?"

"Nothing. He just turned and walked out of the post office. I almost went after him."

"Why?"

She shrugs, holding the parcel of chicken bones against her breast. "Because he looked so bad."

"What could you have done?"

She shakes her head. "The insurance office is going to be some kind of shop. There's a sign. 'Coming soon,' it says. 'Herbs, dried flowers, baskets.' "

"Lyle going to weave baskets?"

She puts the bones in the trash bin, clamps the lid on.

"Dry flowers?"

"Never mind about Lyle. What he does has nothing to do with you."

"It wasn't me brought the subject up."

She's washing her hands, running cold water into the sink. She takes a sliver of yellow pumice soap and rubs it over her knuckles. He can tell she's upset about something. Her cheeks are flushed, her eyes cast down. Something in Hannah's letter? he wonders. Something about him? For the first time it occurs to him that he's not safe, just because she's gone. She could still spill it all out. He feels an excitement that is part sex, part fear. He looks at the rusty circle on the tabletop. It's like a snake stretching to bite its own tail.

"She's in a town called Wollaston," Marilla says quietly. "Staying with friends."

"Is that all she says?"

She shuts the tap off and takes a towel from the rack. "She already found a job. In a hospital. Carney Hospital?"

"There is such a place."

"She works at night."

He feels let down, he's not sure why. Because the possibilities in her life have narrowed to night scut work at Carney Hospital? Or because she doesn't need him to carry on with her life?

"Any messages for me? About selling the Pinto?"

"She doesn't mention the Pinto."

He glances out at the place where her car used to be and sees that the alders are green with catkins. They ripened up some time when he wasn't paying attention.

Marilla dreams that she has gone back to live with Lyle in the house on Poplar Street. Frances is still there but is getting ready to leave. The trouble is that the house is full of born-again Christians, who are there on retreat. Evidently they've been in residence for some time. There's a woman with a child in Lyle and Marilla's bedroom, and the woman's clothes and shoes are in stacks and heaps everywhere. Marilla can't even find a pair of socks to put on her feet.

It's like her old recurrent dream of the messy house she can never get clean, except that this time the mess consists of born-again Christians as well as junk and debris. When she complains to Lyle, he says, "Oh, I'm very fond of that woman." Marilla knows she can't stay here, after all, but she has nowhere else to go. The woman sitting on Marilla's bed says pityingly, "*No*where else?" She's skinny, her stringy hair is pulled back from her face. The child, in overalls, hangs on her, sucking apple juice from a bottle. Marilla tells the woman, "When my mother was alive there was a place, but not now."

When she awakes she's almost surprised to find herself in the loft, with Tucker sleeping peacefully under the blanket. He wasn't in the dream, nor was his house. For a while, as she's dressing, Lyle's house feels like the reality and Tucker's the dream. She shivers uncontrollably, chilly in the damp air.

It's the eleventh of May. During the night it rained, and now fog has settled in. Mackerel comes into the kitchen, dripping. Marilla feeds her, boils water for coffee, pours herself some cereal.

She's picking up a spoon when the telephone rings in the

big room. She goes to the doorway and stares at it blankly. Nobody telephones here at six in the morning. The double rings are shrill, menacing, invasive. It would be possible to silence it by unplugging it, but instead she lifts the receiver.

"It's me," Mittie says. "Have I got news for you."

Marilla stares out into the fog. It has begun to rain again.

"Are you there, Marilla?"

"Yes, I'm here."

"I would've called last night, but I figured you'd probably gone to bed already."

"What is it, Mittie?"

"She's left him, Marilla. Frances has left Lyle."

The dream is still so real to her that she's not surprised, exactly. Still, she feels slow-witted, as though she has a hangover or is coming down with the flu. She sits on the edge of the couch, the phone in her hand. "How do you know?"

"My sister-in-law Connie dropped in last night after supper. We played a couple hands of gin rummy, ate some date squares she brought over. While we're talking about this and that, she just casually mentions she was meeting the Fort Kent plane Monday afternoon—her oldest kid, Stan, was coming home, he goes to college up to Fort Kent, you know—and who should she see standing in the Eastern Express line but Frances Pratt! She was with Bev Purkis, you know—the eighth-grade teacher—and she had about six suitcases she had to pay extra for."

"Sounds to me like she and Bev were going on a little vacation together."

"Bev can't go anywhere—school's not out yet."

"She probably has a sick relative somewhere. Even Frances must have relatives."

"Why wasn't Lyle with her, then?"

"I saw him yesterday in the post office. He didn't look very well."

"I shouldn't think he would look very well. Twice this has happened to him. It's beginning to get monotonous."

"No, I mean that's why he didn't go with her."

"Connie swears she was leaving for good. She has a sixth sense about things like that—I've seen it a lot of times. Like she knew that little Frampton girl was pregnant even before—"

"Well, one way or another, it doesn't have anything to do with me."

"Don't be such a stick, Marilla. Aren't you even curious? You were married to the man all those years. He's the father of—"

"I have to go now, Mittie. I have things to do."

"Why don't you give him a ring? Ask him what's going on?"

"I don't think I want to know."

She hangs up and looks out at the rain. A robin is sitting on the electricity wire, singing. Upstairs, Tucker is moving around, putting his clothes on. It's just an ordinary day, really.

Tucker's boots are muddy. They're dropping hard chunks of clay onto plywood. She hears a clatter and looks at the table. There's a rifle on it. Under the kitchen light the stock gleams like amber. Lyle's father's gun. She'd know it anywhere.

"Where did you find it?" she breathes.

"In the woods."

She leans against the linoleum counter and stares at the gun. In the woods?

"Half buried in a pile of leaves. The barrel was sticking out, pointing right at me."

"It was just lying there, all by itself?"

"I told you. You don't believe me?"

"I believe you."

A long time ago, eleven years ago, before she even left him, she worried about Lyle taking the rifle into the woods. Maybe to kill himself. Maybe to take a shot at somebody else. Even a bumbling man can hurt something with a gun like that. Gradually the tension eased; she forgot about it. Now it's as though those eleven years didn't count at all, never existed. Here's the gun back again, cutting through time like a knife.

"Is it loaded?"

"It was."

He reaches into his pants pocket and shows her a little pile of stubby bullets. In his curled hand they're like the scat of some animal. Some predator. She thinks of the box of bullets deep in a hole behind the tool shed. He must have got more somewhere.

"I have an idea you know who this rifle belongs to."

"How would I know?"

He laughs. "I can tell by the way you look. You look like you've seen somebody back from the dead."

"It's Lyle's," she says, hardly getting the words out.

"Well, well. Careless about his possessions, it seems." He drops the bullets back into his pocket and pulls a chair out from the table. Apparently unruffled, he sits, takes out a cigarette. The weapon looks huge on the table, the sight on the tip of the barrel lapping over the edge. Fingering the unlit cigarette, he says, "I wonder how it happened to land on that particular pile of leaves. Monkey Bay's kind of far out of town. Off the beaten track."

She sits too, scraping chair legs over plywood. "Tucker, listen. I have to tell you something."

"About him?" he asks, almost casually.

"Mittie thinks Frances has left him."

"No shit. Mittie the ferret."

"Tucker, this isn't any joke."

"I'm not laughing."

"So he may be kind of . . . crazy."

"Well, he can't shoot her. Not with this."

"It's not Frances I'm worried about." She touches his arm. The flannel feels soft, supple with many washings. The material is worn through at the left elbow, which he often leans on, smoking.

"You're not worried about me, are you?"

"I am."

"Well, don't bother. He didn't shoot me eleven years ago, why would he now? Anyway, Lyle Pratt has about as much guts as a turnip."

"You know, he once said something like that about you."

"What?"

"Not the turnip part. He said sooner or later I'd find out you have no backbone."

He thinks this over. "Maybe you have poor taste in men, Marilla," he says, showing her his small, gapped teeth.

"Just watch out, that's all."

His fingers are idly stroking the stock. "What do you want me to do with this thing?"

"Bury it. For Christ's sake, bury it."

"I'm dying to see the West Coast," she said. Her breasts hung like flaps on her skinny chest, the nipples pink and rubbery. The sheets were gray, spilling onto the trailer floor. A little rug was kicked into a corner. "I can't wait to get out of this dump."

"How are you going to get there?" Lyle asked. He pulled on his boxer shorts and sat on the edge of the bed, dizzy with the heat. The taste in his mouth was like rotten fish.

"I'll take off like a shot with anybody that asks me."

She fumbled under some magazines on a bedside table wedged between the bed and the wall, came up with a flattened package of Camels with a few bent cigarettes in it. "Want one?"

He hadn't had a cigarette in the ten years since his mother killed herself, but he took one, put an end in his mouth, touched the bunched strands of tobacco with his tongue. It burned without even being lit. He bent and let her hold a match to the other end.

"Or else hitch, if I have to."

"Isn't that dangerous for a girl?"

She laughed. He could see the fillings in her teeth. He'd tasted the metal when he kissed her, his tongue moving around in her mouth. Then she'd pushed his head down between her legs, down into the mess of fish guts. That's what she liked. He'd never done it before.

He thought about Burchard doing it to Marilla.

"I know how to take care of myself," she said.

A shiny smear glistened on her thigh. He looked away. He managed to get the smoke in and out of his mouth without choking. It was good to cover up the other taste. He watched some tiny flies circling a light fixture in the ceiling.

"We could go in your Malibu," she said.

He didn't answer. He didn't like to disappoint her, he felt he ought to be nice to her since he wasn't paying her anything.

"We could have a great time. Stay in motels. Or camp, even. That's cheaper."

He looked around for someplace to deposit the ash, then just let it fall to the floor.

"I know where we could get a tent. And a sleeping bag."

That's something he kept imagining before he married Marilla—the two of them in a sleeping bag for days on end, a whole week maybe, doing it to her whenever he wanted. But of course, it had never been like that. Even when she was his wife she always said she had to get up to go to work, feed the baby, drive to town for groceries. Once he said, just testing the idea out on her, "I heard about a couple that spent a week together in a sleeping bag," and all she did was laugh.

"Hey, Lyle? What do you think?"

"I have a little girl to take care of," he said.

"Aw, come on. You could find somebody to leave her with, some relative. There's Pratts crawling out of the woodwork around here."

"I don't know."

"It wouldn't kill the kid if you took a couple weeks vacation. You deserve it, after all you've been through."

She got up on her knees, wound open the window a crack and dropped her butt out. He passed his to her, and she did the same with it.

"Can't you open it wider? It's hot in here."

"I ain't got no screens. Mosquitoes would eat us alive."

The cigarette was beginning to make him feel like throwing up. She knelt behind him. Her breath was on his neck. Her hand crept inside the elastic, worked around to his dick. He felt it swelling in her hand, shoving against the cloth. He didn't have any more rubbers, he'd only brought one with him. Billy should have said something.

"Tell you what," she whispered into his ear. "Out in Texas we could get ourselves some cowboy boots. Real ones, not like they wear around here. Wouldn't you like that? Wouldn't that be the most heavenly thing?"

All of a sudden he wanted to hit her. He wanted to slap her face until she shut up. He wanted to bash her skinny naked freckly fish-smelling body against the trailer wall.

Instead, he began to cry. She was so startled she let go of his dick and pulled back her hand and the elastic snapped against his flesh.

"Lyle? Did I say something wrong? Lyle?"

He got into his clothes as fast as he could and drove home.

* * *

It's quarter past four in the morning. There's a streak of red across the whole horizon; it must stretch for miles and miles. The tide is all the way out. The trees on the bluff look like they've been cut out of black paper and pasted against the sky.

Marilla sits on the couch in the big room, drinking gin out of a Boston Celtics glass. If you live on the wrong side of the peninsula, you can't have a drink watching the sun set; you have to get up very early in the morning to watch it rise instead. Or maybe you haven't been to sleep at all.

She tries to memorize the view, fix it in her mind like a photograph. But already the rosy color has paled. Herring gulls are squabbling over bits of sea urchin or quahog out on the flat. The trees look more like trees now, three-dimensional. A chickadee is piping up, shrill and monotonous.

She told Tucker to bury the gun. He said, "Things don't always stay buried, you know," but he went out with it. He carried it loosely, easily. Through the window she watched him take a shovel out of the shed and disappear into the woods. When he came back she asked him where he'd buried it and he said, "I'm bit to a pulp, damn it. Black flies hatched out already."

"But where did you bury it?"

"In a bog."

"But where?"

"Planning on digging it up again sometime?"

"No."

"Then it makes no never mind *where,* Marilla."

The gin tastes like a chemical, like toilet-bowl cleaner. She's never drunk much. "A cheap drunk," Tucker called her once, laughing at her. She got pie-eyed on one rum and Coke and had to go to bed. Some Canuck was staying over, sleeping in the lean-to. In the morning he came up behind her in the kitchen and slid his hands onto her breasts. "Amazing boobs you got," he said. *"Incroyable."* She felt his thing pressing into her behind, through his clothing and hers. She turned away from the counter, the bread knife in her hand. "Get away," she said. He didn't know it was dull, wouldn't have cut butter. She didn't tell Tucker. She kept it a secret, an awful kind of secret she took out and thought about sometimes. Awful because she'd liked it: the admiration.

The gin isn't making her sleepy, like it's supposed to. She feels like she might vomit instead, and then she'd be back where she started. She focuses on the glass. Tucker got it for free at a Mobil station in Ellsworth, for gassing up the truck. There a cartoon decal on it, a tipsy Irishman balancing a basketball on one finger. Carefully she turns it around. On the opposite side there's a list of all the years the Celtics were world champions, beginning in 1957. In 1957 she was sixteen, eating Lyle Pratt's fish sandwiches and screwing Tucker Burchard in the weeds. Poor Lyle, stabbed in the back even then and didn't even know it. A little gin dribbles onto her chin when she drinks. The glass is nearly empty.

The sun's pretty high over the horizon now. It's not red anymore, it has lifted into haze. The day may turn out to be overcast, after all, it might even rain later on. She wonders whether to do a wash. It's hard to think of sitting next to Mittie in the laundrymat, listening to her run through all the possible reasons Frances might have had for ditching Lyle. Even if she said, "Shut up, Mittie—I'm not going to listen to one word about it," she'd still have to endure her, her lip buttoned but her eyes glittering like a cat's.

The tide has turned. In five hours or so it will be lapping right below the bluff, depositing rockweed and rubber clamming gloves and shells and plastic bottles in the squashed cordgrass. And then it will drain away again. It makes Marilla's head throb, all that relentless energy, but nothing ever changing, really. A little wearing away of the bank, maybe. A few more exposed roots.

She ought to go throw up the gin. The room is beginning to go around, though, and she's afraid she might fall. She lies back on the couch and closes her eyes, but the room only spins faster. When she opens her eyes she sees the nails, the neat double row that Tucker pounded through the gray carpet in the loft. She'd been furious then. Now it doesn't seem to matter, one way or the other. She thinks she'll be able to sleep, finally.

She dreams about watching the sun rise, the same dream over and over, as though her mind is stuck there, or wants to be stuck there.

Marilla awakes to a sharp grating sound that sets her teeth on edge. For some reason she's on the couch. She sees the Celtics glass on the floor and remembers. Jesus, what a head. She's under a scratchy wool afghan. Tucker must have put it over her when he came downstairs. She wonders what he thought when he found her here.

The telephone begins to ring. Like in a cartoon, it seems to rise a few inches off the table and quiver with the energy of ringing. After a time she struggles out from under the afghan and lifts the receiver.

"It's twenty past nine," Mittie says. "Where are you?"

"It's going to rain."

"Are you crazy? There's not a cloud in the sky."

"Later on it's going to."

"Marilla, what's the matter with you?"

"I can't take the laundrymat today."

There's a brief silence. "All right, so don't tell me."

"I'm sorry, Mittie. I just can't."

"Forget it then, Marilla," she says and hangs up.

She leaves the afghan trailing off the couch and the glass on the floor and goes into the kitchen. But the smell of coffee grounds and stale smoke and half-eaten cat food crusted in the bowl revolts her. Outside, she finds Tucker crouched on the stoop, sharpening the teeth on the chainsaw.

"You look god-awful," he says.

She sits next to him on the concrete and watches him for a while. He files each tooth with practiced, careful ease. "What are you going to use that for?"

"Clearing brush."

"Oh."

Mittie was right, the haze has burned off. The tide's nearly all the way in, and the water's choppy. A stiff breeze whips off the bay. The rusty Atlas Anti-freeze thermometer nailed to the side of the house is registering forty-nine degrees, but it doesn't feel anywhere near that warm.

"There's a dead spruce over by the compost needs bringing down."

That tree has been dead for years, its branches brittle and hung with old-man's beard. "What's the rush?"

He sets the chainsaw on the ground and wipes oil from his hands with a holey undershirt.

"Is something bugging you, Marilla?"

"No," she says, clutching her arms, shivering. The concrete is cold under the seat of her jeans.

"Then what are you hitting the gin bottle for?"

"I was having trouble sleeping."

He's rubbing a greenish smudge of grease on the back of his hand. "Thinking about Hannah?"

"Hannah?" She looks at him in surprise.

"I just thought you might be."

"Hannah's all right."

"You're so innocent, Marilla."

"What do you mean?"

"It's dangerous, working at night," he says, almost angrily. "Hospitals have big, dark parking lots. It's a long walk to the subway. Girls can get . . . bothered."

She feels it now, the tension. It's not only in the throbbing of her head. He's pulling at the rag, twisting it in his hands. At this moment, she thinks, she loves him more than she ever has in her whole life.

"You have to let them go," she says at last.

"What?"

"Kids. You have to quit worrying about them. You have to make your mind go numb. You have to chop them out of your life."

"It's not like you can do it with a chainsaw."

"Yes it is," she says urgently. "Sometimes you have to do it just like that, like the limb off a tree. Or the whole tree down. No matter how much you love them, because once they're grown up, it's too late to do anything else."

"I don't believe you mean that."

"But I do. I've had plenty of practice, so I know."

He flings the rag onto the gravel by the stoop, picks up the chainsaw.

"Maybe it's change of life," she says to his back.

"Are you raving, Marilla?"

"The reason I couldn't sleep. They say it gives you insomnia."

He walks off toward the compost boxes without saying anything more.

It must have been March, because high-school basketball was on the television, the state playoffs. Rolf was watching it, home on leave from the navy. He had a two-day growth of beard and a scrape on his cheek from a fight he'd got into in a bus station in Alabama or somewhere. When Lyle asked him about the service he moved his gum to the other side of his jaw, reached for the television knob, turned the sound up louder.

Marilla went into the kitchen and Lyle followed her. In there you could smell the hair chemicals. Her mother was out playing bingo. Marilla opened the refrigerator and took out a can of beer and gave it to him. He was dying to get his hands on her, more than usual, even. It had something to do with the way Rolf treated him, looking at him like he was a slug or a stinkweed.

He picked up the church key from the table and punctured the can. "Won't you let me see your room?" he said to her. "You've never shown me your room."

She shook her head. "I can't, Lyle."

"Your mother won't be back for an hour, at least."

"Rolf's here."

"You think he gives a shit what we do? You think he'd even notice?"

"I just can't."

She made him so mad he felt like slamming her against the refrigerator. What the hell was wrong with her, anyway? From the things he heard, other girls weren't so fussy about what they did where. He lifted the can to his lips and drank about half the beer in one gulp.

"I just want to see your room, that's all. Where's the harm in that?"

He had a terrible hard-on, it was jamming into his chinos, he thought maybe she could tell. Her face was flushed, her eyes kind of shiny, watery.

"I won't do anything, I promise. I just want to see it."

"Not now."

"When, then? Four years, Marilla—four years this summer. You owe me something for all that time."

"No."

"You do, and you know you do."

Her shoulders sagged. She had on a green dress made of some flimsy, cheap material, he could see her bra under it. She'd been prettier when he first started taking her out. Fresher. Now she was starting to look like one of those housewives in the Shop'n Save, the ones married to tide watchers, with two or three kids hanging on them. Maybe somebody should point that out to her. Hell, his mother said he was too good for Marilla Geary, he almost had a college degree. Her father'd been nothing but a common mechanic, didn't even own his own shop. What was the matter with her—didn't she know a good deal when it stared her in the face? How many more chances did she think she was going to get?

He set the beer can on the table and moved toward her. She just stood there, her eyes on the floor, her back to the refrigerator. He put his hands on her neck, pressed his mouth onto hers. It must have been ten minutes at least they were like that, high-school basketball booming through the wall. He was kissing her so hard it was like he was trying to suck the resistance out of her, maybe even the life out of her. He wanted her so bad he couldn't stand it. He had to have her, just once, or it was going to kill him.

Finally he stopped. She just looked at him. All around her mouth was rubbed raw. "Marry me," he gasped. "You've got to."

"All right," she said.

Seal Neck Road's in bad shape, full of potholes, crumbling at the edges and caving into the drainage ditch. Marilla hasn't been on it in she can't remember how long. It's been raining for a day and a half; now the sky is thickly overcast, and wisps of fog lurk in the swamps and gullies. Shadblow has suddenly sprung into bloom, tiny delicate flowers alit on slender branches.

It's humid in the pickup. She rolls down the window for air and smells the sea.

On the right there's a lawn crowded with painted lawn ornaments, whirlybirds and stooping fat ladies. The little gray house is encrusted with giant butterflies. In winter the old man cuts them out of plywood and glues or nails them together and his wife paints them. In summer they're for sale. Summer people heading for the rent-by-the-week cabins on Seal Neck stop and dicker. The old man has a back injury he got in a boat yard, Marilla knows. It must pain him to bend over the jigsaw. Out back they keep pigs. There's the sign amid the whirlybirds, PIGS FOR SALE.

Without warning the road dips and crosses a rain-swollen stream, and then up on the left is the fish store where Tucker gets the guts for his compost. She thinks he barters, she doesn't know the details. The place is new since Marilla lived on this road. And so is the house a hundred yards farther on, a sprawling olive-green ranch with a TV dish like a spacecraft on the crisply cut lawn.

Now, at the top of the rise, you can see the sea for a moment before the road dips again and twists inland. Scrubby, rock-strewn land good only for blueberries lines both sides of the road for maybe three-quarters of a mile. Marilla raked here a couple of summers, before Hannah was born. Now, in spring, the fields are burned off, blackened, with only sparse patches of green showing, and some clenched fists of fiddleheads. Marilla thinks she can still smell the charred brush and weeds; maybe it's the damp and rain brings out the smell.

Her heart is beginning to thump in her chest. She's near, now. She hasn't been this far down the road in years and years. Never wanted to, never had call to. Out back of beyond, Lyle's mother called it, the one time she visited. Marilla cooked clam fritters that day. The food came out all right, but Lyle's mother hardly ate any. Didn't even take the trouble to push the fritters around her plate. Well, finally she had a heart attack and they could stop pouring money into the old bag and move to Poplar Street.

There it is, a little bit back from the road, next to a swamp maple that's just coming into leaf. She parks the truck in the drive and sits looking at the trailer. Somebody's painted it, but not recently. She hears a dog barking, from a way off, not from the trailer. There's no curtains in the windows, and the things around it look like rubbish people wouldn't bother to haul away when they left: a set of rusty bedsprings, a tire with no innertube, a playpen warped and whitened by rain.

She opens the pickup door and climbs down. There's not much of a breeze, but what there is is blowing papers around in the ditch. On the spot where she once tried to grow lupins from seed she'd gathered there's a crumpled beer can and a couple of lobster traps with missing slats. The white pine seedling she dug out of the woods and planted by the trailer is doing fine, though; the trunk is thick and the tree is twice as tall as she is.

Out back, wild-raspberry brambles have completely taken over, she might as well never have bothered to yank out all those roots. A black fly finds her, then another, then a swarm. It's beginning to drizzle a little, wetting down her hair. The dog's still barking. She can see it now, a big turd-brown animal tied by a rope to a stake, up by Crowley Reese's house. Crowley used to be a kind of caretaker for the trailer, did odd repairs in a half-baked way and collected the rent and mailed it off to some relative in Bangor. Must be dead now. It's been more than twenty years since she lived here, and Crowley was well into his seventies then.

She moves closer to the trailer through a thicket of weeds and peers in a window. The living room. She sees a stick or two of rackety furniture, a paperback open and face down on the floor. It's hard to tell how long the trailer has been abandoned. Might have been months or years ago, might just as easily have been last week, the occupants stealing away in the dead of night to beat the rent.

Suddenly the dog shuts up. She sees a man untying a rope from its collar. The man's old, but not Crowley, not as old as Crowley would be now. The two of them start moving toward the trailer, the dog sprinting in crazed circles and the old man taking his time. He's wearing a Day-Glo-orange cap. As he comes closer she sees that he might be Crowley, after all—Crowley frozen in time.

"What can I do for you?" he asks, slapping at black flies. The dog's trying to sniff her crotch.

"Crowley?"

"He's over to Route 1. Under a stone."

"Oh."

"I'm his boy, Turner. Looking for somebody?"

"I used to live here."

"That right?" He looks her over as if he's not sure whether she's kidding him. "Must have been some while ago."

"The place looks unoccupied. Nobody living in it."

He doesn't say anything. With mild interest he's watching her knee the dog in the chest to persuade it to back off.

"Is it for rent?"

Again there's a long pause. He slaps at a black fly trying to bite him through his stubble. "You interested in renting it?"

"I might be."

"Well, it might be for rent." He grabs the dog by its chain choke collar and pulls it away from her. The dog, half strangled, yelps. "You got a family?"

"There's just the two of us."

"No kids?"

"No."

"Kids tend to mess a place up."

She smiles. As if a dozen juvenile delinquents could do the trailer any more harm than it's already suffered.

"One ten a month. No utilities."

"Kind of steep, isn't it?"

"I don't set the rent. I only collect it."

"I'll let you know," she says, starting back to the pickup through the damp weeds.

Lyle heard her calling. But her voice was so far away. He listened to the sound of his own boots crunching into snow. He needed to peepee, and that made him stubborn. The sun was red in the sky.

He watched a bird flying over the river. Its wings were like long black knives slicing the air. He could see its beak opening, and a noise came out. *Scree. Scree.* It landed on a rock in the river. The second it hit the rock it turned into a different bird, brown and speckled, ugly. Magic.

Big chunks of ice were in the river, knocking into each other. The tide was going out fast, whipping into the bay, pulling the ice with it ass over teakettle. He could hear crackling. The ice chunks weren't white, they were dirty, with seaweed and old grass stuck to them.

She was calling some more. *Ly-ull, Ly-ull,* he heard. It was like something a bird said. It didn't belong to him.

He broke a dead branch off a tree and made marks with it in the snow. Somebody was jumping next to his footprints on a pogo stick. Or now on stilts. Now there was a gigantic snake slithering along just behind him.

He saw something in the river, not ice. Part of a boat, maybe. Maybe somebody drowned. You could, in that river. It would be so cold you wouldn't know what happened. You'd just be dead and nobody would ever find you.

He wiped his nose with his mitten. That made her mad,

when he did it. He thought about making his peepee in the snow. He stuffed his mitten into his pocket and yanked down his snow pants. He dug his weeny out of his fly, but it was so cold, at first he couldn't do anything. Suddenly it sprayed and cut a lot of holes in the snow, like bullet holes. Smoke came up. He smelled it, hot and acrid, like when Pa shot his gun. He wished he could keep on doing it, but there wasn't any more. He pulled up his snow pants.

She wasn't calling now. There was a light on in the kitchen, and another one upstairs, where his sisters were doing their homework. He felt cold. Getting rid of all his peepee made him cold.

He went up the bank in his own footprints, backwards now, toe to heel. He took off his mitten and turned the doorknob. The brass was icy under his bare fingers.

She grabbed him by his coat. She gave him a great push and he went sprawling across the linoleum. He hit his head on the corner of the refrigerator.

Don't you ever do that to me again. He looked at her brown shoes, laced up tight. He was snuffling. *You come when I call you, you hear me?*

She made cocoa, just for the two of them. His sisters didn't get any.

Marilla hangs the towel on the rack and sits down at the table. He's been eating eggs, there are scraps of them on his plate, but now he's smoking. A couple of squashed butts are on the plate with the eggs.

"I have something to say to you, Tucker."

He smiles a little. He's looking outside, at the pale green catkins drooping from the alders, or maybe at the mist, wondering if it's going to rain again before it clears.

"I have to go take care of Lyle."

"Your peas are up," he says. "They're getting strangled in the rockweed."

"Tucker, don't you hear what I'm saying?"

"I hear."

His finger begins to trace around a rusty place where somebody must have parked a house plant before the table came into their possession. His possession.

"I can't be in two places at once."

"When do you think you might be coming back?"

For a long time the only sound is of Mackerel licking her fur. "I don't suppose I'll be coming back," she says finally.

"Did he ask you?"

"I haven't talked to him."

"Maybe he doesn't want you," he says reasonably. "Ever think of that?"

She shrugs. "He doesn't have anybody else."

"He has sisters."

"Don't make me laugh."

He puts his hand on her wrist, holds it so tightly it feels like a clamp. "What about me? Marilla?"

Carefully she says, "You'll be all right."

"That's what you said about Hannah."

"Yes, you're the same. It's almost like she's your kid, not Lyle's."

Abruptly he lets go of her wrist. She pulls back and scrapes it on the rough edge of the table.

"How can you wrench yourself away from your life again? How can you do it?"

"Tucker, I—"

"You're doing this to make yourself miserable, aren't you?"

"No."

"So you can wallow in it, playing the martyr."

"What do you know about martyrs? You've never made a sacrifice for somebody else in your whole life."

"Is that what you think?" He speaks each word as though he's snipping them out of tin. His face has gone white. With shock she realizes he's angrier than she's ever seen him.

"Yes, Tucker, that's what I think. You've always done exactly what you wanted. Got exactly what you wanted." Her cheeks are stinging. She drops her eyes. "Except for me. Maybe you got me without really wanting me."

There's a long silence. "I wanted you."

"Me and my two laundry bags."

"Shit, Marilla. The bags, too."

The cat is in the mud room, mewing. The sound is querulous, insistent.

"You're going to be sorry you did this."

"I don't think so, Tucker. I'm tired of being sorry. I'm worn out with it."

She gets up to let the cat out.

"What about the goddamn peas?"

"They'll need thinning. Pull out every other one."

"And then what?"

"Nothing. After that they can take care of themselves."

33 *down. Monkeys or trees.*

The letters are smudgy, hard to read. He found a stumpy old pencil in the string drawer and sharpened it with a vegetable knife. Cut his finger and had to put on a Band-Aid.

From the words going in the other direction he works out what the answer must be, *TITIS*, but it's a word he's never heard of. They oughtn't to do that, use words nobody's heard of.

She's at the sink, washing dishes. Quite a few have collected. He can hear the water lapping against the side of the dishpan, the faucet turn on and off, the clink of a dish touching the drainer.

14 *down. Leveling wedge.*

29 *across. Use a swizzle stick.*

54 *across. Largest asteroid.*

Now she's upstairs. He listens to her footsteps. She must be crossing the floor between bureau and bed. She does it over and over. He knows there's something he's been wanting to tell her, but can't quite bring it to mind.

30 *down. Compass point.*

She's standing on the linoleum, next to the refrigerator, holding two paper shopping bags by the handles. One is from J. C. Penney's, the other from Porteous in the Bangor Mall. He sees that in the bags are things belonging to him: socks rolled up into balls, underwear, pajamas.

"I couldn't find a suitcase," she says.

Now he remembers. "She left me without saying goodbye."

Her eyebrows bunch together.

"It wasn't my fault."

"You don't have to tell me," she says.

"I want to. I don't want to keep the secret from you anymore."

"What secret?"

"I couldn't tell you, because you would have thought it was my fault. But it wasn't. I didn't know she had the pills."

"What pills, Lyle?"

"I found the empty bottle under her dresser. I hid it in my pocket and the doctor said it was heart failure."

She sets down the shopping bags. One of them tips a little and a sock ball rolls out.

"Lyle, are you telling me something happened to Frances?"

"Not *Frances.* Frances is in Florida or somewhere."

"Well, who then?"

"I felt like it was my fault, because I did things to make her mad. But I never wanted her to die. I loved her."

She picked up the shopping bags. "Come on, Lyle."

"Do you believe me?"

"Sure, I believe you. Get your car keys."

"Where are we going?"

"Home."

June

After Marilla left, Tucker took the money out of the sewer pipe and drove to Ellsworth. He bought vinyl floor tiles, plumbing fixtures, five oak cabinets, and a half-pound of carpet tacks. It took him two weeks to finish the house.

In the garden he planted potatoes, onions, carrots, and beans.

Down cellar he planted a new cash crop.

Now he's waiting for the ice cap to melt and for the sea to rise and swallow up the house and everything else.

FOR THE BEST IN PAPERBACKS, LOOK FOR THE [illegible]

In every corner of the world, [illegible]

[illegible]

In the United Kingdom: [illegible]

In the United States: [illegible]

In Canada: [illegible]

In Australia: [illegible]

In New Zealand: [illegible]

In India: [illegible]

In [illegible]

In [illegible]

In [illegible]

In [illegible]

In [illegible]